THE GIRL IN THE VAN

HELEN MATTHEWS

Copyright © 2025 Helen Matthews

The right of Helen Matthews to be identified as the Author of the Work has been asserted by them in accordance with the Copyright, Designs and Patents Act 1988.

Re-published in 2025 by Bloodhound Books.

Apart from any use permitted under UK copyright law, this publication may only be reproduced, stored, or transmitted, in any form, or by any means, with prior permission in writing of the publisher or, in the case of reprographic production, in accordance with the terms of licences issued by the Copyright Licensing Agency.
All characters in this publication are fictitious and any resemblance to real persons, living or dead, is purely coincidental.

www.bloodhoundbooks.com

Print ISBN: 978-1-917449-6-18

1

LAURA

PRESENT DAY - SATURDAY

I'm running away again – from life; from other people. Let them think what they want. Why should I explain myself?

My heart is thumping, and my right arm feels leaden from waving goodbye to my new 'friends' who have broken off from preparing the communal supper. Emily is gripping a knife in one hand and a tea towel in the other; Bill's gulping beer straight from the bottle and staring at me, baffled. No one is smiling. Today the sun finally came out, so they can't understand why I'm leaving our singles group holiday on this peaceful West Wales campsite where I've paid for three more nights.

I wind up my window, ram the stiff gear lever into reverse, and edge my ancient (but new to me) campervan off its grassy pitch. The van and I aren't yet working as a team, and I'm worried my wing mirrors might not pick up any tiny tots scampering from the playground, following the smell of caramelising meat back to their family's barbeque. It's early July, not yet school holidays, so the only youngsters are under-fours and teenagers who've finished their exams. My t-shirt is damp with sweat, and my foot is shaking as I drive cautiously down the track towards the main exit.

The people I've met on this holiday are harmless. Especially Bill, who seems an okay sort of bloke. He's a fraction the wrong side of forty, like me, but his habit of separating me from the others and starting deep, meaningful conversations has been unnerving. I don't do deep or meaningful. I rarely do conversation. Superficiality and the thinnest veneer of what passes for company suit me fine.

This was my first campervan trip, and it took me half an hour to disconnect the water and gas bottles, unplug from the power supply and trek to the communal bins to dump my rubbish. I'd planned to flee and text the others when I was on the road, but Amy guessed my plan and assembled this farewell party to wave me off, promising they'd see me again soon. I don't think so.

My vehicle crunches over gravel as I reach the gatehouse and pull into the parking bay opposite the campsite office to tell Dave, the manager, I'm off.

"Sorry to see you go, Laura."

"Bush telegraph?"

"That's right." He raises his clipboard and gestures at the main gate. "See that queue?"

I glance towards the road. I've forgotten it's Saturday, so this must be peak arrival time for holidaymakers. Cars towing caravans, engines idling, are queuing to enter the site. "Yes."

"Blasted barrier's playing up. I'll need to raise it by hand for each arrival and queue them in this parking bay. Could you move on?"

"Okay. Sure."

"Sorry." He gives a wry grin.

I restart my engine and swivel round for one final check on my living quarters. The bed fills the whole space. I've left it assembled and covered with cushions, but my backpack has burst open, spewing out clothes and shoes in haphazard heaps so it looks a bit like Tracey Emin's *Unmade Bed* artwork. I notice a lump in the duvet – odd, I don't remember stuffing pillows underneath.

A car beeps its horn. Dave raises the barrier, holds it aloft and motions me out. Cars rev their engines, and it's hard to edge past along the narrow country lane. I glance in my mirror. That bump under the duvet is rippling gently, out of step with the motion of the van. It must be an illusion. Like that fleeting sense of movement you get when you're staring out of the window of a stationary train and the one on the next platform pulls out. All the same it's unsettling, but I can't stop to check because the winding road has deep gulleys, hewn from rock, running along both sides and there are no passing places. I need my eyes on the road and hands clamped onto the steering wheel.

Seeing that bump has spooked me. What if one of the kids from the campsite climbed into my campervan while I was packing up and getting rid of my rubbish? Perhaps they were playing Hide and Seek. The last thing I need is to turn around and drive back to reunite a missing child with their angry parents. But if it is a child, wouldn't they have realised we're on the move and crawled out of their hiding place?

"Who's there?" I ask in a hoarse whisper, glancing in my rear-view mirror.

Silence, apart from the thudding of my heart. Perhaps they're scared.

"You can come out. I won't be cross."

No reply.

I'm itching to check, but tall beech trees leaning across to embrace their neighbours on the opposite side of the road form a dense tunnel and block out light. The road is empty.

I grit my teeth. I won't panic. I'll find somewhere to stop and sort this out.

At last a sign for a picnic area comes into view and I reach a clearing in the trees, with wooden tables dotted around on scrubby grass. A Land Rover is parked in the layby, but no sign of a driver. I ease my van to a halt, wrench on the heavy handbrake, unfasten my seat belt and clamber through the gap next to the driver's seat into my living quarters.

"Whoever you are, get out now." I shove pillows and cushions aside to reveal a mound under the covers. My hand is trembling, and I can't bring myself to touch it. What if it's an injured animal? A horrific image of the decapitated horse's head under the bedclothes in *The Godfather* slips into my mind. Breathing rapidly, I grasp the duvet in both hands and tug. It seems to be tucked in or weighted down. As I slide my hand down the side of the mattress to free it, a skinny arm thrusts out from under the heap of covers.

I freeze. "What the heck!"

The arm is wearing a friendship bracelet and holding up a note as if it's a white flag. Shock forces me to lean in and squint at the scrawled words: *Help me. Don't tell anyone.*

A laugh that's part-hysteria, part-terror catches in my throat as I yank back the duvet and uncover a girl with tangled dark-blonde hair and a nasty gash on one side of her face. She cowers away from me, covering her face with her hands.

"Sit up," I demand, grabbing her arm. She's a teenager, not a small child, and she's wearing a white t-shirt with a faded photo of a band I don't recognise. "What the hell are you playing at?"

The girl levers herself into a sitting position, keeping her face curtained by her long hair.

"Look at me," I say, clamping my hand on her shoulder and turning her to face me.

She straightens her spine, rocks forward and flicks her hair back behind her shoulders so I have my first proper look at her face.

I gasp.
It's her! Ellie.
For the briefest of moments, I allow myself to believe it.

2

LAURA

THURSDAY (TWO DAYS EARLIER)

I'm driving west from London when the bridge across the River Severn, dividing England from Wales, looms into view. My heart lifts. After being uprooted, the pull of Wales is a visceral thing. There's a name for it: *hiraeth* – a kind of call to your inner self from a half-forgotten place or time. I'm surprised it still has this power. When I fled Wales two years ago, I was desperate to escape everything from my old life.

The bridge is painted a pastel shade of green. When she was young, Ellie used to say *It's all minty*. Today the spearmint hue chokes me with memories. I'm making a detour and visiting my mother in Cardiff. None of what's happened is Mum's fault, but she blames herself because it happened on her birthday. She'd love to take away my anguish and carry the burden for me, but she can't do that. No one can.

I've been driving for three hours, rarely accelerating above sixty. The campervan's controls are heavy, and a vibration from the transmission shoots pins and needles through my right leg. At the junction for north Cardiff, I signal to leave the motorway and follow the winding road to the village-turned-suburb, nestled beneath the hills on the city's northern fringe, where my mum still lives.

The driveway is empty, but that doesn't mean she's not home. Mum chooses small cars to fit inside her narrow garage, and cares for each one as if it was a pet or a child. If her car's wet when she arrives home she dries it with a cloth first, before going indoors to change out of her own sodden coat and shoes.

I dawdle up the path to the oak front door, press the bell and wait, noticing the blinds are raised, the sun's rays turning the front windows into a mirror. Mum answers the door wearing fluffy pink slippers and the apron she's kept for baking since I was a child, but there's no smell of baking in the house. Her newly-white hair shocks me, even more than the deeper frown lines etched onto her face, because Mum and her hairdresser always conspired to keep it chestnut brown. As she scans my face, her eyes mist with tears.

"Hello, Mum." I bend forward and kiss her cheek.

She stares at me, this ghost on her doorstep. "Laura, sweetheart. Why didn't you ring?" She rehearses a smile, but it doesn't mask her sadness. And that's understandable when you haven't seen your only daughter for two years and she won't tell you her phone number – or where she lives.

"If I'd known you were coming, I'd have…" Her voice trails off.

"It's just a flying visit, Mum. I can't stop long." I could, of course. It would be easy to abandon my ridiculous holiday plans and stay all week.

She dabs her eyes with a corner of her apron.

"Can we go inside?" I place one foot on the step.

"Of course." She opens the door wider and peers beyond me at the road. "Where's your car?"

"I left it in the car park up at the Deri Inn." If I'd parked my metallic red campervan outside, the curtain-twitchers would have worked out the visitor was me.

"Oh. I see," she says in a flat voice. She leads me into the sitting room, motioning me towards the sofa as if I were a distant acquaintance. The grate is filled with a dried flower arrangement, which she'll replace with logs in November, and the walls are still painted her favourite shade of China blue. Even on this summer's day it feels chilly. The framed family photographs have disappeared from her mantelpiece. She must have packed them away. I can understand that.

We sit facing each other, and I cradle my small backpack on my lap and fiddle with the strap.

"Let's have a proper look at you." Her scrutiny makes me uneasy. "You're so thin!"

She's right. I've lost over a stone. The weight fell off without me noticing. I tell myself I'm happy with a trim waist and thighs that don't bulge, but my jutting collarbone makes me look like I've an eating disorder. I do eat, but sometimes I forget. Most mornings I have cereal. If there's no milk, I swallow it dry. In the atrium of my office building is a sandwich bar, where I buy lunch, but come the evening, I can't be bothered. If I feel faint, I go to the fridge and throw together whatever I find into a makeshift meal. Perhaps scrambled egg, cheese and blueberries, with baked beans scooped cold from the can.

I left home this morning without having breakfast. A piece of cake would be nice, or even a biscuit, but Mum just stares at me so I get to my feet. "Let's have a cup of tea. Stay there, Mum, I'll make it."

"Of course. Sorry." She trails behind me like a puppy scared to let its master out of sight. Through the steam of the boiling kettle I see her shape her mouth to ask a question, but words take a while to come. Finally, she asks, "How's your job?"

I shrug. "It pays the mortgage. I can't ask more."

She flinches, and I feel mean for blanking her effort at harmless small talk. It's the same when I phone her – from the office, because I won't give her my number; our conversations are full of silence and the sound of each other's breathing. I make tea in the brown pot. Mum uses teabags now, so I don't have to faff about with tea leaves and a strainer. In the usual cupboard, I find the barrel-shaped biscuit tin, with a fading picture of Prince Charles and Lady Diana's wedding. Mum always loved fairy-tale romances, and her marriage to Dad was happy, though he died when I was seventeen and she was barely fifty. She doesn't get it when relationships turn sour.

The biscuit tin is empty, and that upsets me. She used to have friends round for coffee to put the world to rights and boast of their grandchildren's achievements. But then, Mum couldn't join in that conversation, could she?

While I was looking for biscuits, she's poured our tea and taken it into the sitting room. She pulls out the hand-painted coffee table she made in one of her arts and crafts classes, and sets the mugs down on coasters. When she speaks, her tone is sharp.

"How much longer are you going to keep up this nonsense, Laura?"

"What nonsense?" I feign surprise.

"Hiding away. Not visiting." She's abandoned the effort to smile, and the corners of her mouth droop.

I shrug. "I'm waiting for things to calm down. If you hear anything, let me know."

"Like what?" She bangs down her mug, and liquid slops onto the table.

"Like Gareth's got a new girlfriend. That he's getting married. That sort of thing."

She gives a tight smile. "Can't you forgive him? It's been almost three years."

"Neither of us can forgive, Mum."

I don't tell her I'm afraid of Gareth and his rages. I never told her the truth about what happened between us. She'd like nothing better than for him and me to get back together. That's why I won't tell her my London address. I know she still sees him, and I can't trust her not to pass it on.

"So where are you heading?" she asks.

"It's a sort-of holiday." I choose my words carefully. "I've been working flat-out, so my boss told me to take some annual leave." I don't tell Mum that alarm bells go off inside an organisation if someone who deals with accounts never takes a holiday. They suspect you're fiddling the books and siphoning off money into your own account. White-collar criminals cover their tracks by being diligent workaholics, and my work pattern ticked all those boxes. Our office's barrier entry system records everyone's arrival and departure times. My boss told me he'd been sent a report showing I was averaging seventy hours a week, hadn't taken any leave for a year, and often went in on Saturdays. I'd have gone in on Sundays, too, if the building wasn't closed. *They're calling in the auditors to investigate,* my boss warned me with a nervous smile. *It's best you take some time off.* To my mum, I say, "I guess they were worried I was working too hard."

"I'm glad your company takes employees' health seriously. Where are you off to? To visit old friends?"

I have no old friends. I left them behind in the chaos of fleeing my past, so I take a deep breath and tell her, "It's a singles holiday on a campsite in Tenby."

"But you don't like camping." Mum's eyes widen in surprise. "You and Gareth always rented a cottage in France."

"Something different will do me good." My answer might sound flippant, but the decision was anything but. When I discovered the holiday was in Tenby, I almost cancelled. Could

I face returning to Wales? But I realised it would give me a chance to see Mum and an excuse to make the visit fleeting. "I've bought a campervan," I tell her.

"What?" Her jaw drops so her mouth hangs open.

"Don't worry, Mum. It's no bigger than the school minibus – I was trained to drive that, remember?" I don't tell her tonight will be the first time I've slept in it. I show her a photo on my phone. She takes it from me, enlarges the picture and squints at it, staring hard for several minutes.

"I'm not keen on that bright red colour. And it's ancient – the registration plate's the same year as that old Astra I had – pre-Millennium. Are you sure it's reliable?" She hands me back my phone.

"I've had it checked over by a mechanic. The engine's fine."

"I don't like the idea of a singles holiday – you being all alone with a group of strangers."

On the scale of bad things that have happened in my life, this barely registers. "A campsite's a public place, Mum. Don't worry."

I excuse myself to use her bathroom. When I return, Mum's sitting at her old bureau scribbling a note with her fountain pen. She doesn't hear me entering the room and flinches, covering whatever she's writing with her hand, then she slips something into an envelope and hands it to me.

"What's this?"

"A small cheque towards your holiday."

I hold up my hand. "Honestly, Mum, I can't accept it. Spend it on yourself."

"I have more than I need. It makes sense to pass some to you before I die. Who else is there, after all?"

"But you're not old, Mum."

"There's nothing I want," she says in a flat tone, and I feel a stab of guilt. Mum used to have a zest for life. When Dad died over twenty years ago she was still young, but she didn't let it crush her. She was a senior librarian, and after she retired she went back to the local branch as a volunteer and worked for free because she was worried austerity cuts were impacting the library service. Later she trained as an advice counsellor and set up a branch of the Citizens Advice Bureau at the library.

"I feel weary," she says, and I notice a greyish tinge to her skin and bruise-coloured circles under her eyes. "I hope I don't have to go on for years."

I stare down at the envelope. If it makes her happy to give me some money, I should accept it graciously. "Thank you." I give her a quick hug.

"What campsite are you going to?"

"Sand Dunes in Tenby. Why d'you want to know?"

"I'll look it up on the internet then I can imagine you there. Can you stay a little longer?"

I glance at my watch. It's nearly four o'clock. "I suppose another thirty minutes."

It seems her gift was a prelude to launching into the only topic she ever wants to discuss. She settles in the chair opposite me and leans forward, hands clasped.

"Gareth came to see me last week. He's good at keeping in touch."

My heart beats a little faster. "How was he?"

"Better, I think. He looked fitter at least; he's been working out at the gym, and he went back to rugby coaching last season."

"Good." The last time I saw Gareth he was a flabby, emotional wreck, his face bloated from alcohol. When she mentions him in our phone calls, I switch off. Mum spent too long on Team Gareth. It felt like she was siding with him against me.

"Anyway, the rugby club's been his saviour. He spends all

his spare time up there, so he's not cutting himself off from people any more."

"Is he working?" I ask. Gareth's a carpenter and had his own successful business building hand-crafted kitchens, but when I left him he hadn't had a commission for months and was sliding down the slope towards bankruptcy.

"Yes. He wound up his company. Now he works as a contractor for someone else, but he seems to have plenty of work. And he's abandoned his mission to investigate – until he finds a new lead."

"Mission! I'd call it an obsession."

"Who can blame him?"

She's right, of course. None of us knows how we'll behave when the worst thing possible happens. My response was to shut down, stay numb and push everyone away. Gareth's grief turned to rage – against the world, against himself, and ultimately against me. He lashed out at the way he was treated by the community and the press, and picked fights with anyone who asked questions or voiced an opinion. When some busybody organised a meeting about keeping children safe, he chucked a brick through the window of the church hall.

I get to my feet and collect up the mugs. I have a long drive ahead before I face a group of new people.

"Did you know," Mum continues, unrelenting, "some of the teachers from your old school belong to the rugby club?"

"Sure, they always did." What else can you do in winter in a small seaside dormitory town if you're not into sailing, and too young to settle for a stroll on the pier or a bracing walk along the pebble beach?

"That teacher who was in your department plays rugby now. What was his name? Gareth spends quite a bit of time with him."

My head aches from her talk of the past. I've cut my ties

with Llewellyn High School, where I taught French for fifteen years and became Head of Department. "I can't think of it at the moment." I've blocked all the memories, not just the sad ones. "I expect it'll come to me."

She glances through the French windows at her garden where deep red and yellow roses are in bud, in bloom and overblown. She'd love me to stroll around the garden with her, but she says, "Off you go. Tenby's a long drive. Make sure you get there before dark." It won't be dark for hours, but her anxiety's a sign of how she's aged, and my stomach clenches with pain and guilt. Surely I could relax my vigilance and spend more time with her? Gareth's threats were angry words when he was at breaking point. If he meant me harm, he'd have tracked me down by now.

"Let's say goodbye here." I stop in the hall and hug Mum tight. I don't want a long goodbye wave on the doorstep in full view of the neighbours. "I'll see you soon."

"Shall I give your love to Gareth when I next see him?"

"No." I didn't mean to snap, but the tight feeling moves from my stomach and lodges in my chest. I ease my backpack onto one shoulder. "Don't tell him I was here. Please."

"Okay," she says.

At the end of her drive I turn and wave, then stride towards the main road and the pub where I parked my van. I'm still clutching the envelope she gave me with the cheque in it, and flip it over in my hands. On the back is a smudged line of text, as if the envelope had been pressed down like blotting paper on top of something she'd written underneath in fountain pen.

The letters and numbers look familiar. With a stab of shock, I realise Mum has noted down my campervan's registration plate from the photograph. But why?

3

LAURA

THURSDAY

As I head west on the motorway I turn up the radio, and Welsh rock band Manic Street Preachers belts out the rasping lyrics of *Design for Life*. I sing along, catapulted back to school discos in the late 1990s, but music doesn't ease my guilt at neglecting Mum. Her haggard appearance shocked me. When we see people regularly, we don't notice changes because we age in tandem.

In Carmarthenshire the motorway ends, and I'm stuck for miles behind a tractor, spilling clods of earth across the carriageway. At the back of my mind lurks an anxiety about the etiquette of singles holidays. Was I meant to bring my own food, or contributions to communal meals? I dimly remember Bill, the organiser, setting up a WhatsApp group and messaging to say he'd added me. Occasional notifications pinged onto my phone but I never looked at them. Shit! Maybe that was where they organised the nuts and bolts.

In a village outside Tenby I drive into the car park of a small local shop and scroll through WhatsApp. Sure enough, there's a list of what each person should bring, and I'm down for breakfast items. The store's still open, so I hurry inside and weave through a narrow aisle of fruit and veg, grabbing punnets of blueberries and strawberries. What do people even eat for breakfast? Cereal? The shop only has those fun-sized boxes of sugary brands, but I grab some, along with granary bread, croissants and eggs. I don't eat sausages or bacon – how am I meant to know if the pigs have had a happy life? I pick up some packs marked *Local Produce* and hope for the best.

I join the queue at the checkout. What about tea bags and coffee? Checking the group tells me Bill is bringing those, along with plentiful beer and wine, if I'm translating his row of emojis correctly. I push my sunglasses up onto the top of my head to hold back my unruly red hair. Why didn't I have it cut? I hate it hanging past my shoulders. The customer in front is searching for her debit card, but no one complains because here the pace of life is slower. People take time to breathe, smile at their neighbours and pause for a chat.

"Hosting a big brunch, love?" asks a man behind me. He's wearing a flat cap but he doesn't look elderly. It must be in fashion round here. "Give us your address. I'll be round."

I smile. It's good to practise. "I'm going camping at Sand Dunes," I tell him.

Other customers join in. "Family break is it, love? What's the campsite like?"

"I've never been there before." I mean the campsite, not the town, which I know well.

"We haven't been to that campsite, have we Dai?" says the dark-haired woman.

"Well, we wouldn't, would we, love? We've our own beds to sleep in."

Everyone laughs. Their accents comfort me, as does being back in Wales, until my mind circles back to thoughts of Mum. I pay and wheel my trolley outside, where I stash the chilled food in my plug-in cool box and join the road for the final stretch.

As I turn into the campsite the manager is locking the office, but opens it again when he sees me and I follow him inside.

"You're just in time." He shows no hint of irritation, though a notice says the office shuts at six-thirty and it's well past seven. At the side of the building is a static caravan, behind a wattle fence woven from branches, a vegetable patch, a couple of hens pecking about, a paving-slab patio, a garden table and a couple of chairs. That must be where he lives.

"I'm Dave," he tells me. "Your mates are here already." There's a computer on his desk, but he ignores it and refers to a clipboard. Campsite life must be one of the last bastions of pen and paper. I'm oddly comforted by that.

Dave hands me a key to the barrier and a map of the site, pointing out the shower block and washing up area. "You're pitch number fifty-six," he tells me, colouring it in with a highlighter pen. "You take this main drive, follow the curve of the road and it's at the far end beyond the children's playground."

My heart sinks. I wasn't expecting there to be children.

"Now, will you be needing anything in the morning?"

"Um?"

"Milk, eggs, local newspaper...?"

"Of course." I forgot milk. "Yes, please, two large semi-skimmed."

He notes my order down in neat block capitals.

"Do I pay you now?"

He shakes his head. "Pay when you pick up."

I watch from my van as he lets himself in through a gate in the wattle fence, and wonder if there's a Mrs Dave waiting. The main drive is full of potholes filled with gravel chippings, and the first field has tents in every shape and hue. Some are just a crawl space of conjoined tunnels, others have vast awnings with a field kitchen set up. A young woman, in a leopard print onesie, opens her car boot, takes out fresh flowers and arranges them in a vase on a folding table. Beyond the tented area an open gate leads to a field of campervans and caravans, and I can just make out the blue poles of playground swings.

Why have they put a singles group in a family area? All the courage that's brought me to this place evaporates. There's still time to turn tail and head back to my London flat and my solitary life, shuttling to the office by tube and returning home to empty walls and silence.

My work colleagues think I'm snooty for not joining them in the pub to celebrate birthdays. I've cut ties with my old friends and I'm about to mix with strangers. Am I ready?

A dark-haired man with a full beard is strolling down the gravel track towards the gatehouse. He's very tall, at least six foot three, and walks with a slight stoop. With his hand up to shield his eyes from the low sun he doesn't appear to notice me, but as he draws closer he picks up his pace and heads straight for my van. He mimes a hand gesture telling me to wind down the window.

"You must be Laura?" His beard hides his mouth but his eyes crinkle so I guess he's smiling.

"That's me. How did you guess?"

"Process of elimination. You're the last to arrive, so unless you've hidden someone in the back, I'd say you were a single camper, like the rest of us."

"Of course. So you're … Bill?"

"Yep." He sticks his arm through the open window and we perform an awkward handshake. "I was getting worried about you. I was heading down to ask Dave if you'd sent a message."

"I'm here now, as you see." Why do I have to be so curt with everyone? It's my way of closing down, fending off questions I don't want to answer. Even harmless ones.

"Come on, I'll show you to your pitch."

"No need," I begin, but Bill opens the passenger door and jumps in, gathering up my map, wine gums and water bottle and holding them on his lap.

He rubs his palm over the dashboard, buffed to a high shine by my mechanic. "How long have you had this old girl?" He sounds like he's admiring a pet, and I stifle a giggle.

"Just a few days. I found it on Gumtree. If it's not for me I'll sell it when I get home."

"You'll love it. When you're a city-dweller like me – and you – escaping at weekends keeps you sane."

"How do you know where I live?" Even here, I'm paranoid about privacy.

"Erm – your holiday registration form. I collected them all and lodged them with the campsite. But your accent sounds Welsh."

"I am Welsh, but I live in London now."

"You must be glad to be home, then."

I ease out of the parking bay and drive along the track, through the narrow gate into the second field. I don't look at pitch numbers because I know Bill will tell me. And he does, with plenty of hand gestures and pointing to a wide, grassy space with a brown patch where the turf has been worn away by vans that came before. "This one's yours."

He points out the electricity supply. "Think where you want your awning – the sun rises over there." Again he points, and I duck out of range of his circling arm. "I suggest you drive in forwards."

Awning? I think that's a kind of mini-marquee that attaches to more upmarket vans than mine to add living space. Whatever it is, I don't have one.

I drive in and pull over to the left. "Thank you." Perhaps now he'll get out of my van, but he lingers.

"Mine's the white Vauxhall, three along. Anything you

need, come and find me. Supper's over at Emily's pitch." He points along the field to a circle of chairs and tables set out under the spreading branches of an oak. Through a gap in the hedge I can just make out a youngish, balding man with a pinstripe apron tied over his t-shirt and shorts, tending two kettle barbeques. A fair-haired woman, holding a bottle of wine, appears on the steps of a massive motorhome that looks brand new.

The journey's left me sticky with perspiration and I'd like some time to chill out, but it seems everyone's waiting for me before having supper. So I connect my water barrel, check the power is working, and go to join the group.

Bill rises from his chair and introduces me to Sam, the barbeque chef, whose bald head is shiny from his cooking exertions. He wipes his mouth and shows me his greasy fingers.

"Sorry – can't shake just now." We elbow-bump instead.

"This is Emily..." The blonde woman flutters her fingers in a wave. "Welcome."

"... and Delia." A woman with short spiky hair chomps on a mouthful of food, her cheeks puffed out like a hamster. She raises her eyes to look at me, then focuses back on her plate.

"And Amy." A woman with coppery hair and a light dusting of freckles says, "Hi."

"Everyone – this is Laura from London but originally from Wales."

"Please carry on. Sorry I delayed you."

Emily fetches the bottle of red wine, wrapping a piece of kitchen roll around it before touching it with her greasy fingers, and pours me a glass before I can mention I prefer white. Sam beckons me across to the barbeque, hands me a melamine plate and serves up skewers of mushroom, onion, red pepper and courgette with a jacket potato.

The two men and Delia have chicken and burgers. Three of

the six of us are vegetarian, so I needn't have bothered with bacon or sausages. I sip my wine and tune into the ripple of chatter, wondering why they're here and what made them choose campervanning.

Amy finishes her food and turns to me, as if reading my mind. "Bill said you've just bought your van. Beware. It can become addictive. I've had mine two years." She points with the end of her fork at her VW camper – iconic and stylish. "Mine's not just for camping. Back home in Shropshire, I commute to work in it. My younger step-sister used to come on trips with me, but she's at uni now so I go alone." She shoots me a fierce look. "At Easter I was camped out in Snowdonia when I met Bill, and he was on his own too. That's what got us thinking up this idea of a campervan holiday for singles." She reaches under her seat for a pack of cigarettes and clicks a silver engraved lighter. I haven't finished eating, so her smoking surprises me. "So what activities are you up for?"

"Activities?"

"Like water sports? Tenby has kayaking, jet skis, paddle boarding. Perhaps wind surfing if the conditions are right. Have you brought your wetsuit? It's cold, even in summer."

When I lived by the sea in Penarth, Gareth used to sail and I occasionally crewed for him, but I no longer have a wetsuit. The memories, happy ones, flood back. I sit with them for a while, then realise Amy's waiting for my answer.

"I was thinking of walking the coastal path."

She gives me a curious look. "I'm sure we'll do that, too." She tugs on Bill's sleeve and he turns towards her. "We need to discuss plans. Laura, here, wants to walk the coastal path."

Bill signals for quiet and makes a little speech about what there is to do in the area, reading from a list.

"Do we need voting slips?" asks Amy.

"Nah. We'll have a show of hands."

I watch as every hand, except mine, shoots up in favour of increasingly extreme choices from paddle boarding to quad biking. Hiring a boat for mackerel fishing gets the most votes. I sit on my hands and cast my votes for walking and a pub supper.

"That's settled then," says Bill. "Mackerel fishing tomorrow."

Everyone whoops and shuffles chairs so they're sitting next to someone different. I stay where I am on the outer fringe. Emily strolls around topping up glasses. I accept a glass knowing I won't drink it and put it down by my feet. Bill turns his chair to face me at an angle that blocks me in. Perhaps because I don't talk as much as the others, he's chosen me to regale with his plans for extreme camper trips. I learn he's covered most of accessible Europe and wants to go further afield.

"Scandinavia," he says. "Or North Africa. Imagine driving down through Spain to catch the ferry from Tarifa across to Tangier." He takes another swig of beer and wipes his beard with the back of his hand.

Sam has produced a small firepit and a box of logs. The wood is smouldering, sending puffs of smoke in different directions each time the wind changes. Bill grabs another beer and wedges it between his knees but doesn't open it. He spreads his hands in front of me, palms up.

"I'm a freelance photographer, but I've made my name so I can pick and choose commissions. When I'm travelling, I pitch to magazine editors before I set off and they always say 'yes'. So I don't need to stay in one place. I can live on the road and work along the way."

His brown eyes reflect the soft firelight and he leans closer, his hand brushing mine in a movement so subtle it could be accidental. I feel the strangest tingling sensation, as if he and I have made some sort of connection. "You'll love campervan life when you get into it."

"I doubt it." I shake my head. I can't see myself turning into a seasoned road-tripper. The feeling of comfort fades, and a shiver creeps along my spine. Is Bill secretly auditioning for someone to join him in a weird, nomadic life?

4

LAURA
FRIDAY

A clanking sound pulls me out of sleep. I yawn and kneel up to look out of the window to see Dave steering his ride-on mower across the adjoining pitch. The smell of freshly-cut grass reminds me where I am – and I'm breakfast chef. I spray on deodorant, wriggle into my jeans and top, and sprint across to Emily's pitch which has become the centre of our little community.

The first raindrops hit my head while I'm laying out juice, bread and croissants on the communal table. I'm squinting up at the sky when Emily sticks her head out of her door and grimaces. "I've just caught the weather forecast. Not good."

As the others emerge, yawning, the rain gives notice of its serious intent.

"I'm not going out on a boat in this," Emily grumbles.

Bill and Sam are still up for mackerel fishing, but I'm guessing Amy and Emily were planning to don bikinis and work on their suntans on the boat. No one knows what Delia's thinking because she doesn't say. The sky is a gloomy shade of greyscale, and sets the tone for the day. Huddling over breakfast under Emily's marquee-sized awning, everyone is grumpy. We don cagoules and anoraks to tramp along the coast and down to North Beach, a crescent of brownish-gold sand with a vast rock rearing up in its centre like a stranded onshore island.

"That's the Goscar Rock," I tell the others, showing off my local knowledge. "It's named after a Welsh legend." The salty breeze stings my face, and it's a struggle to blink the sand away.

"The paddle boarding shack's this way." Bill points to the far end of the beach. "Why don't we book a group session for tomorrow?"

The heavens open. Emily's jacket has no hood, so her hair is soon plastered to her forehead as thick clouds swirl overhead.

"Let's head round to South Beach," I suggest. "There's a beach café where we can get coffee."

On the way everyone admires the Georgian architecture, and I try to remember Tenby's connections to famous people my dad used to tell me about when we came here on family holidays. "That's the house where George Eliot was staying when she wrote her first novel."

"I've read *The Mill on the Floss*," says Emily, but it seems no one else has heard of her.

We walk along a street of shops, and I point out the house (now painted a deep Wedgwood blue) where Admiral Lord Nelson stayed with Emma Hamilton. Sam makes a Kiss-me-Hardy joke. When we reach South Beach it stops raining, and everyone wants to know about the island, a short distance off shore.

"That's Caldey Island, where there's a monastery owned by Cistercian monks. Years ago, I went there with my parents. I think the monks make and sell violet perfume."

"Let's go there today," says Emily. But snarly clouds are building again, so we stay in the café and Sam produces a pack of cards. We finish our coffees and move on to fish and chips for lunch.

Afterwards we mooch around the museum's exhibits of local geology and archaeology and the collection of paintings by Welsh artists Gwen John and her brother Augustus. I thought they were famous, but the others look blank when I mention them. On the way back we visit a supermarket to buy food for supper. All of us have hotplates in our vans, and some have ovens, but despite the rain the consensus is for another barbeque.

The rain has slackened to a fine drizzle when Sam dons his navy-and-white striped apron, rolls up the clear plastic sides of Emily's awning and sets up the barbeque. It's hammered down all day, so the canvas roof is bowing under a huge puddle. Sam pokes it with a broom handle; water floods down and swamps the table, missing our food but drenching the giant box of matches. Sam stands by the barbeque, striking one dud match after another. Amy digs into the pocket of her jeans and hands him her posh cigarette lighter. A flame flickers but the firelighter won't catch. In a fury, Sam grinds the heel of his trainer into the damp turf.

"Hang on a minute." I push back my chair and stand up. "There's a gas lighter in my van." I inherited a box of tools with the van: drill bits and devices whose purpose I had no clue about, along with crockery so scratched that I bought a new set. But I kept the tools. I head over to my van and scrabble around in the cupboard under the sink until I locate the lighter in a metal bowl full of bits and bobs. I take it back to Emily's pitch and hand it to Sam.

"There you go. No idea if there's any gas in it."

Sam holds it close to his ear and gives it a shake. "It's full, I'd say." He points it at the barbeque and a thin column of flame shoots out, igniting the firelighter tucked beneath the charcoal. "Woah! You didn't say it was a bloody flamethrower! The button's stuck." He carries it outside the awning and jabs it deep into the soggy grass until the flame fizzles out.

"Be careful with this." He hands it back to me. "It has a mind of its own, and this switch is stuck." He points out a miniscule slide button on the side.

"Thanks. I won't use it inside my van for sure."

While we wait for the charcoal to heat up, Bill hefts a case of beers out of his van and carries it over. By the time our food's ready, twelve bottles are gone.

"Thirsty work, barbequing," grins Sam, serving up platefuls of charred steak and sausages for himself and Bill and veggie burgers for the rest of us. I fill my plate up with coleslaw and couscous, but finish long before the meat-eaters, because their knives can't saw through the tough steaks.

"Anyone up for Xbox?" Sam asks as we finish eating. There's an awkward silence. Emily goes back into her motorhome and fetches an armful of board games.

"How about one of these?" she suggests.

"We've drunk too much," Sam grumbles, but Emily ignores him and sets up a quiz game with impenetrable rules. We split into two teams, and I'm with Bill and Amy who are uber-competitive. My attention wanders. There's so much to learn about campervan life. I didn't even know what to bring. Not just food, it seems, but music, packs of cards, board games and tools.

After we've won, Amy and Bill high-five and she goes off to her van and returns with a celebratory bottle of Cava. My fellow campers' voices amplify with every glass. The sun daubs fiery colours across the sky, and as it turns dark I stroll across the field and climb a small hill so I can see the stars. As the light pollution from the campsite fades, I take a deep breath and feel calm – at one with the darkness and a universe teeming with stars.

On my way back I hear voices and a splutter of giggling coming from the children's playground, and sniff the distinctive aroma of marijuana. In the thick shadow I make out a small group huddled around the swings. One of them looks up and notices me. There's a murmur of alarm, some scuffling of feet across bark chippings, and they scatter in all directions. The red glow of a spliff picks out the dark shape of one remaining teenager sitting on a swing, heels anchored in the earth, rocking back and forth.

"Hi! Who goes there?" she calls out. She has a long thick plait, running down her back almost to the base of her spine.

Her greeting makes me smile. "Hi. I'm Laura. And you?"

"Pippa. Want some?" She holds the spliff out towards me.

"No thanks. Is it half-term?" I've noticed a few teenagers hanging out together on the site.

"Nah – GCSEs," replies Pippa. "Me and my mates have finished our exams. We wanted to go to Ibiza, but our parents wouldn't fork out the airfare so we've come here. We're having a wicked time."

"Of course. Nice to meet you, Pippa. Have fun and good luck with your results when you get them." I wave and stroll on back to my campervan.

So she's sixteen – the same age as Ellie. How could I have forgotten so soon what sixteen looks like?

5

LAURA

SATURDAY

Next morning, sunshine tempts us back to the beach. Mackerel fishing has been brushed aside, and paddle boarding is on trend. The men have brought their own wetsuits. Amy and Delia decide to join in, and at the hire shack on the beach Bill helps them search through the rack for a wetsuit in the right size.

"The fit should be like a second skin," he says, holding one out to Amy. She tries it on and her body transforms into a sleek, dark sea creature. They rent boards for half a day and book an hour's tuition. Emily and I wave them off, then climb the worn steps leading up from the beach to the cliff where we'll join the coastal path.

Emily is wearing a chunky-knit sweater and shorts, and by the time we've toiled up to the narrow lane, fringed with ferns and ivy, her cheeks are pink with exertion. "Stop a minute." She swigs water from a bottle, tugs the sweater over her head and knots the sleeves round her waist.

"Ready?" I ask.

She nods, and we set out in the direction of Saundersfoot. Emily's the easiest to talk to because she's not interested in me; she wants to talk about herself and her recent divorce. She's venting because it's a form of release for her. Some people react to trauma in that way; others – like me – block it out and never speak of it again.

"We'd only been married two years," she begins, "but Mark was having an affair with a colleague." We've reached a grassy part of the track and I'm staring at the ground trying not to crush wild flowers under my heavy walking boots. "But I got the motorhome. He was hopping mad about that."

"Is that something you did together?" I ask. "Weekend trips away? Like Amy and Bill?"

Emily seems puzzled. "Amy and Bill? Are they an item?"

"Who knows?" I brush seed-heads from my sleeves.

"The motorhome was our only property," says Emily. "Our flat in Bristol was rented, so when I left him, I piled all my stuff into it and drove down the M5 through Somerset with no plan of where I was heading. After I crossed into Devon, the sense of freedom and the adrenaline drained out of me. I found a car park near a beach, shut myself inside the motorhome and slept for two days."

"I can understand that."

Emily pushes her blonde hair out of her eyes and shoots me the look of a fellow-conspirator. "I guessed you would." She bends down to untie her boot and tips out some stones. "Ouch, that's better."

I wait for her to retie her laces.

"Mark was fuming – kept sending me angry texts, calling me up all night, screaming at me down the phone."

My body tenses, because that behaviour sounds familiar. Perhaps all men act the same, regardless of who's right or wrong. When I told Gareth I was leaving – and that I'd be selling the house – his threats ratcheted up. The man I thought I knew had been wearing a mask all those years – the person underneath was raw and angry with a brooding violence.

"Mark didn't hurt you, did he? Physically, I mean?"

"No. He was weak and pathetic."

I touch her hand lightly. "I'm glad."

"I knew Mark wouldn't fight me for the motorhome. He couldn't afford it. He'll struggle to pay the rent on our flat in Clifton. Neither he, nor his new woman, Anna, earn as much as me."

"What do you do?"

"I'm a business analyst."

"Oh." Where I work there are swarms of analysts. Some do complicated mathematical modelling and clever geeky stuff, but there are also business analysts tasked with streamlining processes, who come and bother us back-office people about our working methods. Then they go away and make processes supposedly slicker. And cut more staff.

"And you?" she asks.

I clear my throat as I wonder how to answer. Nothing I do now feels like any part of my identity. Once I was a teacher and a mother, but I've left those roles in the past.

"I'm an administrator for a hedge fund firm," I say, wondering if she'll tell me hedge fund managers are responsible for all the evils of society. Since working for one I've discovered many people think that. Emily's smile prompts me to continue. "It's boring but well paid."

"I bet you get huge bonuses, don't you? They say everyone does in the city."

"The bonuses are welcome," I agree, remembering when my boss called me into his office and handed me an envelope and I honestly thought he was giving me my notice. *Don't look so worried*, he'd said. *It's your bonus.* I was stunned at the amount in the letter – five figures – because the firm had had a good year. Bonuses weren't something that happened much in teaching. Working hard suited me. No task was too onerous, no late night too inconvenient, and the work was just demanding enough to keep my brain engaged and silence the ceaseless chatter of my mind.

"I had a bonus this year," says Emily. "Nearly a grand. It was a huge help."

It's five miles to walk to Saundersfoot by the coastal path, so we don't have time for the round trip. After ninety minutes we turn and retrace our route so we're in time to meet the others. We've parked Emily's motorhome in the cliff top car park, and unload a case of beers and the cool box with the picnic lunch to carry down to the beach. We spread out two picnic blankets, and I weight down the corners with pebbles to stop the rugs flipping sand in our faces. We sit side by side sharing coffee from her flask, and scan the expanse of sea. Sam and Delia are rounding the point as they paddle back from the neighbouring bay. Amy and Bill are nowhere in sight.

Emily's restless fingers plait the fringe of the tartan rug and she turns towards me, away from the blustery wind. "Have you ever been married, Laura?"

Without thinking where the conversation might lead, I say, "I was with someone for eighteen years. We never married, but we had a daughter – Ellie. We were too young. I'd hardly done a year of teaching when she was born…" My voice trails off.

Emily's luminous blue eyes study me with renewed interest. Perhaps she thought I was some sort of shrivelled-up old hag. "A daughter, how wonderful! Where is she now?"

I open my mouth to reply, but only a gulping sound comes out as I choke on my coffee. My eyes sting and it feels like I'm peering through a mist, and then a cheerful voice interrupts.

"Shift up." Bill slots himself into the space on the rug between me and Emily. She shoots me a look of irritation, as though guessing she was on the verge of prising out my life story, but Bill's arrival has spared me from sharing painful memories. For now. I'd underestimated the power of a company of strangers: the temptation to share, the urge to reveal secrets. Bill's hopeful but clumsy attempts to break through my defences, to spark a closeness between us, pose a risk. I've been starved of human interaction for so long. If I stay, either Bill or Emily will nudge me into confessional mode – and I don't want that. As soon as we get back to the campsite, I'll pack up and leave this evening...

6

LAURA
SATURDAY

Shock loosens my grip on the duvet, and the frightened girl tweaks it from me and covers her lower face. She's still holding the torn-out page of a notebook with words scrawled on it, her narrow shoulders are hunched, and she draws her knees up to her chin.

"What the hell are you doing in my van?" I demand of this stranger with dirty blonde hair, tumbling down her back just like Ellie. But nothing like Ellie.

She lets the covers slip down and stares at me. Her dark blue eyes have mascara smudges underneath, and the cut on her left cheek looks recent but seems to be scabbing over. She offers me the scrap of paper again.

I brush it out of her hand. Part of me wants to grab her by the shoulders and shake her, but she's so skinny I'm scared she might break.

"What's wrong with you? Can't you speak English?" That's ridiculous, of course, because her note is written in English. Unless someone else wrote it for her.

She nods and puts a finger to her lips like a child playing a game. Does she have learning difficulties? My anxiety soars. She scribbles more words on the back of the paper: *I'm in danger. Help me get away.*

My patience is wearing thin. "If you mean out of the campsite, it's five miles back up the road." To underline my statement, a caravan rattles past us heading in that direction.

She scribbles again. *Out of Wales*, she writes. *To London. Please.* She underlines *London* and *Please*.

"How do you know I'm going to London?" I push past her towards the rear of the van. "I'm going to open this door and you can get out." I fiddle with the catch. It's stiff.

When I glance round I see she's trembling, and her eyes silently beg me. I would be strong enough to drag her out of the van, but she looks frail, as if she hasn't had a proper meal in months. Perhaps she's an addict. What if she starts shooting up in my van?

I remember seeing a Land Rover parked in this layby, and stumble back to the driver's seat in time to see a track-suited woman open her rear car door for a spaniel to jump in. She slams the door, nips round to her driver's seat and reverses out of her space.

As the Land Rover approaches, I wind down my window and call out, "Hey!" waving to attract her attention. She waves back, but doesn't stop, churning up grit and dust, her wheels spinning as she pulls out onto the road.

"If you don't get out, I'm calling the police," I tell the girl, tapping 999 on my mobile's keypad and holding it up to show her I'm serious. If I report seeing a young woman who seemed to be in trouble, they'll send someone to check up on her and I can drive home with a clear conscience. As her dark wide-set eyes plead with me, the fleeting resemblance to my daughter is beyond unsettling. My heart thuds inside my ribcage. When Ellie was in trouble, did she turn to some stranger and ask for help? And did they pass her by?

The girl kneels up, leans her arms on the back of the driver's seat and touches my shoulder lightly. A sinking feeling tells me I can't leave her here – she claims she's in danger. What if I abandon her and she comes to harm?

I twist my head round and scowl. "I'm not happy about this, but if you're determined to get out of Wales, I'll drive you across the border to the first motorway services. When we get there, you either tell me what's going on, or I'll leave you there."

She nods and offers a wan smile.

"Now, come and sit in the passenger seat next to me and put on your seatbelt."

Shaking her head, she shrinks back under the cover of my black-and-white-check duvet. I sigh. I know I shouldn't carry a passenger without a seatbelt. What if we're in an accident? My head aches from thinking through all the permutations that could happen. It's not too late. I could drive back to the campsite and leave her there, but I don't. I sling her a bottle of mineral water and watch her twist off the cap and gulp it without pausing for breath.

I drive on, but the back of my neck prickles. What if she has a knife? If she stabs me in the back, I'll veer into the fast lane and we'll both be killed. But if she has a death wish, would she make this effort to escape?

The thing is, I believe her. She's in trouble, and she's asked me to help her. I can't let her down.

7

LAURA

The sign for the motorway services looms like a beacon of safety. I'm breathing heavily when I pull into the car park and twist round in my seat. My stowaway is sitting up on the bed, leaning against the side of the van. She looks more alert than me.

"I'm stopping here for the loo," I tell her, fishing my purse out of my bag. "You'll have to come with me."

She doesn't move.

"Come on." I urge. I'm desperate for the loo and still she's playing games. "Well, I'm not leaving you in my van," I snap, though my clothes and camping crockery aren't worth stealing.

Our silent battle of wills lasts several minutes, and she wins. "You are a blasted nuisance," I tell her as I drive across to the petrol station on the exit road. I fill up with fuel, then move the van to a parking bay outside the shop so I can keep an eye on it while I pay.

"Could you watch my van for five minutes while I nip to the loo?" I ask the cashier, pointing at it through the window.

He stifles a yawn and looks at me as if he thinks I'm nuts.

I improvise. "Some kids were prowling round it just now."

"Okay, sure."

It's a unisex washroom, and I hold my breath because the strong-smelling disinfectant doesn't quite cover the ammonia stench of men who'd waited too long for a pee. On the way out I buy two coffees from a machine. One is supposed to be cappuccino, the other's a flat white, but they look identical. Back in the van, I give the cappuccino to the girl and sit beside her on the fold-out bed. The cardboard cup is too hot for my hand to hold, but my confused brain doesn't decode the signal, and when I take a sip it scalds my tongue.

"Wait for it to cool down," I warn her. Something about her passivity has turned me into a solicitous mother hen. "This is Leigh Delamere services. We're out of Wales, so you can tell me what the hell you're doing in my campervan."

The sky is pale grey with puffs of cloud, tinted pink by the setting sun. Vehicles whoosh past on the service road with their headlights on. Inside the van it's already dark. The leisure battery is fully charged so I could switch on the internal lights, but perhaps the girl will open up and talk if I can't see her waiflike face.

"What's your name?" I ask.

She hesitates, scrabbles in her shoulder bag, and produces a notebook. As she tears out yet another sheet of paper and hunches her small shoulders preparing to write, I snatch the book from her hand.

"Talk!"

And then it occurs to me that maybe she can't speak. I wait and the silence lengthens.

"Miriana," she says, finally, in a London accent. For some reason I wasn't expecting that.

"And when we get to London, Miriana – if I agree to drive you there – what are your plans?"

She shrugs. "Find a place to stay and a job." She swirls the coffee in her cup and keeps her eyes on that.

"Do you have friends in London? Or family?"

"No."

"Tell me why you're running away. Has someone hurt you?" The cut on her face isn't a knife wound. It's more like a deep scratch, the kind you see on people who've been living rough. "Do you need a hospital or the police?"

"No and no," she replies, but she's noticed me examining her wound and shields it with her hand. She pushes back the duvet covering her legs. She's wearing dark blue skinny jeans and sandals. My eyes have grown accustomed to the dim light, and I notice that her feet are dirty, as if she's walked a long way.

"I'm not hurt," she says, meeting my eyes for the first time. "Just scared. When I get to London I'll be safe."

"How old are you anyway?" She looks about sixteen.

"Eighteen. You needn't worry. I'm not a child."

"Can you prove that?" I ask with a shiver, because it dawns on me that I could be in deep trouble here. Years ago, when I was a student living in a shared flat with no garden, I took my books out to a nearby park to revise. Three young children were playing nearby, and whenever I looked up they were watching me. After a while, they came over to chat, surrounded me, told me their names and their ages: two were eight, one was ten.

"You should be in school," I told them.

"Nah. School's boring."

"Your whole life will be boring if you throw away your education," I warned them pompously.

When I packed away my books they followed me home and asked if they could have a drink. Foolishly, I agreed and left them waiting on the doorstep while I fetched beakers of lemonade and tap water. While I was in the kitchen they must have darted inside, because later I discovered several small items missing from my room: mascara, perfume, and a purse full of small change. They must have split up and worked a room each, because jewellery belonging to my flatmates also went missing. If it had been just my stuff I'd have chalked it up to experience, but my flatmates wanted to make insurance claims. So I reported the sorry incident to the police, who found the culprits easily – the children had told me their real names and ages. When an officer came to update me, he told me the ten-year-old boy was already known to them, and worked on distraction techniques for his older brother. When the police had turned up at his school, the boy's pockets were bulging with stolen car keys. The memory that's stayed with me was the dressing-down I was given by the officer: a grown woman inviting children back to her flat? Did I think that was a good idea? I hadn't invited them, of course, they'd followed me, but it clearly was a bad idea – then and now.

"I'm not a child," Miriana repeats. She rummages in her woven shoulder bag – the sort made in India and sold in street markets across the world – and takes out an envelope. Inside is an official-looking letter. She holds it out to me. "See, this is my National Insurance letter. I take it with me everywhere so I can find a job."

"Where does it show your date of birth?" I ask. It's too dark to read the small print.

"This is the envelope it came in." She jabs her forefinger at the postmark and I see that, even if the card was issued long before her sixteenth birthday, she'd be at least seventeen by now. "Do you believe me now?"

"Do you have a passport?" I ask. A young runaway who's taken the trouble to bring proof of her National Insurance would surely have brought her passport too.

"No," she replies. "I've never travelled abroad. I don't know if I can get one."

This conversation is going nowhere. "Do you have a phone?"

"Yes." She produces a cheap-looking mobile, probably a Pay-As-You-Go.

"Call your parents and tell them where you are. That you're safe."

"I have no parents. Not here. They have left me."

A two-hour journey lies ahead, and I'm tired of riddles and being enticed down roads to nowhere. "There must be someone who needs to know where you are?"

"No. There are people who must **not** know where I am, but no one who needs to know."

"So what are you running away from?"

She flinches and looks away from me. "A man."

I sigh. What a cliché. It's always a man. Perhaps she and I have something in common.

"Why don't you just leave him?" I suggest. "You don't need to run away. What about your job? Were you working?"

"Yes. In a café in Penarth. The Green Kitchen."

"Penarth!" My stomach lurches because Penarth in South Wales was my home too. My family home in the little pebble-dashed house I shared with Gareth – and Ellie.

8

LAURA

I drain my coffee, crumple the cardboard cup in my fist and look around for a bin bag that isn't there because I cleared my rubbish before leaving the campsite. The coffee tasted bitter, but it warmed me and sharpened my thought processes. It didn't boost my energy. If I don't set out soon, I'll be too exhausted to drive to London.

This weariness isn't just from the grinding effort of interrogating Miriana. The time with my singles group, pretending to be upbeat, has drained me. On top of this is the shock of Miriana saying she was living in Penarth, the small seaside town I fled two years ago. Did she attend the school where I taught? But surely I'd have recognised her, or she'd have known me. If she was living in Penarth with a man she wanted to escape from, why did she run west – in the opposite direction from London – and choose my campervan to stowaway in?

I remember meeting Pippa on the campsite. Perhaps Miriana was with that group? Maybe she overheard someone saying I was heading for London and decided to hitch a covert lift. Nothing else makes sense. What harm will it do to drive her to London?

"Come on, sit in the passenger seat. It's almost dark; no one will see you."

To my surprise she agrees, and clambers through the gap between the seats to sit up in front beside me. I'm hot from the coffee so I turn up the air conditioning, but I notice she's shivering. "Don't you have a jacket? Or a sweater?"

She shakes her head. "Nothing."

"Grab a blanket from the back."

She leans over and hauls my duvet onto her lap, pulling it up to her chin and fastening her seatbelt on top like cabin crew tell you to do on a night flight. There's an old-style music system in the van, but I didn't bring any CDs so I turn the radio on low and hum along to the music. When I glance over at Miriana she's asleep.

It's after eleven o'clock when we reach my south London street, and there's nowhere to park. I drive twice around the block, but unless someone has friends round for supper no one's going to move their car until morning.

"Damn." I must have sworn out loud, because Miriana's eyes flicker open and she gazes at me with a rabbit-in-headlights stare. "We're here," I tell her. "There are no bloody parking spaces. I'll drive you to the main road and show you where the night bus goes from."

"Oh." She pulls a face when I mention the bus stop. "Is this your street? Which house?"

"The one with the red front door." Why am I telling her this? What the hell did she expect me to say?

"Okay." She fumbles beneath the folds of duvet, finds her bag and gathers it up.

At the far end of my street, a supermarket delivery van starts its engine and pulls away. Yes! I know they deliver till 11.30 pm, but this is a minor miracle – not just a parking space, but one large enough for a campervan. I can't drive Miriana to the bus stop now. I rev the engine and speed along to claim it. It's too late to unload, so I grab my backpack and a small handbag containing my wallet and keys, plus a shopping bag with food I bought for tomorrow's breakfast. My breakfast-chef rôle became permanent – too bad the others won't have fresh bread or eggs in the morning.

I clamber out of the van while Miriana folds the duvet neatly and leaves it on the seat. She gets out, slams the door, and waits, shivering, under the sallow street lighting, while I lock up. When I turn towards home, she follows a pace behind. I reach my gate, stop, and put down the shopping bag on the mosaic-tiled path while I fish inside my handbag for the keys. The former owner restored the front garden to its original Edwardian glory, and my path has alternating black, white and terracotta tiles, set on the diamond, with a low hedge lining each side. The hedge looks shrivelled and dehydrated after the recent dry spell. I'll water it tomorrow.

Miriana's hand is on the wrought iron gate, swinging it back and forth so my porch light sensor picks up the movement and bathes her in lemony light. I raise my arm to point in the direction of the main road and bus stop, but her haunted expression silences me.

"Come on." I sigh and gesture to her to follow me as I unlock the door and rush inside to punch in the burglar alarm code. "You can stay with me. Just for tonight."

9

LAURA

SUNDAY

I'm moving into a new house and someone is helping me shift furniture around. I smell coffee brewing and inhale deeply, knowing the next scent will be freshly-cut grass as Dave, the campsite manager, drives his ride-on mower around, pimping up vacated pitches. I yawn and stretch my arms above my head, luxuriating in the best night's sleep I've had in years. My bed feels so soft. I pat the mattress with the flat of my hand – it's springy, not hard like the one in my campervan. Then I remember – my minibreak's over and I'm home in my own bed. So who is making the coffee?

Memories of yesterday crowd into my mind, and I remember that girl who stowed away. Miriana. I let her stay here – what was I thinking? My eyelids snap open. I reach for my turquoise bathrobe and shrug it on.

I pad, barefoot, out of my room and notice the guest room door is closed, but the one leading to the kitchen-diner is wide open and there's a cafetiere of freshly-brewed coffee sitting on the countertop. The pot's still warm, so I pour myself a mug and take it to the bathroom. Two days of shivering in chilly cubicles in a communal shower block and I'm desperate to stand under a cascade of hot water, but I should check on my guest first. I splash water on my face and re-knot the belt of my bathrobe.

It's almost nine o' clock, and a wedge of sunshine is pushing under the half-drawn kitchen blind. A bunch of lilies on the windowsill have wilted in their vase, and the water is green with a sulphurous stink. I empty it down the sink and parcel up the dead flowers into the bin. It's rare for me to sleep this late. The holiday did me good in that sense at least.

I pour another mug of coffee and knock on the spare room door. "Miriana?" I call in a tentative voice.

No reply.

I thump louder. I've lived here for two years – first renting, then buying when my landlord decided to sell. No one has ever slept in my guest room before.

"Miriana, open the door."

Still no answer.

I rattle and turn the handle and push. It's stuck. There's no lock – how can that be? Angrier by the minute, I hammer on the door till my fist throbs, and I hear footsteps cross the floor and something heavy being slid across the floorboards. The door opens a crack and Miriana peers out.

"Please wait. One moment." The dragging sound starts again. Slowly the door opens, and I see she's barricaded it with a heavy pine chest of drawers.

"For goodness sake." The door swings open. "What did you do that for?"

"Sorry. I needed to feel safe."

"Safe from me? I didn't leave you out on the street all night." Perhaps I should have done.

She casts her eyes down at the floor. "No. Not you. And thanks."

I sigh. "Come out and have breakfast then."

She's wearing the same t-shirt and skinny jeans she had on

the day before, and has her bag slung over her shoulder. She follows me to the kitchen, and we sit facing each other across the table. Eye contact is hard for both of us, so I fetch the food that should have been breakfast for Bill and the gang, turn the oven on low and put four croissants on a baking tray to warm up. The coffee is lukewarm now so I make a fresh pot. When I put the plate of warm croissants on the table, Miriana grabs one and crams it into her mouth without waiting for jam. Crumbs scatter across the table and she chokes on the last mouthful and coughs, but it doesn't stop her dabbing up flakes with her fingertip and swallowing them.

"When did you last eat?" I ask, gently.

She covers her mouth with her hand until her coughing stops. "Maybe Thursday?"

"But weren't you with those students?" Now I come to think of it, every time I saw them they were drinking, so perhaps they didn't bother with food.

Miriana ignores my question, takes a sip of coffee and reaches for another croissant.

"May I?" Her phrasing sounds quaint, and despite the London accent, I wonder if she's foreign. Her hair is that shade of dark blonde that looks dirty if it isn't washed every day, but I notice dark roots running along her parting so her natural colour must be brunette. Her face has an unnatural pallor. Blonde hair doesn't suit her.

I tear my own croissant into segments and dab apricot jam on each piece. The sun picks up, and my kitchen heats like a glasshouse. If only the weather had been like this in Wales. I raise the blind, but the glare's too strong, so after opening the window I pull the blind back down.

"It's so peaceful here." It's the first thing Miriana's said without being prompted. Up to now every word has been a painfully-extracted answer to a question. Is my street peaceful?

I've never thought about it, but it's Sunday morning, so there are few lorries and my flat's in a leafy residential road near the common and far enough from the roar of traffic on the main road. In summer, the cloud of pollution drifts this way and you can taste and smell exhaust fumes.

"Where in London are we?" Miriana asks. "Is it the part they call south of the river?"

"This is Streatham. Do you know London?"

"Yes. I was born not far from here. In Croydon."

Her admission takes me by surprise. I'd assumed she might be from another part of Europe, perhaps Poland or Romania.

"That's good." I use my brisk former-teacher's voice. "Croydon's a short bus ride from here. It'll be easy for you to get home."

Miriana examines her flaking purple nail varnish and picks off some more. "I'm never going back there, Laura."

I stare at her, confused.

"How did you know my name was Laura?"

10

LAURA

Miriana twists her shoulder bag strap around her fingers, tugging it until her fingertips turn waxy-white.

"I asked how you know my name is Laura."

"Perhaps I read it from the name plate by your doorbell?"

She can tell from my expression that I don't buy that. My doorbell says: *L. Lister*.

"Or on a letter?"

"Hmm." When I came in last night, I picked up the small pile of mail and put it on my radiator shelf. I suppose she could have read my name on an envelope. She'll be on her way soon and I can forget about it.

"Do you want a shower before you go?"

She looks sullen, but nods.

Why should I let this stranger make me feel bad in my own home?

"I'll find you something to wear. You can put your clothes in the washing machine with my holiday stuff." In my bedroom I find a blue t-shirt and a pair of cut-offs I bought in a sale but have never worn. Miriana's petite and skinny, but I've lost more than a stone and dropped two jeans sizes so these should fit her.

"Thank you." She accepts the clothes and the fluffy white towel and opens the bathroom door a few inches to drop her clothes in the hall.

I tip my backpack contents onto the kitchen floor, and sand spills out with my laundry. After loading the washing machine I lean back in a chair, watching the water swirl. It's not my fault she chose my campervan to stow away in, and I've more than met my part of the bargain by driving her to London. But it bothers me how she knows my name, because I'm certain I didn't tell her.

The scent of my favourite Moroccan Rose shower gel precedes Miriana into the room. The cut-offs look great on her. She's draped a towel around her shoulders and her hair is dripping, but she refuses my offer of a hairdryer.

"Tell me your plans. If you're not heading back to Croydon, where will you go?"

She produces a wide-toothed comb from her bag and drags it through her damp hair, gritting her teeth against knots and tangles. With her damp hair scraped back she looks much younger than eighteen.

"There's not much to tell. I'll find a job and somewhere to live."

"Do you have money for a deposit on a flat?" I ask, though the voice in my head nags me not to get involved.

"I have money, but not enough for a flat. I'll look for a room in a hostel." She takes a worn leather wallet out of her bag, opens it and counts out some twenty- and ten-pound notes on the table. There looks to be over a hundred pounds. "I have this, too," she says, showing me a plastic card, "but I can't use it because it's linked to his account." She bends the credit card until it snaps, then folds each piece again and drops the sharp-edged postage stamp-sized fragments into her bag.

It's not for me to ask if that was wise. If she has waitressing experience she should find a job easily.

I've figured out how she knows my name. I'd introduced myself to Pippa. "You were with those students on the camp site, weren't you?"

"I told you," she says, stiffening. "I'm not a student. I'm eighteen years old, I was working in a café, and," she sounds as if she's speaking from a memorised script, "I was living with a man, who let me go out to work but was always watching me."

Inside my head, alarm bells sound. When I was a teacher, a teenager making an announcement like this would have galvanised me into action: police, social services, the works. But Miriana's not my responsibility and claims she's eighteen, so who she lives with must be her own decision.

"Did he harm you, this man?"

"No. He was my protector."

"How do you mean, 'protector'? Don't you mean boyfriend?"

She shakes her head vigorously; her hair's not yet dry and a fine spray of droplets mists the air. "No. It wasn't like that. Many people took advantage of me, for sure. But not him. He helped me."

My head spins with the effort of comprehending her. "Last night you told me you had to get away from a man. You were so scared that you hid until we were out of Wales, yet you say you were living in Penarth, you wanted to go to London, but you ended up further west in Tenby. I don't get it."

Miriana gapes at me as if I'm simple. "What if he was watching me? I sometimes thought he asked someone to watch me while he was at work, because he used to message me and say *Miriana, I know you're in Tesco, get me some cigarettes*. He'd guess I was going to London, so I left while he was at work and travelled in the opposite direction, to a place where he'd never think of looking. I hoped to find someone to help me, and I found you."

Her hair is almost dry, and the darker layer, beneath the blonde, gives her face more definition. Colour has returned to her cheeks, and apart from the scab, which is slowly healing, her complexion is perfect. The sun has moved round to the back of the house, so I open the door to my patio garden. The air's so still I can hear a blackbird singing high up in a neighbour's tree.

"Let's sit outside." I open the storage chest and take out striped cushions for the garden chairs and the rope I use as a washing line. "Bring the washing out, and then you can tell me the rest of your story. I'll try to understand."

While I'm erecting my blue sun parasol Miriana pegs clothes on the makeshift line. When she's finished, she moves a chair out of the shade into the sun and sits down. "It's a long story," she says. "Too long for a girl who must soon be moving on." She bends to loosen the straps of her sandals and kicks them off. "If I tell you my story – the whole truth – will you let me stay for a while? You make me feel safe."

I shiver. Not because my chair is in the shade, but because her offer to trade her story for safety brings the legend of Scheherazade to my mind. For a thousand and one nights Scheherazade fended off her execution by telling fascinating stories to her husband King Shahryar, and ending at dawn on a cliffhanger. Is Miriana really in danger, or is she playing me? I used to be a good judge of character, but no longer. Her story had better be good.

"I'll have to think about it."

"I trust you, Laura, so I'll tell you." She leans forward in her seat and clasps her hands together. "My story begins a long time ago, during the war in the Balkans. Perhaps you remember it?

Most people in this country have forgotten because wars in Iraq, Afghanistan and Syria have wiped it from their memories."

"I remember," I say. "Though I was a child at the time."

Sunlight picks up natural blonde highlights along with the bleached ones in Miriana's hair, and her voice drops to a whisper. "A long time ago, many years before I was born, my parents came to this country as refugees..."

11

MIRIANA

ONE YEAR EARLIER

Miriana stared up at the grey walls of the Croydon tower block where she lived with her parents. The open windows seemed to be winking like sightless eyes as the sun caught the glass at different angles. It was a humid windless day, and the air was stagnant and thick with traffic fumes. Music poured out of the flats: drum and bass, rap – pumping, grinding and booming. She pushed the heavy door and went inside. The lift was out of order. A battered pram stood, abandoned, fastened to the stair railings with a flimsy bicycle chain – as if that would stop anyone who wanted to steal it. She adjusted the straps of her school bag so it sat flat across her back and clattered up the concrete stairs, pausing on the fourth- and seventh-floor landings to catch her breath. On the tenth floor, she turned along the communal balcony and let herself in with her key.

The blare of afternoon TV greeted her: one of those endless quiz programmes her mother watched, though her grasp of English wasn't good enough to follow it. Above the TV noise, Miriana heard sniffing and wailing like an injured animal. She went into the empty sitting room, and through the open door to the kitchen she could see her mother, standing by the sink and sobbing.

"Mum, what is it?" Miriana dropped her bag by the sofa and crossed the room in three paces. Her mother turned; her hands were bleeding, and the sink was full of broken glass.

"Miriana!" Her mother's eyes were red and swollen.

"How did this happen, Mum?" Miriana collected the glass from the sink and put it in the bin. Her mother seemed in some kind of daze. After checking there were no glass splinters in the wound, Miriana pulled sheets of paper towel off a roll and pressed on it until the bleeding stopped. The cuts weren't as bad as they'd seemed.

"A letter came." Her mother shook her head and dabbed her eyes with paper towel.

"Speak English, Mum. What letter?"

Her mother picked up a brown envelope that was lying on the counter top – the edge was jagged where it had been ripped open roughly – and held it out to Miriana. "That letter. I couldn't read it. Your father figured some of it out, then took it next door and Mr Brian read it out to him."

"You should have waited for me to read it. Why did you bother Mr Brian?" Brian Simpson, their eighty-five-year-old neighbour, was in poor health, but he never minded helping her father with official forms.

The envelope was empty. "Where's the letter, anyway?"

"Your father's taken it. When he came back he was so angry he took a drink and smashed his glass in the sink. Then he went out. Mr Brian told him there was an advice centre at the library, and he should go there to ask what he must do."

Miriana's heart galloped, remembering the last time her father was angry. It was when the factory where he'd worked for seven years suddenly laid him off. He found casual work, but it didn't fill his time and he wasn't built for a life of idleness.

Before he was made redundant, he rarely drank alcohol. Now Miriana often saw him drinking beer or raki – sometimes both – and stomping around the flat smashing things: a framed photograph of the stooped grandmother Miriana had never met, dressed in black and looking like an angry crow; a miniature bust of Mother Teresa; and a lantern that held candles and was her mother's favourite ornament. Often he shouted at Miriana and his wife. Late at night, strangers came to their flat. Men he called friends, who Miriana had never seen before. Those evenings always ended in raised voices and more arguing.

"Come and sit down." Miriana led her mother into the sitting room and perched beside her on the sofa. "This letter – was it something bad? Tell me."

Her mother stopped crying. She looked solemn. "Very bad. The letter was from the immigration people. It said we don't have a right to stay here any longer. We have to leave the country. If we don't leave, we might be sent to a detention centre and then de... de... something."

"Deported," said Miriana. Something knotted inside her stomach. She remembered a boy called Kamal, who was at her school for a while. He didn't speak much English, but was an ace goalkeeper everyone wanted on their team and was quickly accepted. Kamal learned to swear in English and he was getting good grades. His family had hoped to rebuild their lives in Croydon, but out of the blue they were told there'd been a 'safe country review' and it was now fine for them to return to their home country. The whole school held a protest. Photographers from the local newspaper turned up and took pictures of students outside the school gates holding placards. Miriana's said *Justice for Kamal*. Parents wrote letters to their MPs protesting about Kamal's family's safety and their son's right to finish his education. No one listened. Soon after, Kamal stopped coming to school and Miriana heard rumours that 'they' had come for him in the night. Who were 'they'? she wondered. And would 'they' now come for her family, too?

"That can't be right, Mum," said Miriana. "Remember when Kamal from my school had to leave? His family had only been here two years, but Dad told me you came to England in 1998."

Her father often told her the story of how Britain had opened its borders to save refugees fleeing conflict in Kosovo. "Britain had great compassion," he'd said, and whenever the former prime minister, Tony Blair, appeared on TV her father would tell her, "That man is a true hero." If ever he heard one of Blair's opponents calling him a war criminal, he'd hurl his slipper at the TV screen. "Why do they say that? What an opportunity he gave to our family. I, myself, am working three jobs and your mother is working two. One day we'll save enough money to buy our own flat. And you, my Miriana, will go to university and become a doctor. I am sure of it."

"Perhaps not a doctor, Dad," Miriana had replied. Her grades in Maths, Chemistry and Biology were stuck stubbornly at C.

"How can they make us go to another country, Mum? I was born here. That means I'm from here, yeah?"

Her mother caught her in a fierce hug. "You were, my precious. In the Mayday Hospital, and you've never travelled anywhere outside England."

Miriana got to her feet and grabbed the remote to turn down the TV volume. She had a History test tomorrow, but any hope of a quiet evening to revise was gone. "I'll make a start on supper. What are we having?"

"Oh. I haven't been to the shop. I was too upset."

"Aren't you going to work?" Miriana's mother was a care worker, and every evening she visited two elderly clients to dole out their tablets and put them to bed.

Her mother clapped one hand over her mouth. "Yes, I must go. Mrs Kennedy relies on me. And Mr Bannon, too. But I can't go like this. How can I?"

"Okay. I'll go for you."

Later that evening, when her father came home, Miriana smelled whisky on his breath, but he seemed upbeat. The adviser at the library had put him in touch with a firm of specialist immigration solicitors.

"Come here, Daughter." He frowned so his thick black eyebrows knitted together. "Has your mother told you about this injustice?"

She nodded. "Yes, Dad."

"We'll fight it." He pulled back his shoulders like a soldier heading into battle, and his chest puffed out. "Now we have a lawyer we'll win, I'm sure."

His confidence transmitted to her mother, and when Miriana returned from putting Mr Bannon to bed (an hour-long session for which her mother would be paid for fifteen minutes) her parents were sitting on the sofa watching TV.

In the weeks that followed, Miriana's father was buoyed by their solicitor's confidence. When he came home from the first meeting with reams of forms to fill in, he took out a battered red tin of documents that he kept locked with a key and set it on the coffee table. Miriana sat beside him and watched him rummage through the contents.

"The lawyer needs all our papers, Miriana," he told her. "But your mother and I have none except what we've been given here. Everything was lost when we left our country. Only you have papers. See – here is your birth certificate." He held it up to show her.

"Can I look at it properly, Dad?"

"Sure." He handed it to her and returned to his sifting of what looked like mostly bank statements. Miriana took a photo of her birth certificate on her phone. Two days earlier, a letter giving her National Insurance number had arrived in the post and was waiting for her when she got home from school. Her parents were out at work, so she hadn't mentioned it to them. School friends with birthdays earlier in the year had already received theirs, and some had gone straight out and found Saturday jobs. You didn't even have to apply for it, her friend Jade had told her. The number found you.

Miriana was convinced this would be her passport into work, but the timing of its arrival taunted her. What if they had to leave England? She knew she'd never be a doctor, but maybe she could be a veterinary nurse. She loved animals, and had been feeding the neighbours' cats and walking small dogs since she was twelve. She slipped the card into a zipped compartment of her backpack and never mentioned it to her parents.

The solicitor took charge of their appeal process, but he didn't keep them updated. Miriana's father wasn't comfortable speaking English on the phone, so he'd head to the law firm's office in Southall, a long journey by train and underground, only to find a different team member had taken over their case. He turned up without making an appointment and no one was ever free to talk to him, so they fended off his questions with booklets about processes, written in formal language he couldn't understand. He brought the leaflets home and gave them to Miriana. "What does this one say, Daughter?"

Miriana scowled as she studied the latest leaflet, and kept her head turned away from her father so he wouldn't notice she'd been experimenting with gold eyeshadow and had three coats of mascara on her lashes. "I need time to study it," she said, and took it into her room. She closed the door, inserted earbuds and turned up the volume on her favourite singer, Dua Lipa.

The booklet was written in simple language and she understood all the words, but the concept of immigration law was alien to her. She read it for a second time. It was so hard to grasp why her parents were being asked to leave when they'd lived here more than twenty years. There was one section about children born in the UK. She studied it extra-closely, but there were so many conditions: where your parents came from, whether you'd lived in England and not left to live elsewhere for more than ninety days in your first ten years. Many different rules might apply.

She headed back towards the sitting room. Her mother was in the kitchen making coffee, and her father was shouting at her to hurry up. He was standing up, eyes trained on the kitchen door, shoulders hunched, and rocking on the balls of his feet.

"Dad," she called out to him.

He spun round and stared at her like a tiger preparing to pounce. "What?"

"Did the lawyer say anything about me? Because I was born here. I think I have a right to stay." She held out the booklet, pointing her finger at the relevant section. "But we would need to apply."

Her father, a short thickset man, seemed to grow taller. He loomed over her, fixing Miriana with furious dark eyes, and raised his hand as if to hit her. She took a step back. His hand dropped to his side.

"Nothing," he shouted. "He said nothing about you. Don't ask me again."

The immigration process rumbled on. The law firm said it could take a year, to be patient and wait. Then, suddenly, they heard it was due to be decided in the next month. Her father paced the room, pausing to pick up the plaster bust of Mother Teresa he'd smashed, now stuck back together with Superglue, and passed it from hand to hand like a stress ball.

"Once I loved this country. Now I hate it. So many taxes paid, working so hard it feels like my back will break. What does this government care? Come here, my Miriana."

She dawdled towards him. He'd been so unpredictable lately that she never knew if he was going to hit her or caress her, but he wrapped his arms around her and pulled her so close she could hear his heartbeat and smell stale tobacco on his pullover.

"You're suffocating me, Dad."

"Sorry." He released her and a sob escaped his lips. "If they don't want us in this country, we'll leave. We'll go with our heads held high. We won't wait for the appeal."

Once again, Miriana felt that knot of panic hovering between her chest and her stomach. "Where will we go?"

"Back home. To Tirana."

"Is that in Kosovo?"

Her father shook his head. "No, Daughter. We're not from Kosovo. We're from Albania. And that's why they are making us leave."

"I don't want to go to Albania!" She struggled to suppress a wail. Her head felt like it might explode with rage and fear and grief. "Why must we?"

Her mother was out putting Mr Bannon to bed. Her father took her hand and led her into the sitting room. "Sit."

He sat down so heavily on the leather sofa that it made the farting noise she used to laugh at as a child, but today neither of them laughed. He hung his head and patted the seat beside him. Miriana noticed how his receding hairline exposed his large brow and gave him the look of an intellectual. Perhaps, if he'd been born in different times, under a different star or another regime, he might have had the opportunity to study. Lately his face had settled into a permanent scowl and he picked arguments without provocation.

"It was my fault." He spoke quietly in a mix of English and his native language. "In the late 1990s, when the UK opened its borders to refugees, fleeing for their lives, we saw it as an opportunity. Your mother and I aren't from Kosovo, we're from a village near Kukës in the north of Albania. Back then, our country was in chaos. Our communist dictator was long gone. Under Hoxha, people had lived in terror but they always had work, but after the economy collapsed there was no work, and the only food we could get was what we grew for ourselves. Many people lost their life savings."

Miriana shifted on her chair. This was sounding like a history lesson. "Speak English, Dad. I can't understand you."

He sighed and switched into English. "Your mother and I were sweethearts at school. When we finished our studies we moved from our village to Tirana, but we couldn't find work. Friends told us they were leaving for England, so we decided to come too."

"But that was for Kosovans escaping persecution, Dad."

"Exactly. But how would people in England know any difference? We all threw away our papers and joined the exodus. When we arrived in England we told officials we were fleeing ethnic cleansing and violence. They believed us at the time, but—"

"You broke the law!" Miriana was shocked and impressed.

"To save our lives – and yours, although you weren't born until many years later. People here welcomed us. We were treated well, given a place to live and a small allowance. As more people in our country heard about it and wanted to come, the controls got tougher. But we were in the first phase, so we were allowed to find work and encouraged to settle. A few years later I was given an indefinite right to remain."

"Why did we never go back there to visit?" Miriana asked.

Her father stared down at the floor and mumbled, "It was to protect ourselves and the life we had built over here. We didn't want to risk crossing borders."

"I don't get it." Miriana felt her face growing hot, as ugly thoughts and anger at her father swirled inside her. "If we've been here so long and you were given a right to stay, why are they telling us to leave?"

"Sometimes they investigate. We knew there was a risk, so for all these years we've kept separate from the Albanian and Kosovan communities to stay safe," he said. "Some years ago a newspaper investigated fake asylum seekers, and many people were hounded out. A few months back I began meeting up with some old friends."

"Were those the men who came to the flat, Dad?"

He nodded. "I think someone betrayed me to the authorities."

Miriana thought of the photographs she'd been shown of an old woman, who, she was told, was her grandmother and lived in another country, but she'd never thought to question why they didn't visit. Since finishing primary school, none of Miriana's school friends had ever seen her parents. Her mother worked evening jobs, so her friends had forgotten her halting command of English. Miriana used to beg her mother to come to school parents' evenings, but she always refused, saying she had to work. She secretly suspected her mum found the teachers intimidating.

Now, though, she was glad her parents had kept a low

profile. She dyed her hair blonde and spoke with her natural south London accent, and if anyone asked her where she was from, she always said Croydon.

12

LAURA

SUNDAY

The sun has dipped and is scorching my right cheek, so I adjust the angle of the umbrella while trying not to interrupt Miriana's storytelling. It's intense yet impersonal, as if she were looking back on a girl she once knew and narrating that other girl's experiences. Her descriptions feel so real I could be there, in the Croydon flat, as Miriana's father goes to war with faceless authorities and bottles his anger until it explodes and alienates his daughter. I empathise with her mother, seeing everything she's worked for slipping from her grasp. Their lives came to a halt, and their only route forward was to go backwards to a home country where they'd severed their ties.

"So you see," says Miriana, "I couldn't go with them. Albania is nothing to me. I couldn't even find it on a map."

"But your mother!" Empathy tugs on my maternal heart strings. "How could she survive without you?"

Miriana hangs her head while her hands frantically twist a strand of hair around her forefinger. "She pleaded with me to accept it. I don't think she realised I'd run away, but my father was already changing. When I stood up to him, he reminded me I wasn't British and yelled that nobody here wanted me.

Albanian girls and women must know their place, and when I was back in their country I'd have to obey him."

"But you were born and educated here, so that would be impossible."

"Exactly. When I was a child, he used to tell me about a place he called the 'old country'. He never said it was Albania – to me it was a nameless place beyond the seas. I took for granted we all came from Croydon."

"What were his stories about?"

"Many of them were about faith and shame from the olden days' culture. In parts of Albania, like the north where my parents were born, the old traditions run deep."

"D'you mean honour?" I ask. I'd heard something similar at a teachers' training day about welfare of pupils from overseas. The school where I taught had a mix of nationalities, and some were refugees or asylum seekers. The course tutor had explained cultural practices, and told us to be alert for signs girls were about to be shipped off for arranged marriages.

Miriana nods. "Dad's stories came back to me and gave me nightmares, so I searched the Internet and read about an ancient code of law from the fifteenth century. There were two types of honour, and if someone loses it the shame sticks to the whole family. It can never be forgiven..."

She lifts her solemn eyes to look at me. "One story was about a girl who had a secret boyfriend and was killed by her family because of shame."

"But how could shame attach to you? You haven't been living there."

Miriana scratches the cut on her face until the scab opens up and bleeds. I pull her hand away from her face. There's blood under her fingernails.

"Don't do that, Miriana. It'll get infected. I'll get you some cream." I go into the kitchen and rummage in a drawer to find my first aid kit. While I'm there I boil the kettle and pour some water into a bowl and take it outside with a clean flannel. "Bathe the cut first." I slide the bowl across the table towards her and hand her a wad of tissues.

"Thanks." Her gratitude for the smallest kindness overwhelms me.

"You were telling me about your dad," I prompt.

She presses the tissues to her wound and winces, but the bleeding soon stops. "Oh yeah. He fretted that my western ways and lack of deference would lead to trouble when we were back there, so he tried to retrain me as if I were a dog. If he noticed me wearing shorts to go out, he'd send me back to my room to change. If I used makeup, he said I looked like a slut. I took no notice." She pushes her hair back from her face. "Then, one evening when I was meeting friends, he blocked my way to the front door, grabbed the strap of my bag and yanked it off my shoulder." Her voice trails off, and she's visibly upset. "When he searched my bag he found a half-bottle of vodka, so he slapped me and locked me in my bedroom."

"No!" I've been holding my breath so long it hurts to exhale. I know as well as most parents how challenging teenagers can be. Most families navigate tricky adolescent years, battle-scarred, and make an uneasy truce to propel their kids to the safe shores of adulthood.

Most families, but not mine. Because Ellie played us. She kept silent, so everything we thought we knew about her teenage life turned out to be false. When our lives imploded, it was too late – Gareth and I were left thrashing around, not knowing the truth and totally ill-equipped to deal with the fallout.

Tears glimmer in Miriana's eyes, and she rubs them away with the blood-smeared tissue. "My father's violence shocked me. He never once slapped me when I was young. I thought he doted on me..."

My chest feels tight. I lay a hand on her arm to comfort her.

"So you see why I couldn't go to Albania with them. Better to take my chances here."

"Weren't you forced to leave with your parents if they lost their permission to stay here?" I ask. "How old were you?"

Again she ignores my question about her age.

"My father didn't wait for the appeal," she says, with a shrug. "He was so angry at how Britain was treating him, he told his caseworker he'd make his own arrangements to leave voluntarily. He contacted the Albanian embassy to organise travel documents, and when he came home he boasted that he'd proved he had plenty of savings and they'd promised we'd get our papers soon. Everything happened so fast. My parents emptied our flat and sold everything apart from our clothes. Mum was excited when she realised their savings would buy a house back there. In Croydon it wasn't even enough for a deposit on a flat."

"What did your friends say?"

She rolls her eyes. "I didn't tell anyone. Except Jamie."

"Who's Jamie?"

"My boyfriend." She pauses, as if to see how I'm taking this, then adds, "My **secret** boyfriend."

Finally, everything she's been saying about her father's strict attitude makes sense.

"Jamie said I could stay at his. I got on well with his mum, Frankie, and it was cool with her. Every day I packed a few clothes and other stuff into carrier bags, and he took them to his mum's flat. If my dad had suspected I was seeing a boy, he would have killed me right then and there."

"But if you ran away, your parents must have searched for you."

Miriana shrugs her shoulders. "I didn't think so. My father made it clear I was a burden to their new life. If I'd left home too soon, he might have asked for police help to search for me. But I knew if I waited until the day they were leaving, he wouldn't waste the cost of their tickets."

"But your mother must have cared," I protest, upset on behalf of this woman I've never met.

"She was caught between us. She used to tell me he'd calm down once we were back over there. *There are universities in Albania*, she said. *You can continue your studies*. But I couldn't see my father allowing it.

"On our last day, Mum and I went shopping to buy gifts for their family, and she took me for lunch in a French brasserie – the smartest restaurant I'd ever been in. Before we only ever went to McDonald's." She lifts her head, and her eyes lock onto mine. "I couldn't keep my secret inside." She places her palm on her chest, close to her heart. "I told her my plan to run away."

I gasp. "That was bold. How did she react?"

Miriana sniffs, and tears well up in her eyes. "Mum didn't try very hard to stop me. I think she'd secretly guessed, but I didn't tell her where I'd be staying in case she weakened and told Dad. She agreed to cover for me. *Promise me you'll come to us if you change your mind, darling,* she said, and gave me a piece of paper with her parents' address on."

"So your escape had her blessing?"

Miriana nods. "I crept out of the flat at four o'clock in the morning and went to Jamie's. His block was close by. A few hours later, he and I sat on his balcony and watched my parents leave on foot, wheeling big suitcases along the pavement to East Croydon station to catch the train to Gatwick Airport. Dad wouldn't even spend on a taxi. Poor Mum was struggling, lagging behind and looking around, perhaps hoping I'd change my mind. My father left his cases and went back for her. He caught hold of her arm and dragged her forward, faster than she could walk. When I saw her stumble, I cried. That's my last memory of her."

Her restless fingers tear the tissues into shreds. "So you see, Laura, when I told you I didn't have any family, I was telling the truth. My family left me."

How could any family leave their precious daughter behind? Why didn't the authorities question Miriana's whereabouts?

But why would they? It sounds like it wasn't a deportation or an administrative removal, if her family had agreed to leave voluntarily and organised their own travel documents and air tickets. I doubt there's record-keeping for that, because when it works in reverse, people come here on tourist visas, look for work in the black economy and fall off the radar.

"What about Jamie's family?"

Meeting Miriana's gaze is like looking into the eyes of an old soul. "In Croydon, kids moved around all the time," she says. "Taking in other people's kids was normal. Girls who couldn't get on with their parents went to live with grandparents; boys moved in with their pregnant girlfriends' families, and others just dossed wherever they could find a bed."

"You mean like sofa-surfing?"

"What?"

I blush. Stupid of me to use a middle-class idea. What Miriana's describing I'd seen in my own school, with grandparents stepping in to head off family breakdown, because in my part of South Wales people didn't travel so far from their roots.

"So how did you get on? Were you safe at Jamie's?"

"I thought I was. Jamie and his mum were fine with it. Then his brother Liam came out of jail, and everything changed…"

13

LAURA

SUNDAY

Miriana gets up from her chair and strolls indoors, her sandals slip-slapping on the patio. Guessing she's gone to the loo, I lean back in my seat and stretch my eyelids to keep my eyes from closing. The sun beats down and even my sun-hardened geraniums are turning brown, so I get up and dead-head a few, then find the watering can and plunge it into the water butt which collects the rain from the gutter. My skin feels itchy as I give the plants a quick soaking. I remember I haven't showered yet, but if I'm going to catch the supermarket there's no time. Before I left for Wales I emptied my fridge and chucked away pre-washed salad liquefying in its cellophane bag, manky tomatoes, and yoghurts lurking beyond their sell-by dates. There are times when I ask myself why I bother going to the supermarket just to create food waste for landfill, but I have a guest and it's my duty to feed her.

Miriana nudges the door open with her shoulder. She's carrying two tumblers of water. As she sets them down on the table, I notice she's gripping something else in one hand.

"Who's this?" she asks holding out a silver-framed photograph. "She looks a bit like me."

I don't need to look at the picture to know it's Ellie – the one taken on holiday in France when she was fifteen. She's on the beach, wearing a white bikini, her skin bronzed, a touch of pink in her cheeks and freckles on the bridge of her nose. It's a happy photo. The only one I can bear to look at. All the others I tore to shreds and burned or threw away.

"It's Ellie. My daughter." I steel myself for her to ask: *Where is she? Why doesn't she live here with you?*

"Oh," she says, and hands the photo back. I put it on the table. Face down.

"I must go to the supermarket," I tell Miriana. "Come with me."

She shrinks back and shakes her head. "I can't go out. Sorry."

"What do you mean? We're not in Wales now." These drama-queen antics are making me snap at her. "You can't still be hiding from that man?"

"Not him. Another man."

"Miriana – you're being ridiculous." I plonk down my glass and it clinks on the metal table. Is she a fantasist who thinks every man in the country is on her trail?

Miriana dips her head – her old trick to make her hair shield her face. "This place is so near Croydon. Jamie might see me. Or his brother."

"It's hardly close," I protest. "At least five miles."

"But the main road through here leads to Croydon. I remember Jamie's brother Liam driving here in his black BMW. When I left, he was extending his territory. What if he now controls this area too?"

"Controls?" The meaning of her words sinks in. "Are you saying what I think you're saying? That Jamie's brother's involved in drugs?"

She nods. "That's why he was in prison."

What new trouble have I brought to my door?

"Stay here if you must. I have to go shopping." I slam the door behind me. There isn't time to walk to the supermarket, so I drive the campervan and break out in a sweat trying to park in a regular-sized space. Half an hour later, when I emerge with my shopping, an angry man stomps towards me.

"Is this yours, Miss?" He points to my van, and I realise he's not been able to open the door of the Honda in the space next to mine.

"Sorry."

His expletives ring in my ears as I climb into my van from the passenger side. When I've got the engine running, I wind down my window and tell him to fuck off.

At home I carry the bags through to the kitchen. Miriana has brought the dry washing in from the garden and folded it in a neat pile on a chair. There's no sign of her outside, so she must be in her room. I'll let her know I'm back and ask what she'd like for supper. Her sad family story is still looping in my mind. Her parents made a false declaration to enter the UK – I get that – but, after years of paying taxes and contributing to society, it seems barbaric they were forced to leave.

The guest room door is shut, and I hesitate. Has she barricaded herself in again? But it's not her room; this is my flat, my guest room. As I raise my hand to knock, I hear what sounds like a radio. Perhaps she took the one from the kitchen to keep her company. I bend close and in the split second before my knuckles connect with the door, I realise it's not the radio. Miriana's voice is raised and I can make out every word.

"I told you," Miriana is saying, in an angry tone. "Write it down... No, I'm not going to text it to you. It's 25 Balmer Road, Streatham. I don't know the postcode."

Rage engulfs me. How dare she recite my address to some stranger! As I push the door, my head feels about to explode.

This time there's no chest of drawers blocking it, so I burst into the room.

Miriana turns towards me, colour draining from her face. She flinches, taps her mobile screen and ends the call. Her hand drops to her side and she lowers her head, just as my students used to do when expecting a telling-off.

"Who the hell were you talking to?" I yell. "Giving my address to some drug dealer? Is that it?" I can't believe it. An hour ago she was claiming to be too terrified of Jamie's brother to go out to the supermarket; now she's telling someone where she's staying and inviting him to come here.

Why did I help her? My instinct warned me not to trust her, but even as I think those thoughts, I know it's because she reminds me of Ellie – and when my daughter was in trouble, I wasn't there to help her.

"I... err... haven't, I wasn't... I mean it wasn't him," she stutters.

"Tell me who it was, then." I make a grab for her phone and try to wrest it from her, but her reactions are quicker than mine. She thrusts it into the pocket of her cut-offs – my cut-offs – and keeps her hand over it. I grab her by the shoulders and shake her so hard her head judders on her frail neck. I know I shouldn't do this. It's a form of assault, but my anger spills over and comes again in waves.

"Laura, stop – you're hurting me."

I let my hands drop and take a step back. She rubs her neck. I don't say sorry.

"Right," I say. "Are you going to tell me or not?"

"I c-can't," she stammers in a quiet voice. "I'm sorry."

The room is stuffy and unbearably hot. I stride across to the window, flick the catch and slide it open, thinking how easily an intruder could climb in. Many of my neighbours have fancy window grilles, but I couldn't bear to be trapped behind bars. I have my burglar alarm, but that's all. A chorus of birdsong reaches me from the garden, and I yearn to be outdoors because my flat no longer feels like a sanctuary.

"Is there one single thing you've told me that isn't a lie?" I yell. "There was no man in Wales, was there? You were just looking for some sucker to give you a ride back to London."

It's obvious to me now. She must have been a courier working for Jamie's brother, taking drugs down from London to Wales. Perhaps she was delivering to Pippa and her friends on the campsite for their post-exam partying. They had weed – Pippa offered me a drag on her spliff. I've read how easy it is for youngsters to get supplies from the dark web or a simple phone call. Kids much younger than Miriana are sent to prowl around university campuses and hand out business cards with dealers' numbers on them. I've heard drugs can be delivered to a university hall of residence faster than a takeaway pizza – and if university students can get supplies, so can vulnerable schoolkids. When I taught at Llewellyn High, staff had to exercise constant vigilance to keep drugs off the premises.

"You were the courier, weren't you?" I say, quietly. "And Jamie or his brother, or whoever, sent you to deliver drugs to those students on the campsite."

"No." She shakes her head emphatically so her hair spins across her face. "It wasn't like that. When Liam tried to force me to be his courier I ran away."

Running away seems to be Miriana's answer to everything.

"I don't believe you."

Miriana hangs her head. "Laura, please..."

But I'm no longer prepared to listen. All the energy I've invested in my young guest has ebbed away. I feel used. The sight of her shoulder bag lying on a chair, along with the clothes I washed for her, enrages me. I gather them up and try cramming them into her too-small bag.

"What are you doing?" Miriana asks in a small voice.

"You're leaving. I won't have you in my home any longer. And you can tell your drug-dealer mates I'll be alerting the police in case they're thinking of turning up at my door."

I doubt I'll ring the police. I just want this to be over.

"Please, Laura. I want to explain but I can't." She hangs her head.

I lay my hand on her shoulder and swivel her around to face the door. "Have you left anything in the kitchen?"

"N – no."

"You've got your money?"

She swallows and nods. I frogmarch her along the hall and she doesn't resist. I open the front door. As she hovers, trembling, on the step, I remember all the groceries I bought at the supermarket. Enough to feed two people for several days. Why didn't I just do a circuit of the supermarket, picking up cans, and put them straight into the foodbank crate?

"Wait." I jog back down to the kitchen, empty one of the carrier bags and repack it with crisps, biscuits, croissants – Miriana seemed to like those – a sealed pack of Cheddar cheese, a couple of cans of Coke. Not the sort of food I normally eat – I bought it for her. I take the bag to Miriana and push it roughly into her hands. "Make sure you eat something," I tell her, in a gruff voice. "Good luck. Try to stay out of trouble."

She nods and accepts it from me without looking inside. I follow her to the gate and watch her trudge along the street, round-shouldered, head down. At the corner, she turns and looks back. I dodge behind the hedge but she's seen me watching and lifts her hand to wave.

"That's it." I slam the front door so the stained-glass panel rattles. I'll never see her again.

A shiver creeps over me and I feel cold, then clammy. Who the hell did she give my address to?

14

LAURA

SUNDAY/MONDAY

Alone in the kitchen, I rummage through my shopping bags and find the giant bar of fruit and nut chocolate. I break off four squares and cram them into my mouth, followed by another row, and another, until I'm choking on crushed nuts, and chocolate is leaking from the corners of my mouth. I don't stop bingeing until the whole bar's gone. I grab a green apple from the fruit bowl and take a bite. The acidity stings my palate. My stomach growls. I put a carton of soup in the microwave. When it pings, I don't wait for it to cool but spoon it into my mouth straight from the carton.

I prowl from room to room. Should I ring the police? What would I say? That I'm worried a young woman who is – or was – involved with local drug dealers has given my address to someone? But who? The gang leader? A client? And how would I explain to the police how I came to meet Miriana? Would they regard me as a kidnapper?

With a sigh I conclude there's no intelligence I could give them, and set about erasing all traces of my visitor. I drag the sheets off the bed, bundle them into the washing machine and sit watching the drum fill with foam while the laundry flops around. Minutes later I'm back on my feet, pacing, unsure what I'm searching for. I open my fridge and see a pork pie. What's a pork pie doing in my fridge? More snack food I bought for Miriana. I toss it in the bin.

I can't settle to Netflix, so I stand with the controller in my hand, surfing channels. The news is depressing. I pick up a book, but it's historical fiction and needs my concentration. I put it down again. By ten o'clock I'm exhausted from doing nothing. I check the windows are double-locked and put the chain on the front door.

All night I fidget, clammy with terror, dreaming armed drug dealers are surrounding my home. Faceless men yell they've come to get Miriana and won't believe me when I say she's not here. Someone's threatening me. I'm tied up. I struggle to free myself, and find it's the sheet twisted around my legs. I check the time on my phone – seven o'clock – and remember I'm still on leave from work. My exhausted head drops back on the pillow and sleep grants me oblivion.

The ring of my doorbell drills through the flat and I snap awake. It'll be a delivery for Callum upstairs, who's a bit of a recluse, like me. Callum's front door is around the side of the house. A sign with an arrow points to number 25B, but his delivery people are forever pressing my bell.

Pulling on my bathrobe, I ram my feet into slippers and head to the door. What if it's not the postman? What if it's Jamie's brother, the drug dealer? I creep the last few paces, flattening my back against the wall. My flat is the converted ground floor of an Edwardian house, and through the original stained-glass panel I make out the shape of a tall man who doesn't have the lanky build I'd associate with a young drug dealer. The silhouette turns sideways. He's holding something that looks more like a florist delivery than a sawn-off shotgun or a book. Callum must have a secret admirer. Pulling the belt of my robe tighter, I snatch the door open. The man has turned his back, preparing to leave. When he swivels round, my mouth drops opens.

"Bill!" I gape. When I fled Tenby on Saturday evening, I never thought I'd see him again.

Bill smiles, and the part of his face that's not hidden by his beard reddens. The bouquet is huge, practically a pop-up herbaceous border, with stems in a cellophane bubble of water.

He glances from my slippered feet to my dishevelled hair, and his forehead creases. "Sorry, Laura. Are you ill?"

"I'm okay. Just surprised."

"I messaged you and left a voicemail saying I was in London and would stop by—"

"My phone's been charging. I haven't looked at it. What are you doing in London, anyway? Shouldn't you be in Wales?"

He shrugs. "After you left it fell flat, so I packed up early this morning."

"Don't you live in Birmingham?" Slowly it dawns on me that his arrival in London didn't just happen. He's travelled all this way to see me. "How did you get my address?" I stammer, then laugh – didn't I ask him something similar at the campsite? "Oh yes – you had everyone's addresses on their booking forms." Isn't that a breach of data protection? If I said that I'd sound pompous as well as paranoid. "It's Monday morning," I point out. "I could have been at work."

"Erm, Monday afternoon, actually," he replies with a grin. "I took a chance that you'd still be on leave from work."

I check my watch. He's right – it's almost two o'clock. How did that happen? I glance down at my dressing gown and blush.

"I suppose you'd better come in." I stand aside, stiff and awkward, as he steps into the hall, tilting the flowers sideways so water leaks over my polished wood floor.

"Sorry." He looks mortified, cups his hand to catch the drips, then thrusts the flowers at me. "These are for you."

"Thanks." Now the water's seeping into my dressing gown. A nervous giggle forms in my throat as Bill follows me to the kitchen, where I put the flowers in the sink. "Do you want a drink?" I ask, opening the fridge. "Or are you driving?"

"I am, but not till later." He sits down before I invite him to, and accepts a beer.

I make myself a coffee. "I'll have to go and get changed. I can't sit here, unkempt in my dressing gown."

Bill puts down his beer. His eyes meet mine and his craggy face softens. "You look fine," he says. "To me."

A sensation of warmth sets my pulse racing. With my crooked nose and hollow cheeks, how could anyone think me gorgeous? Then my heart sinks. More complications. How am I going to get rid of him?

15

LAURA

On the singles holiday in Wales, there was a brittle tension among our group that I'd assumed was due to me and my social awkwardness. I'm used to being the one who doesn't fit in – I actively choose it. Thinking back, I see everyone had issues: Emily overshared; Delia rarely spoke but constantly hummed tunes under her breath; Sam wore his geekiness like a badge of honour, telling us he'd married his childhood sweetheart, divorced at thirty-five and moved back home with his parents. From what I could gather, he'd reverted to an existence of online gaming and 'a bit of gambling' behind his childhood bedroom door. No wonder his wife wanted to unshackle herself.

Amy and Bill were the only two of our group who'd known each other before, but even an outsider like me could see the imbalance in their relationship. If Bill chatted to me for too long, Amy treated me to her trademark hard stare. And now Bill's here, in my kitchen, drinking beer. After my weekend with Miriana, he represents relaxed normality.

"We all went to Laugharne on Sunday and visited Dylan Thomas's boathouse," he says. "I remembered you wanted to go there."

"I did. I ran out of time, didn't I?"

"Afterwards we ate in Brown's Hotel – the pub where he and his missus used to drink."

"Not a barbeque? You surprise me."

He laughs and makes a face. "The barbeques were getting a bit much. I'd had enough of the group dynamic, so I set off this morning at seven-thirty."

"How did the others take it?" I ask, wondering how Amy reacted.

He shrugs. "We're all grown-ups. Free to leave or stay. I doubt Amy and I will be organising any more meet-ups. But it was an interesting experiment – and I met you."

His eyes lock onto mine and my cheeks grow warm. "Let's go for a walk," I suggest. If he hadn't turned up, I doubt I'd have left my flat today. "We could get something to eat. How about pizza?"

"Excellent idea."

The rain has stuttered to a stop, leaving a damp sheen and puddles across the pavement, but there's a hint of sun behind the clouds and the air feels clammy. We walk alongside the Common until we reach the main road, where we turn right and pass a parade of small shops. It's hard to converse above the rumble of traffic, so we stroll along in comfortable silence to St Leonard's junction and I lead the way down a leafy road of large houses where the noise finally abates.

"At the end of this road is Tooting Bec Common," I tell him. "We can have a walk around there."

Bill is wearing a blue denim shirt and knee-length khaki shorts, probably the same ones he had on every day on the campsite. Compared to the groomed London versions, his beard has an untamed look, as if he's an explorer or a naturalist. As we cross the road he makes a grab for my hand, and I surprise myself by not pulling it away. We stroll through a belt of woodland and catch the sound of children's laughter floating towards us on the air.

"Where's that coming from?" Bill asks. "A playground?"

I shake my head. "The outdoor swimming pool. We can have a look if you like."

As we approach, the high-pitched laughter grows louder. Despite the earlier rain, the lido is packed with mums – and nannies – watching small children splash around. I persuade the cashier to let us in through the gate without paying. "We're not swimming, we just want a quick look," I say, and she nods us through.

Last summer, my first in London, I came here whenever I was adrift with nothing to do. I didn't swim, but camouflaged myself behind a book and watched families having fun. The pool looks larger and more turquoise than I remember, and the layout is utilitarian with functional paving slabs, but the changing huts lining the poolside, painted red, green, yellow and orange, give off a cheerful vibe. Small children, and older ones who must have been brought here after school, are bobbing around clinging to vast inflatables. This isn't the time of day for serious swimmers.

"People swim here all year round," I tell Bill, "but outside of summer it's only open to club members. Some even come when it's snowing."

Bill is entranced. "It's magic!" He takes a few shots with his mobile. "Wish I'd brought my camera. Let's come back tomorrow and swim."

It's hard to squirm when you're standing up, but I manage. "Tomorrow? Won't you be heading home after we've eaten? Birmingham's a long drive."

He waves a hand dismissively. "I told you – I don't have to be in Birmingham. I can work from anywhere." He turns his head slowly from left to right, as if mentally filing a panoramic view, then glances down at the photos he took on his phone. He holds it out to show me, and I can see he's captured the essence of the place: sun sparkling on water, the vibrant changing huts, the symmetry.

"That's good." I hand the phone back.

"I could take some great pics here. It's given me an idea for a feature on open-air swimming pools across London. I might call up an editor friend and pitch it. I've heard there are several. Do you know where they are?"

"Um, Brockwell Park, close to here, Hampton, and Hampstead Heath." My mind is racing – he's talking as if he's settling in London for a while. "But where will you stay?"

He laughs, clasps my upper arm and squeezes it. "Don't panic, I'm not moving in – my trusty campervan's parked in a side street around the corner from you."

I exhale. That's all right then. He's not expecting me to invite him to stay. All the same, I worry if his van's safe. What if the locks aren't secure? I hope he hasn't left valuable camera equipment on view, because it could be a target for thieves.

We complete our stroll across the Common and cut back to the main road along one of the streets which was blocked to through traffic in the days when this area was plagued by kerb-crawlers.

There's a wide choice of restaurants, but I head for a pizza chain in a building that was once a bank. It's late for lunch, but too early for dinner, so we almost have the place to ourselves. Without asking what I'd like, Bill orders a bottle of Barolo. Our voices echo in the empty space, so every word sounds like an announcement over a public address system and our easy conversation trails off. Heavy red wine gives me migraine, but I sip it to fill the silence. When our pizzas arrive, I snatch up the circular cutter and slice my Margherita into quarters, then eighths, grateful for something to do.

Bill watches me over the rim of his glass. "I've booked into the Crystal Palace campsite. My van will be safer there and I can use their showers."

"Good, I mean great," I reply, then recklessly overwrite his solution by offering, "You can shower at mine tonight if you need to."

"Thanks, Laura, that's kind, but I don't want to impose." He attacks his pizza – some kind of hot spicy sausage – while I leave mine to go cold. The wine has stained my glass purple. I expect my lips and teeth are discoloured too, and I rub my mouth with a tissue. I can't drink any more, and I guess Bill's rationing himself so he can drive later.

"I'll pay," I insist, as I head off for a comfort break. When I return from the cloakroom I discover he's cheated and already settled the bill, and feel cross for no reason. Our walk home is flat and moody, as if clouds were hanging heavy above us, yet the sky is forget-me-not blue and the air's been scoured clean by the heavy showers. In the last two days I've had more conversations than I'd normally have in months – perhaps I've spent my word allocation. With nothing to say, I don't bother taking quieter side roads but stride along the high road, in tandem with cars unable to travel further than us between each set of traffic lights.

We leave the main road and reach the street running parallel to mine, where Bill stops and points out his parked campervan. "I'll head off to the campsite," he says. He doesn't suggest meeting up again.

"You can come in for a coffee." My voice sounds stiff and ungracious. "Bring your camera. Don't leave it in the van."

"Fair enough." He strolls along to open his van and leans inside, while I wait at the end of the road. When he returns he's carrying a black canvas bag, and we walk the short distance to my flat. I unlock my front door and realise I didn't set the alarm.

Panic sends me scouring the flat for signs of an intruder. Did I leave the guest room door open? Was that rug rucked up? But nothing's out of place, and the atmosphere inside my home is serene. As I come out of the sitting room, Bill is looking bemused and lays his hand on my arm.

"What is it, Laura? Why are you so anxious?" His attempt to calm me has the opposite effect. I jostle past him to the kitchen and fill the kettle. As I'm spooning coffee into the cafetière he comes to stand close to me, and the hairs on the back of my neck prickle. He slips his arms around my waist and I feel his body pressing against my back. I don't tense or shrug him off, not even when he bends to nuzzle my neck and plants a kiss on my cheek.

"Why did you run away?"

I twist round to face him, holding my hands up to show they're empty and I don't have an answer. He pulls me close and kisses me gently on the lips. A tingle travels along my spine and breaks the veneer of self-control that's been holding me together. When I touch my face with the back of my hand, it comes away damp with tears.

Bill steps back, shocked.

"It's not you," I sniff, as he tears off a sheet from a roll of paper towel and hands it to me. I dab my eyes. My face feels hot and tight, but my body is relaxing.

"I'm sorry. I didn't mean to upset you."

"You didn't. You've helped me, I think."

The kettle clicks off, but I've lost interest in coffee. I grip Bill's hand tight. "Come." I lead him into my bedroom where the rumpled covers look squalid, but I don't care. I sit on the edge of the bed and tug his hand, and when he sits down beside me I turn to him and say, "Make love to me. Please."

"Are you sure?" He looks stricken, and I can't blame him.

Perhaps he thinks I'm unbalanced. My behaviour has shifted from stiff rejection to an open invitation.

I nod and pull him closer. He holds me tight and we kiss until seconds become minutes and then we're fumbling to unfasten belts, buttons and zips. My heart thuds, and feelings I thought I'd left behind in another life slowly stir. For the first time in years, I allow myself to accept some comfort.

16

LAURA
TUESDAY

The dawn chorus of robins, thrushes and blackbirds wakes me. A greyish light creeps into the bedroom and I lie on my right side, facing the window, realising I didn't draw the curtains last night. The mattress shifts beneath me, and I inhale the musky scent of another human. In my bed. I haven't forgotten last night. I know it's Bill, but I lie still and stiff, collecting my thoughts, before I roll onto my back.

Bill's awake. He props himself up on one elbow and gazes down at me. It's hard to see his expression, but when he speaks I hear the smile in his voice.

"Good morning." He takes my hand and strokes it. "You were sleeping so peacefully."

He's right. A calmness radiates through me like the endorphin-fuelled relaxation you get after a run and a revitalising shower. My breathing is even, and the hopelessness crushing my chest when I wake most mornings isn't there. It's like a miracle – a tiny part of my burden has been lifted.

More light seeps into the room, and I return the gaze of the only man who's ever been with me here. His lips find mine and we kiss. His beard scratches my chin but I don't care. I wrap my arms around his back and pull him close.

After a while, we lie side by side, holding hands. There's enough light now to see the chaos of my bedroom. It looks as if someone's sorting clothes for a jumble sale. Yesterday's jeans and t-shirt are balled up on the floor, next to Bill's shorts and denim shirt. Suddenly aware of my nakedness, I slide one hand under my pillow and fumble around for the baggy shorts and strappy vest top I sleep in. While I'm struggling into them Bill slides his legs out of the bed and stands up, giving me a view of a pale but well-toned backside and tanned muscular legs.

"Don't leave." I lunge across the bed and hook my arms around his waist.

He turns and hugs me back, grinning. "I'm going nowhere. Except the bathroom. And I'll finish brewing that coffee you started on last night."

"What time is it?" I grope on the floor for my mobile, but find only the charger cable with nothing connected.

"Don't panic. You're not going to work today. Remember? You told me last night. We can stay in bed and make love all day long."

I blush, because I've been thinking the same, but I don my familiar poker face. Bill might be perfectly comfortable with no clothes on and discussing a sex marathon, but it's years since I had close contact with anyone.

While Bill is in the bathroom I interrogate my feelings. When we were in Tenby, he was just a fellow-camper, annoyingly intent on getting my attention. Was I attracted to him? Did I encourage him? I don't think I was even open to the possibility. Something has happened to me since I fled the campsite – I've stopped focusing on my own misery. It must be because of Miriana.

Thinking of her sparks my guilt. I didn't let her explain. Her parents abandoned her – is it surprising she was groomed as a drug courier? By giving her a lift to London and listening to her story, I became involved – and I should have protected her but I've let her down. She's gone. I don't even know her surname, so there's nothing I can do about it.

I prop a pillow behind my back and sit up, hugging my bony knees. How could Bill think me beautiful, with my crooked nose and skeletal figure? Whatever happens from now on, I vow I'll eat properly.

The aroma of fresh coffee wafts into the room and Bill appears with a couple of tea towels tied around his waist. When he hands me my mug and gives a mock bow, I'm reminded of the male stripper at a hen party I once went to, and burst into giggles. He keeps a straight face until I've set my mug down on the bedside cabinet, then unfastens the knot and whips the tea towel away. "Ta-da!"

"Idiot! Come here." We kiss for a long time, and my coffee is cool when I reach for it. Above the traffic hum, footsteps pound down the stairs and Callum's front door slams.

Bill puts his head on one side. "You didn't say you had a housemate?"

"That's Callum upstairs."

"Does he share your front door?" His expression is mildly perplexed.

"No, his is round the side."

"Ah. That's good." He traces the contours of my face with his index finger. "You have the most expressive eyes. I'm sure they could tell me things you'd never say."

I should be embarrassed by such intense scrutiny, but there's a telepathy between us as if he's looking beyond my vulnerability into my actual soul. We slide further down the bed until we're lying on our sides, facing each other. Slowly and tenderly, we make love.

An hour later, still damp from the shower, I push open the door leading into my garden and feel the sun's rays on my face. After yesterday's storm my geraniums have revived, and their blossoms are ketchup-red and healthy. I'm glowing inside.

Bill follows me out with toast and coffee on a tray.

"Do you want eggs?" I ask. "They're the ones I bought for you and the gang. I felt really bad when I realised I'd fled with your breakfast."

He laughs. "We had plenty of bread, and you left butter and milk in Emily's fridge. No one starved." He kisses me again. "Forget the eggs. Let's sit here together and enjoy your last day of freedom."

Yesterday in the pizzeria, when our conversation was faltering, I'd told him I was going back to work on Wednesday, though I'm not due in until Thursday. Sad person that I am, I was thinking of ringing my boss and cancelling my last day off to return to the comfort-blanket of my office. "Let's make the most of today," I say.

"By staying in," Bill adds. "Who needs to go anywhere when the company and the weather are perfect?"

"I thought you wanted to swim at Tooting Bec Lido?"

"No. The pool will still be there another day." He spreads my butter-substitute, and a thick layer of homemade marmalade I bought from the campsite shop, onto a slice of toast and bites into it. Crumbs cling to his beard. It ought to annoy me, but it doesn't. I nibble on a slice of toast, remind myself I'm changing my relationship with food, and take a bigger bite. I didn't go off food; I went off life. Not eating was a symptom of apathy.

"Tell me about yourself." Bill reaches for another slice of toast. "You know all about me, but you've hardly told me a thing."

I shrug. "Not much to tell. I work for a hedge fund firm in the City." For most people this would be a conversation stopper.

Either they don't want to admit they know little about investments and financial markets, or they have preconceived ideas of how hedge funds operate and the iniquities of vast bonuses. Bill sweeps my current life aside.

"Yes but you told me you moved to London two years ago. So you must have had a life before the hedge fund. Were you living in Wales?"

"Yes." I choke.

"So what did you do there? Are there hedge funds in Wales?"

I take a sip of orange juice and it turns acid in my stomach. "Hedge funds aren't really me. It's just a job. I'm a French teacher. I mean, I was a teacher. Not any more. Obviously."

His hand – sticky from the toast – reaches for mine. "What is it, Laura? You seem so sad. Confide in me. Maybe I can help you."

A cloud blocks the sun. I shiver in my sleeveless top, and press my lips together to lock my story inside. As I glance up, calculating how many seconds before heat breaks through and I'm warm again, instinct tells me the time has come to break my silence.

I reach for my sunglasses. It will be easier to talk if Bill can't see my eyes, because telling him will peel away protective layers. "It's a pathetic story. You'll understand why I don't talk about it."

"Try me. It might help."

"Maybe. I used to live near Cardiff, in a coastal town called Penarth, with my partner, Gareth, and our daughter, Ellie. She was sixteen, and no one in the world was more precious to me. But I lost her. And I'm to blame."

Bill doesn't flinch. He keeps hold of my hand and waits. Telling Bill will take me back to that dark time, but shutting it out hasn't worked. Maybe if I revisit the past, I can move forward again?

17

LAURA

THREE YEARS EARLIER

It was a Thursday – my mum's seventieth birthday – but Mum was adamant she didn't want a big celebration.

"What is there to celebrate?" she'd said, when I mooted it. "Why broadcast how ancient I am? I'll keep my head down and battle through the day, and when I come out the other side no one need be any the wiser."

I was relieved because, being a teacher, spending a Thursday with Mum outside of school holidays would have been impossible. But she reassured me she was going out to lunch with her oldest friend Susan, and we agreed on a family meal on the Sunday.

"I feel bad about not seeing Mum on her birthday," I said to Gareth and Ellie at breakfast time. It was a miracle to find all three of us sitting around the kitchen table together in our semi-detached house, but Ellie had finished her exams and Gareth was working on a local job.

"Well, that's not your fault," Gareth pointed out. "Why don't you go over and see her this evening?" He leaned back in his chair and stretched, his long legs kicking my foot. He was anxious to get to work, but his client didn't want him in her house before ten o'clock.

I sighed. "Don't you listen to anything I say? It's Year Eight parents' evening tonight – the one postponed from March because so many teachers were off with flu." For some reason our school had decreed that parents' evenings must always be held on a Thursday, and July was the next available date. "I'll be lucky to get home much before ten."

"What's for tea?" Gareth asked, getting to his feet. His brown hair was curling past the collar of the navy-blue polo shirt, emblazoned with his company's logo. Part of the lettering had rubbed away so now it read: *Kitch Dreams*. When he set up the company I'd argued the name Kitchen Dreams was naff, and suggested he used a strong word with 'kitchen' – like 'artisan' or 'hand-crafted' – but he ignored my advice, and his clients don't seem bothered.

"That's up to you. And Ellie. There's plenty of food in the freezer."

Ellie stayed silent in her private world, her phone inches away from her face.

"Right-o," said Gareth. "I'll sort it."

"I could go," said Ellie, yawning. She lifted her head and tossed back her mane of dark-blonde hair.

"Go where?" asked Gareth. "The supermarket?"

"To Grandma's this evening."

"Oh darling, would you? She'd love that." Mum doted on her only grandchild, and I wished Ellie would visit her more often.

"Yeah. But let's make it a surprise," she said, laying her phone face-down on the table and challenging me with her unfathomable blue eyes. "It would be cool to turn up and surprise her. What time will she get back from lunch with Susan?"

"About four-thirty, I expect. But I won't be able to drive you. My appointments are back-to-back." Why was nothing ever simple for teachers? Our working lives have zero flexibility and we have to shoehorn family commitments into the holidays. "I could drop you at Cardiff Central around four. You'd have to change at Queen Street. How would that be?"

Ellie made a face. "You don't have to tell me how to get there. I've been taking that train on my own since I was, like, twelve years old." She stirred cereal around her bowl without ever raising the spoon to her mouth, and I knew she was working up to telling me something.

"Guess what?" She flipped her phone face-up as if it was a card in a game of Patience.

Gareth and I exchanged a glance. He was at the sink rinsing his orange juice glass under the hot tap. We waited for her to tell us.

"Remember Hubert?"

"The boy whose family you stayed with when you went on the French exchange?"

"He's hardly a boy, Mum. Hubert's, like, seventeen. Anyway, he told me he was coming over this summer with his mates, and they arrived in London on Tuesday. Look." She held out her phone and showed me a photo of three lads, balancing on the parapet of the Trafalgar Square fountain.

I smiled. "Funny they should choose Trafalgar Square to start their sightseeing. Next you'll be telling me they're staying at a hotel in Waterloo."

She wrinkled her brow "Why?"

"Napoleon?" Sometimes I worried about the standard of history teaching at my school. "Never mind. I'll explain later. I must get going. Meet me outside the staffroom at ten to four and I'll give you a lift to the station."

"Thanks, Mum." Her smile was unusually radiant. Lately,

she'd been morose. I'd put it down to the pressures of her exam year, but something else nagged me. I'd always tried not to pry into Ellie's life. When she was younger we were close, so I knew she'd confide in me in her own time. I'm hyper-sensitive to the pressures on teenagers in this age of social media. We've had problems at Llewellyn High, but the Head's always taken a firm line, and bullying was stamped on. Under his regime, victims are protected and it's always the bullies who are suspended or made to leave. Those policies have kept our students safe. They know they can speak up and will be listened to.

I didn't think Ellie was being bullied, but she'd grown apart from her closest friends. It troubled me, but I tried to keep it in proportion. She still had a large circle and often went to music gigs at weekends, but since she turned sixteen she no longer invited friends over. Was it because I was a teacher, and they didn't want to come to our house and fall under my beady eye? I was a tolerant parent. Some would call me lax – and, later on, they did. I knew Ellie and her friends had fake IDs, and I didn't want to be the only parent who stopped my daughter going to city centre pubs and night clubs – I used to go when I was her age. What's the harm? Ellie wasn't a heavy drinker; she didn't do drugs. When Ellie went out in town, she stayed with her friend Zara who lived with her mum in a flat in Cardiff city centre. They could walk back safely without needing to get a cab.

Gareth took a dim view of my liberal parenting style. He was scornful, and accused me of not prioritising our daughter's safety. One winter Saturday his rage had erupted and I saw another side of him.

"Where's Ellie?" he'd asked me when he came home late from the rugby club.

"She's out in town and she'll be staying at Zara's," I told him. A couple of weeks earlier I'd phoned Zara's mother to check she was happy about Ellie staying so often. I didn't know her personally, but she'd assured me that Ellie was welcome to stay, any time.

"What were you thinking?" he'd hissed. "You know there was a Wales v France rugby match on. The city centre will be heaving with drunks."

"Ellie speaks good French." I hadn't intended to rile him. "She'll be fine."

"For Christ's sake, Laura," he'd yelled. "I'm going to pick her up. Now." When he bent towards me, I could smell beer on his breath. "Where the hell is she?"

"It's eleven o' clock," I protested. "And you've been drinking. Let her enjoy her evening."

"I'm warning you, Laura. Tell me. Now." The naked anger in his eyes unnerved me. I didn't mean to say anything, but it slipped out.

"She's gone to Phantasia with Zara and some others."

"What time's she coming home?"

"I told you – she's sleeping over at Zara's."

"Right." He turned on the tap but couldn't aim it straight. Water splashed against the sides of a glass and slopped over the draining board. He gulped it back and wiped his mouth with the back of his hand. "I'm off."

"Don't be daft. You're in no fit state to drive." He'd walked to the rugby club. I needed to stop him getting into the car.

"Make me a black coffee, then," he said.

"Make it yourself."

He glared at me, but I knew dismissing his worries wouldn't make them go away, so I put the kettle on and tried to negotiate. "Listen, I'll message her. She can tell you she's okay." I fired off a WhatsApp asking Ellie to give us a quick call. No reply. After ten minutes, I phoned, knowing she'd never hear it ring if she was inside the club but perhaps it would vibrate in her pocket.

Gareth gulped his coffee standing up and stared at me over the rim of the mug till I felt anxious too. Minutes ticked away. "She's not answering, is she? Message her again. Tell her I'll be outside Phantasia at midnight to pick her up."

"No, Gareth, please." Where were his car keys? He must have noticed me checking the hook where we intend to leave keys but never do. He produced the keys from his pocket, pushed back his chair and waved them in my face.

"Listen, I'll drive you," I offered in desperation, though I'd polished off a third of a bottle of white wine earlier in the evening while he was out.

He was already striding along the hall, not looking back. "She'd better be there."

I ran after him. He slammed the front door in my face. When I wrenched it open, he'd started the engine and was pulling away from the kerbside. Ellie would be mortified. I messaged to warn her he was on his way.

> Wait outside for him. Think Cinderella. Be there.

To my surprise, Ellie messaged me straight back.

> What's up? String of messages and a missed call from you.

I dialled her number again and this time she answered, sounding slightly out of breath.

"Hey, Mum."

"Your dad's on the warpath. He's driving into town to pick you up. Now."

"I'm not in town. I'm at a friend's house. I'll be home soon. Before midnight definitely."

"Thank goodness. I'll let him know."

As my fingers fumbled to tap in Gareth's number, I glanced

around at the outdated green-and-cream MDF units and wondered why the family of a high-end craftsman lived in a kitchen that belonged in a skip. Gareth had been promising to upgrade it for years – I could have gone round IKEA, loaded up new units and installed the damn thing myself. He didn't answer my call – probably still driving. I fired off a couple of messages and when I judged he'd have arrived, I tried phoning. No reply.

Defeat descended on me like fog. Neither my daughter, who was umbilically attached to her phone, nor Gareth, who was forever scrolling through rugby scores on his, could be bothered to respond to my messages. I turned on the TV, flicked through the channels and kept on clicking until I reached soothing music. I leaned back on the sofa and closed my eyes.

A shuffling sound in the hall jolted me awake. Ellie appeared, in a sodden jacket, shaking rain from her hair.

"Didn't you take an umbrella?" I was turning into my mum.

"Don't fuss, Mum. I walked home. It wasn't far."

"Where were you, anyway?" She was wearing jeans and a t-shirt, not her usual clubbing garb of mini skirt and stilettos, and her face was flushed from the walk in the rain.

"A few of us decided to stay local. We went to Jono's house and played board games."

"Board games?" I think of all those Christmases when we'd begged her to join us for a round of Monopoly to please my mum, who yearned for an olden-days Dickensian-style Christmas: families gathered round the hearth to sing carols and roast chestnuts, instead of staying split into separate atoms by mobile technology.

"Yeah, we sometimes do that now," said Ellie. "Jono said in London they have board game cafes."

"Who knew?"

"Where's Dad?" Ellie's eyes flicked nervously around the room as if he might be hiding behind the sofa.

I glanced at my watch: half past midnight. "I hope he's not still outside Phantasia, waiting for you."

"He didn't!" Her eyes grew round with alarm and her voice trembled. "Mum – I thought you were joking! Why did you let him?"

I shrugged. "I tried to stop him. But you know what your dad's like once an idea's lodged in his head. I'll message and let him know you're home."

"If he's going to start harassing me, I'll..."

A headache pressed in on me. "What will you do, Ellie?" I snapped. The stress of my row with Gareth had shredded my nerves. "Ring Childline? Run away from home?" I wished I could bite back the words, but Ellie flounced out of the room and the stairs creaked as she stomped up to bed.

I waited up for Gareth. I'm a night owl, and even on school nights I'm rarely in bed before one, but my eyelids felt heavy. When he lumbered into the room I was dozing on the sofa.

"What time is it?" I asked, yawning and lowering my feet onto the carpet.

"Three-thirty..."

"Where the hell have you been? Ellie got home hours ago." I lifted my bleary eyes to look at him properly, and saw streaks of dried blood on his face. "What happened?"

Gareth's mouth was set in a grim line and his face had a greyish tinge. "I was arrested," he said. "For causing a breach of the peace."

18

LAURA

Despite what he told me, Gareth wasn't actually arrested. He was held and questioned for two hours in a police van, but no further action was taken. He wasn't even breathalysed because the officers didn't realise he had a car parked nearby, and – so he told me – assumed he was among the rugby supporters, carried away, celebrating Wales's victory over France. If only it had ended there. But the fallout sent ripples through our small community, until everyone, from the postman to the youngest Year Seven pupil at my school, heard about it.

Gareth had waited outside Phantasia. When Ellie didn't show up by twelve-fifteen, he'd pushed through a queue of youngsters who were still hoping to get in, and forced his way past the door manager and into the night club, calling out Ellie's name. He was followed and quickly apprehended by one of the security team, who frogmarched him to the entrance. He was still shouting when they slung him out onto the street, where he staggered and bashed his head on the pavement, but his ejection coincided with a police vehicle doing a drive-by check.

"What's up?" the police officers had asked door staff, who'd pointed out the oddball bloke who'd forced his way in and was now scrambling to his feet with blood pouring down his face.

Zara, and some of her friends, had happened to be coming out of the ladies' cloakroom and witnessed the incident. Although Zara didn't know Gareth, she'd heard him calling Ellie's name and made the connection, but before she could walk over and tell him Ellie wasn't there, the door manager had grabbed him. Jeering clubbers joined in a chorus of heckling "Sick fuck" and "Dirty old man" – or so I was later told – while Zara stood by and watched the ungainly spectacle of her friend's father being ejected and led away to a police van.

By Monday morning, the story was all around my school. Gareth had told me a version that seemed to ring true, but in the lurid version, shared with me by my colleague Val before I'd had my first coffee of the day, Gareth single-handedly fought off a team of burly door staff, decking several of them, before the police were called to subdue and handcuff him.

With my arms half-out of my coat sleeves, I leaned against a chair for support. "Do you think I should talk to the Head?"

"Good idea," said Val. "Joanne was in her office when I came past. You can catch her before the bell goes."

In all the years Ellie and I had both been at Llewellyn School there'd never been any conflict, but now my family seemed to be creating scandal. Why didn't I send Ellie to a different school and keep my home and professional life separate?

I'd asked Joanne to book me an appointment with the Head at first break. I perched on one of the purple vinyl armchairs meant to jazz up the dingy waiting area, while a radiator blasted out tropical heat. My palms grew sweaty, my face red and shiny.

"You can go in now." The secretary summoned me and I leapt to my feet, the seat making a rude sucking noise as the backs of my legs peeled away. We both pretended not to have noticed.

"Thanks." I pushed the door open and caught sight of the Head, leaning back in his chair, one hand smoothing a few strands of hair across his balding crown. Why didn't he shave his head and be done with it?

"Take a pew, Laura." He waved his hand at the upright chair opposite his desk. It was lower than his own, reminding me of the naughty seat, where generations of students and parents had sat to receive a ticking off from him and his predecessors. I ignored the chair and stayed on my feet so I could get out of the room fast.

I stuttered out an apology. "Gareth went to collect Ellie from town," I explained, trying to smile through gritted teeth. Why had Gareth put me in this humiliating position? "He was concerned about the crowds on Saturday night because of the match."

When I finished speaking my knees were shaking, so I sank down onto the chair after all, hoping he wouldn't notice me trembling.

It turned out the Head already knew about the night club incident. "Don't fret. No one's been hurt; nobody died. By next week it'll be history." His cliches were meant to be reassuring, but the gleam in his eye told me he secretly thought it was hilarious.

I dropped my gaze and noticed my skirt had rucked up when I sat down, exposing my black tights up to thigh level. I squirmed. Why hadn't I worn trousers, today of all days? Flustered, I stood up to leave, but the Head cleared his throat and force-fed me his wisdom. I was head of Modern Languages, but there was no doubt he was my boss.

"You might want to think about where Ellie spends her evenings. She's only sixteen."

The Head and I locked eyes. I looked away first. I should have heeded his warning, but instead I rebelled. He had no kids; he wasn't even married. Why should I stop Ellie doing things her friends were allowed to do?

Gareth took the opposite view, and the rift between us deepened.

19

LAURA

The Thursday of my mum's birthday, I felt like I was trapped in Groundhog Day, sprinting between classrooms and into meetings, scurrying to stand still. At three-thirty, the head of Year Ten called me to join her for a chat with parents who wanted to dispute their daughter's projected exam grades – especially in French. When I joined the meeting the atmosphere was tense, as if all the oxygen in the room had been used up. The chairs in the classroom were sturdy enough for grown-ups, but the father had perched his massive backside on a table with spindly legs, and I watched in fascination wondering if it would collapse under his weight.

"Miss Lister," he said, offering me his hand without getting up. The classroom windows magnified the intense July sunshine, so it was hard to concentrate on what the man was saying, though his voice boomed louder than the laughter of homebound teens passing along the corridor outside.

I opened my computer and showed the parents their daughter's records from the previous two years. Whichever way you looked at it, the estimated C grade was generous. The man let his glasses slide down his nose and peered over them for a couple of seconds, but the mother's eyes flicked over the screen then she turned her cold gaze on me and said, "We've been paying a tutor to come every week and talk French to her."

I was tempted to tell her they'd been wasting their money. "I expect she'll do well in her oral exam," I said, snapping my laptop lid shut.

That's when I discovered the father was a barrister, and could argue for hours without pausing for breath. I kept one eye on the wall clock, then realised the hands hadn't moved: time had stood still at three-forty. I rolled back my sleeve to check my wristwatch: four o'clock. Ellie would be waiting for me to give her a lift. By offering to spend the evening with her grandma she was doing me a huge favour, but this meeting had made me late.

"Sorry, I have to go." I stood up and briskly pushed back my chair. As I reached the door, the barrister's voice boomed in my ears, suggesting my team was incompetent. Seething, I put my head down and strode along the corridor.

Outside the staff room Ellie was leaning against the wall with a languid, unfocused expression. "You're late."

"Sorry darling. Late meeting. I couldn't get away."

"Whatevs. Let's go." I noticed a backpack at her feet and she bent down to pick it up.

"What's in the backpack?"

"A present for Grandma. It's a surprise." She hugged the bag tight against her chest and I smelled perfume: Sea Siren, the one Ellie uses herself. If that's her birthday gift for her grandma, it's generous, though a bit brash for Mum's taste.

I tapped my foot as I explained my predicament. "I was wondering if you could get the bus to the station?"

She didn't reply, but a subtle shift in her posture showed she was annoyed that I'd let her down. A draught caught the side of my face as the staff room door opened, and my colleague Bryn stepped into the corridor. He must have noticed Ellie glaring at me.

"Hi – is something up?" he asked.

I shrugged. "Not really."

Ellie scowled, and I raked my hand through my hair and sighed. "Ellie's off to visit her grandma and I'd promised to drive her to Cardiff Central, but I'm out of time. My first appointment's at four-thirty."

"No problem." Bryn glanced from me to Ellie. "I've no one booked in till five-fifteen. Why don't I drive her?"

"Would you?" Ellie's sulky expression shaded into a grin. "I'd hate to disappoint Gran on her birthday."

"Well, if you're sure..." I said. It was typical of Bryn to come to my rescue. Since joining the school in September, he'd often stepped up to take on more responsibility, unlike the rest of my team in Modern Languages. When he'd offered to lead the school exchange to Nantes back in October it got me out of a predicament, because Ellie had point-blank refused to go if I was in charge. The two other teachers signed up to accompany our group were from the Sports department, because football and netball matches against the host school were part of the programme. It was essential one of the staff was a fluent French speaker, but Jess had a one-year-old daughter, and Val was downright pig-headed and argued it wasn't her turn.

When Bryn volunteered, I ducked out and Ellie opted back into the trip, but by that late stage all the French host families with daughters had been allocated, so Ellie was billeted with the family of seventeen-year-old Hubert.

What I wasn't told at the time was that Hubert had been held back a year, not just for failing his exams, but for anger issues and fighting.

20

LAURA
TUESDAY

The angry whine of a chainsaw from a nearby garden rips through my concentration.

Bill has been sitting quietly, his clasped hands resting on the metal table, as he listens to me unwrapping my past. When the noise distracts me, I'm so detached from my surroundings that Bill has faded to a background blur. I'm locked inside my nightmare, running down corridors to nowhere, searching for a door that will open and lead me to Ellie. A scream is forming in my throat. To stifle it I bite down hard on the heel of my hand, and a metallic taste fills my mouth. There's not much blood, but I stare at my hand where my teeth marks make a neat circle.

Bill takes my injured hand and examines it. "You'll live," he says, and kisses it better like a parent soothing a child.

Suddenly I need a shot of alcohol. "Fancy a drink?"

"I'll get it." He disappears into the kitchen and returns with two beers and the remains of a bottle of Petit Chablis. Even when my cupboards are bare, there's always alcohol in my fridge. "Which do you fancy?"

I point to the wine bottle and he fills a glass up to the brim. I curl my hand around the stem but don't raise it to my lips. It's comforting to know it's there: my familiar medicine.

Bill takes a bunch of keys out of his pocket and uses the edge of one to prise the cap off his beer and swigs it from the bottle. He tries to catch my gaze, but I reposition my sunglasses from where I've put them on top of my head like an Alice band and cover my eyes.

"Take your time, Laura. I want to hear the rest."

I take a sip of wine and it gives me courage to continue. I dread seeing Bill's pity, but the slow pace of my story is agonising, so I jump forward and tell him the end. "I said goodbye to Ellie outside the staff room that day and went to set up my table in the hall for parents' evening..." I pause. "That was the last time I saw her."

There, I've said it. Behind the sunglasses my eyes well with tears as Bill's hand inches across the table to touch mine, but I snatch it away.

"You don't need to tell me any more if it's too painful."

I nod. "I know, but I want to. Give me a minute." I sniff and get to my feet, walking a few circuits of my small patio garden to calm myself, and stopping to stroke an Acer's dark red leaves between my finger and thumb. It must have been a tiny shrub when the previous owner planted it; soon it will be a tree. Isn't this what happens in life? Growth, death and renewal. Last winter I hung a bird feeder from its branches and watched the sparrows and blue tits flock to it when food was scarce. The privacy of this tiny garden preserved my sanity until Callum, who's in his late twenties and has no outside space, took to climbing out of his bathroom window onto the flat roof of my kitchen extension. When I asked him what he was up to, he held up a stripey beach towel and a tube of sun cream.

"You're actually going to sunbathe up there?"

"That's my plan," he replied, and he seemed to be smirking

because he must have known it would be hard for me to stop him. "Where else is there?"

"The Common or the Rookery gardens." I glared at him, but he ignored me and yawned as he spread out his towel, removed his t-shirt and exposed his dough-coloured flesh. Can't I even snip dead heads off my plants without being watched? Callum rarely comes out when I'm there, but I know he still sunbathes because I've had to clear his empty beer bottles out of my gutter. Today his window blinds are all drawn, and I know he's out at work so won't be spying on me and Bill.

I shuffle back to the table, sit down and gulp my wine. Bill takes a drink and waits, his face solemn. Agitated, I pick up the threads of my story.

"Bryn dropped Ellie outside the main station and drove back to school. Later, we were told CCTV cameras showed her walking to the ticket office and buying a ticket."

I can't look at him so I swallow more wine. All those trivial details that plagued me while the police were searching for Ellie, flood back.

21

LAURA

THREE YEARS EARLIER

I understand how time is critical when a young person goes missing, and one of many things I blame myself for is stopping for a swift drink at the King's Arms with my colleagues, Val and Bryn. While we were mulling over the highs and lows of parents' evening, Ellie was slipping out of sight. When I arrived home it was after ten-thirty, and Gareth met me at the door.

"Did Ellie ring for a lift from the station?" I asked.

"I haven't heard from her."

"Right, I'll message her." I tapped out a WhatsApp and stared at my phone, waiting for the two grey ticks to turn blue and show Ellie had read it.

"Tough day?" Gareth filled the kettle to make tea. He didn't seem concerned about Ellie.

I grimaced and pushed my hair behind my ears. "The worst. I'm frazzled." I checked my mobile again. No message. I tapped on the phone icon and heard a faint ringing somewhere in the house. "Listen. It sounds like her mobile's in her room. Perhaps she came back while you were out or watering the garden."

"Yeah. She's probably fallen asleep."

I ran upstairs and tapped on Ellie's door. "Hi, darling. Are you awake?" I waited a few seconds, then edged the door open. Ellie wasn't there, but her phone was, in its pink sparkly case, lying in the centre of her swirly-patterned duvet. When I picked it up, a list of missed calls and messages, mostly from me, appeared on the front screen. I shivered. Ellie went nowhere without her mobile.

"She's not there," I called out to Gareth as I clattered down the stairs to ring my mum from the landline. I'd phoned Mum at first break to wish her happy birthday, but kept Ellie's planned visit a secret, as we'd agreed. Mum's a night owl, like me, so I knew she'd still be up, and one mystery was solved – Ellie couldn't ring for a lift if she didn't have her phone. Yet in my heart I knew she'd have noticed hours ago and phoned us from Mum's.

Mum answered sounding slightly out of breath, and I felt guilty because a late-night phone call can be alarming. "Did you have a good birthday, Mum?"

"Lovely, thanks. Susan treated me to lunch at Celtic Manor—"

Without waiting for her to finish, I asked. "Can I speak to Ellie? Or has she left?"

"Ellie?" There was no disguising the surprise in Mum's voice.

Cold fingers of fear clutched my heart, but I forced a laugh. "Yes. How was your birthday evening together?"

"I haven't seen Ellie today, darling, but she messaged me at breakfast time before she left for school. Wasn't that sweet?"

What was going on?

I flumped down on the sofa, covered the mouthpiece with my hand and mouthed to Gareth, "Ellie didn't go to Mum's."

"What did you say?" He stepped closer, his voice booming in my left ear, while Mum talked, in discordant stereo, into my right. How could I shut her up without making her anxious?

"Sorry, Mum." I faked a laugh. "My mistake. I'm just home from parents' evening and Gareth's updating me on Ellie's change of plans." I patted the air with my hand, signalling to Gareth to lower his voice. "I'll call you tomorrow."

"Yes, but, darling—" Mum was still asking questions when I ended the call.

"Where's she got to, Gareth?"

He must have detected a note of panic in my voice, but if I expected him to share my anxiety, I was wrong.

"How the hell should I know?" He furrowed his brow. "You're the one who encourages her to do exactly as she pleases. When have you ever bothered about her staying out late? If something's up, it's down to you." He stomped out of the room.

In the slipstream of his vitriol, I gasped. Ever since the nightclub incident Gareth had kept a brooding silence about Ellie's socialising. Their once easy-going relationship turned tense, and Ellie often left the room when he came in. While she was revising it wasn't so noticeable because she shut herself in her bedroom, but she still went out every Saturday night. And some Fridays, too. *It helps me deal with exam stress, Mum.* It made sense to me – I encouraged her, but all that time Gareth was nursing a grudge and saying nothing. Inside my head, a soundless scream clamoured to escape.

I ran back upstairs to check her room. Her pink and black duvet draped onto the floor on one side of the bed; she hadn't plumped up her pillow, and the indentation from her head was still visible. On her wall was a poster of singer Ariana Grande, wearing a strapless ballet dress in grey chiffon, heavy black mascara, eyeliner flicked up and out – catlike. Before nights out, Ellie used to spend hours peering in the mirror copying that look.

Where could she be at half past eleven on a school night? A friend's house was the obvious answer – they'd all finished their exams – but why would she say she was going to visit her grandma? I wasn't an uptight, killjoy mother who stopped her going out, but my chest felt tight as I jotted down her friends' names and reached for my phone.

I started with Zara. She wasn't a long-standing friend, but I had her home number from when I'd rung to check that her mum was okay with Ellie staying over. I tapped the number and paced while I waited.

Zara's mother was polite but firm. "No, Mrs Lister, Ellie's not here, and you can't talk to Zara because she's asleep." Perhaps she didn't mean to be so abrupt, because she quickly added, "Is everything okay?"

"I hope so – sorry I disturbed you." I swallowed as I ended the call. This was going to be difficult; most families, especially those with younger children or long commutes, would already be in bed and wouldn't thank me for waking them.

I trawled back through my list. Some were families I knew when Ellie was at junior school. I tried the Davieses but they didn't pick up. Next, I dialled her one-time best friend's house. Rosie's dad answered, and was even brusquer than Zara's mum. "Rosie's been home all evening, and we haven't seen Ellie for months. I don't think they're talking to each other. Rosie was quite upset about it. For a while."

A lump was forming in my throat. I dropped my mobile on the bed next to Ellie's, thinking her phone must hold a clue. Perhaps she used the phone calendar. Perching on the edge of the bed, where I'd read her stories and listened to her prattling happily about her day, an inexplicable sadness came over me. I tapped different numeric combinations of her birthday. Nothing. Would Gareth know her passcode? I was too angry to ask him a favour. Then I heard his voice calling from the bottom of the stairs. Bone-weary, I dragged myself out to the landing.

"Sorry, Laura. I shouldn't have yelled at you." The harsh

hall lighting picked out worry lines etched on his face. "Who've you tried?"

"Zara's mum; the Davieses; Rosie's dad..." I clattered down the stairs and held Ellie's phone out to him. "D'you know her passcode? It isn't her birthday."

Gareth took it from me and tapped 1,2,3,4 and other simple combinations. He shook his head. "If I do it too many times, it'll lock up. Have you tried Adam?"

As children Adam and Ellie were close, but lately I'd suspected he was keener on her than the other way round. "Could you ring?" I asked. It was now past midnight, and I was losing my nerve. It was too late to ring, except in an emergency – was this one? My thoughts were spinning as I searched for the number. My knees felt wobbly, so I clung to the bannister as I listened in to the call. There was a throat-clearing sound of someone snatched from sleep, then Adam's dad's voice came on the line. He wasn't rude, but it was obvious he had no idea where Ellie might be. "I'll wake Adam," he offered, but Gareth declined.

"We'll carry on ringing round."

"Good luck, mate. I'm glad we don't have daughters!" Perhaps he regretted that remark, because he added, "Maybe think about giving the police a call?"

As Gareth thanked him, I felt oxygen draining from my body and from our home. I tried telling myself it wasn't even late. If Ellie hadn't told us she was visiting Mum, we'd only be mildly anxious.

"Ellie's running late, that's all." I tested the idea on Gareth by saying it out loud. "She can't ring because she doesn't have her phone." As excuses go, it sounded thin.

"I'll go out and drive around." Gareth laid his strong, reassuring craftsman's hand on my arm. "She'll be walking home."

"But where would you look?" In Penarth, young teenagers congregate near the pier, or in the playground by the cliff path, but Ellie and her peers are too cool for that now. They've moved on.

With an effort I formed words I didn't want to say. "I think we should call the police."

22

LAURA

We argued. Gareth insisted the police would treat us as timewasters. He'd heard they wouldn't respond to a missing person report for forty-eight hours unless there was reason for concern. "In this country people have a right to go missing," he informed me. Why must he be so bloody pompous? He rammed his feet into trainers, strode to the door and went out, without tying the laces. When I caught up with him, he was staring at his car with a bemused expression as if he'd forgotten his plan.

"You're wrong about that, Gareth. Forty-eight hours only applies to adults. Ellie's a child, so she's vulnerable. Let's report it to the police so they can look out for her."

He nodded and put his arm around me. Together, we bumbled back to the kitchen, where I made the call. Shifting some responsibility onto professionals felt like a sugar-rush. I craved chocolate to extend the sense of relief, but there was none in the house, so I made tea, handed Gareth a terracotta-coloured builder's brew, and watched an insipid peppermint teabag float around in my mug.

"Eurgh." Herbal tea wasn't what I needed. I tipped it down the sink and poured a glass of wine.

When the doorbell rang, I jumped to my feet and put the half-finished glass of wine into the fridge. I couldn't see flashing blue lights through the opaque glass panel in the door, but any neighbour on a night-time bathroom expedition would spot the yellow and blue patrol car and the rumour mill would kick into action. After Gareth's nightclub antics, our dubious celebrity status had lasted for several weeks. Tongues were wagging at school, but in the wider community fingers pointed, and the only place Gareth felt comfortable was the rugby club, where being slung out of a nightclub when you're almost forty was a badge of honour.

For Ellie, our family's notoriety was torment. *How d'you think I feel? Now everyone knows my dad's a dickhead.* Doors were slammed, angry words exchanged, but Gareth's effort to curtail Ellie's freedom backfired so spectacularly that he'd ceded his authority over her and blamed me. He became morose. Our conversations were brittle, and I'd catch him looking at me with contempt. Our lives were running on parallel tracks.

I snatched a breath and opened the door. The motion sensor had detected the officers walking up the path and activated a light. I was dazzled by their hi-viz jackets and faces bleached by the floodlight. Both officers were in uniform and at first I thought they were two men, but as they came closer I realised one was a woman. Her pale hair was scraped back in a tight bun, so she looked almost bald.

I led the way to the sitting room and noticed Gareth scrutinising them, perhaps to see if either had witnessed his previous brush with the South Wales force. The female officer made the introductions: "I'm PC Jenkins, and this is my colleague, PC Hughes. You must be Mrs Barton."

"Ms Lister," I replied, and Gareth scowled. We'd met at uni and been together almost twenty years, but we weren't married. Gareth's degree was in Law, but he regretted his career choice, and after a year in a solicitor's practice he'd ambushed me with his plan to retrain as a carpenter. This would have been fine if I hadn't been pregnant with Ellie.

"Please sit down," I said, remembering my manners, but I didn't offer tea.

"We've had a report of a missing sixteen-year-old, Ellie Barton. She's your daughter, Ms Lister?"

"Our daughter," said Gareth.

"What makes you think she's missing?"

I swallowed, but my throat was still dry. I croaked my way through the reasons we were worried.

"Ellie told us she was going to visit my mother this evening because it's Mum's seventieth birthday today." I remembered it was now tomorrow. "I mean yesterday. I had a parents' evening at school – I'm a teacher – so I couldn't go." Every few words, I paused to run my tongue over my parched palate.

"Did she go missing on her way home from her grandmother's?"

"No. My colleague dropped her at Cardiff Central station but she never turned up at her grandma's house."

"You've asked your mother to confirm this?"

"Yes. I rang her as soon as we realised Ellie was overdue."

"We'll take her details in a minute. What's your colleague's name? The one who drove her to the station?"

"Bryn Jones."

"And did Mr Jones see her go into the station?"

"Um," I mumbled, remembering Bryn swinging by my table in the school hall and giving a thumbs-up sign above the head of the parent I was talking to. Later, in the pub, he'd told me the time he'd dropped Ellie. "He reached the station at around four-twenty, but I didn't think to ask him if she went inside."

"If she changed her mind and went elsewhere, where might she go?"

Three pairs of eyes bored into me. I was in an armchair and the two officers were sitting on the sofa opposite me. Gareth was leaning against the doorframe, one foot in the room and one in the hall, noncommittal – as if this was nothing to do with him.

My hands trembled and I pinned them in my lap so the others wouldn't notice. "Sometimes she goes out in town. Or visits friends."

"What time does she usually come home?" PC Jenkins pushed a loose strand of pale hair back into her bun. One side of her mouth was slightly twisted, as if years of listening to reports that weren't quite credible had stamped her face with scepticism.

I prevaricated. "By midnight. Unless she's arranged to stay with a friend."

"What have you done to locate her?" asked PC Hughes. His deeper voice stirred Gareth to attention. Sometimes I wondered if he was deaf to the pitch of female voices.

"We've rung around some of her friends." Gareth listed the names, counting them off on the fingers of his left hand, and PC Hughes solemnly noted them down. "No one's seen her."

PC Jenkins' radio crackled, and I felt a stab of alarm. What if they had to rush to another incident, leaving us with platitudes like *We'll keep a look out for her* or *Call us when she turns up?*

"We should establish whether or not Ellie caught a train," she said. "What was the name of that teacher who dropped her at the station?"

"Bryn Jones." I repeated, certain I'd already told her.

"Does he live here in Penarth? D'you have his number?"

Bryn was a colleague, not a friend; I was his boss. I shook my head. "I'm not sure where he lives. As far as I know, he's renting. He joined the staff last September."

Her voice turned brisk. "Who will know it?"

"Um, the school secretary. I have her number." With a sinking heart, I realised Joanne would never forgive me for being woken from sleep, and she'd make sure everyone at school heard about it. "Joanne sometimes works from home – her daughter's been ill with ME – so she can access school records remotely."

"Give her a call, please. Once we have that intel, we'll speak to Mr Jones and pinpoint the exact place he dropped her, then I'll call Control so they can make arrangements to pull the CCTV footage from the station area. The station closes after the last train departs, so they may need to seek help from British Transport Police."

My heart drummed in my chest. Far from accusing us of wasting their time, they were taking us seriously. My emotions were in turmoil – I didn't want this. Why didn't they tell us we were worrying needlessly?

"We'll split up," said PC Jenkins to her colleague. "You take the car and go and talk to Mr Jones when we have his address, and I'll make an initial search of the house." She gave me her lopsided smile again, but her face didn't relax.

I rang Joanne and waited. My first call rang out. I dialled again. This time she answered on the fifth ring.

"Who is it?" She sounded sleepy, breathless and upset.

Explaining took a while. Ripped from sleep, Joanne seemed to think this was some languages department jape, and went on and on about how giving me Bryn's address would be a breach of data protection.

"Listen," I begged. Surely she could hear the desperation in my voice? "Ellie's gone missing. The police are here."

Her tone softened. "I see. I'm sorry. Give me a minute." The phone went silent. How long did it take to log on and retrieve a single piece of data? The hands of the antique clock my mother gave me moved painfully forward.

Finally Joanne spoke. "I have Bryn's address but I shouldn't really give it to you." Her voice was a mix of officiousness and concern.

"Right – I'm handing the phone to PC Jenkins. Talk to her."

"How do I know she's really a police officer?"

"Stop it, Jo!" I passed over my phone, crossed my arms and let my chin sink onto my chest. Time dripped on past two-thirty.

PC Jenkins had a calm authority as she noted down the address and reassured Joanne she wouldn't get into trouble. "Can you get us some recent photos of your daughter?" she asked me, ending the call and handing back my phone.

My face began to crumple.

"Don't worry. It's routine."

"What do you mean?" Gareth was tapping his foot. It was his way of releasing pent-up energy, but it made him look shifty.

"Most runaways are found, or come home of their own accord, in a couple of days," said PC Jenkins.

Her words hit me like a blow to the stomach. *So that's what my daughter is. A teenage runaway.*

23

LAURA

The front door slammed as PC Hughes headed off to talk to Bryn. I stood motionless, like a child awaiting instructions, and feeling as if my kitchen walls were closing in on me. I'd always loathed the black and white tiles – they reminded me of a crossword grid I'd never complete. When PC Jenkins asked me to hand over Ellie's phone, I flinched but slid it across the table towards her and watched as she placed it in a plastic evidence bag.

"Aren't you going to examine it? There must be a clue."

"They'll do that back at base. I'll take a look around. Do you have outbuildings?" The word sounded ridiculously grand for our road of suburban semis.

"Only a shed and a garage."

"I'll fetch the keys," said Gareth, and went to grab them from the hook inside the door.

"Thanks." PC Jenkins slipped them in her pocket. "I'll have a look around upstairs first." I stood up to escort her, but she waved me away. "No need."

A sudden stomach-dropping feeling came over me. I'd checked Ellie's room and mine but not the guest room. Was it possible she'd come home while we were both out and gone to lie down in there?

Our house was a typical 1930s semi with two decent-sized bedrooms and a box room hardly big enough for a child's cot, but PC Jenkins examined our upstairs rooms as if inspecting a mansion. Floorboards creaked as she tramped from room to room, opening and closing doors, while I stood in the hall, stretching my neck like a meerkat, and listened to her pulling out drawers and sifting for clues. How Ellie would have resented the intrusion into her space. But she'd put us in this position – and if she was fine, why didn't she ring?

"Stop foot-tapping," I said to Gareth. His prowling and fidgeting was fraying my nerves. "Do something useful. She wants recent photos of Ellie."

He nodded and headed to the study, and soon I heard the printer whirring into life. To occupy myself I went to the kitchen and unloaded the dishwasher, but as I put the plates in the cupboard I realised everything was still dirty. Gareth hadn't switched the dishwasher on.

P C Jenkins came downstairs and strode straight past me to the back door. "I'll check outside."

"There's no light. You'll need a torch."

"I have one, thanks. I'm equipped with everything, as my aching back reminds me at the end of a shift." As she selected it, I noticed her bulging pockets and the implements dangling from her belt: handcuffs, a phone, a radio, a canister of gas, an extending baton and a body-camera.

Watching through the window, I saw her unlock the shed and train her torch into a space so cramped that a five-year-old would struggle to find a hiding place. When she moved on to check the garage, I turned away and put the kettle on.

PC Jenkins returned and took off her boots inside the door, though they weren't muddy.

"Find anything?" Gareth asked, laying a sheaf of photo printouts on the table.

She shook her head. "No. But you'd be surprised how often we find younger children hiding out in an attic or shed, after their parents have been searching for hours."

I made tea and toast, spreading it with a thick layer of butter, not caring about transferring burnt crumbs back into the tub. I couldn't eat, but Gareth managed two slices and PC Jenkins had one.

"What do you think has happened to her?" I repeated, though PC Jenkins had no more chance of knowing than me.

"Honestly?" She gave her lopsided smile. "I'd say she's most likely at a friend's, so try not to worry. I know it's hard." Narrowing her eyes, she glanced from me to Gareth and asked in a casual tone, "You didn't have a row, did you?"

Thinking of Ellie's long-running feud with her father, I dropped my gaze and waited for Gareth to speak, but he carried on munching his toast. "No, we were all fine this morning. And no one forced Ellie to go to Mum's. She volunteered."

"Is that in character?"

"Yes. Ellie's fond of her grandma and sometimes visits on her own."

PC Jenkins sifted through the prints Gareth had made and examined each in turn. One was a holiday snap of Ellie, in her white bikini, looking more mature than her years, her pose bordering on provocative. I leaned across to whisk it away and tore it into pieces. "Not this one – sorry." I shuddered.

PC Jenkins took a last gulp of tea and stood up. "Excuse me. I must check in with Control." She strolled out to the hall, moving silently in her thick black socks. When her colleague returned, she opened the door to let him in and the two of them huddled together, talking in low voices. Gareth and I waited in moody silence. I half-expected him to lash out at me, but he stayed mute, his eyes red-rimmed with incomprehension and defeat.

"We're off," said PC Hughes, coming to find us in the kitchen. "It's shift changeover."

I felt a tug of panic. These officers were my comfort blanket – they were going to find Ellie. *Don't leave me*, I wanted to shout.

"What did Bryn say?" I asked. "Where did he drop her?"

"He was very helpful." PC Hughes wasn't the type to give anything away. His stocky frame seemed to fill our kitchen, but he was aloof, with none of the emotional intelligence of his female colleague.

Gareth had his elbow on the table, resting his chin on splayed fingers. Why was he leaving all the talking to me?

"So what happens now?"

"Try and get some sleep." PC Jenkins collected her boots from inside the back door. "We've made a full report, and arrangements are in place to pull the CCTV footage from cameras around the station area. You'll hear from Investigations in the morning. They'll keep you posted."

"It won't be you?"

PC Hughes shook his head. "We're Response. If she doesn't show up, Investigations will take it forward. I doubt they'll appoint a family liaison officer because, there's been no crime, has there? As far as we know. So look on the bright side."

24

LAURA

I sat with my fingers curled around my cold, empty mug. "Sleep! They must be having a laugh."

Gareth nodded and continued pacing, the soles of his trainers squeaking on the kitchen tiles until I wanted to chuck a plate at him.

"Say something,"

"Like what?" His eyes were raw and bloodshot. "That it's my fault?"

Both of us were floundering in guilt. Did he think Ellie was staying away to punish him? Angry tears stung my eyes, and I stumbled to the fridge and found the half-glass of wine I'd stashed there hours earlier. With a shaky hand, I topped it up.

"What are you doing?" Gareth demanded, with no hint of irony as he poured himself a Scotch. "It's half-four in the morning."

"So what?" It was the wrong time to antagonise him, but something was niggling me. "This morning, after I'd left for school and you weren't starting work until ten, did anything happen between you and Ellie?"

"What do you mean?"

"Did you have a row?"

He glared at me. "Did Ellie say something to you?"

I shook my head. "She was in a foul mood when I saw her at school, but I thought she was angry because I couldn't drive her to the station."

Gareth shrugged. "It's down to you then." He knocked back his Scotch and poured another. I pushed blindly past him and went to the sitting room where I stretched out on the sofa, leaving my wine glass on a table just out of reach. Much as I craved a drink, there was no comfort in the bottle. If there was a development, I might have to get into my car and drive somewhere to pick up Ellie. My frenzied mind made a collage of the photos Gareth had given PC Jenkins, especially the one I'd censored: bronzed, bikini-clad Ellie, aged fifteen, gazing steadily into the lens. I'd never noticed before, but she had the look of a young woman ready to shrug off her close-knit family.

I must have dozed, because the next thing I remembered was a hammering on the front door. The room was bathed in lemony sunlight as I levered my body off the sofa and trudged to the front door. Gareth was talking on the phone in the study. "Why didn't you answer the door?" I asked as I passed him. His clothes looked as creased as his face. I sighed and opened it myself, pushing sleep-tangled hair out of my eyes.

A grey-haired woman in a pin-striped trouser suit was standing on the step. Something about her nondescript hair-and-suit combo made me reel back – Social Services? She showed me her warrant card.

"Hi. Mrs Lister?"

I nodded. Now wasn't the time to insist on Ms – our non-married status was getting a hostile response.

"I'm DS Jane Tranter from Investigations."

"Come in." Her presence calmed me like a painkiller, numbing a physical ache I couldn't handle. "What news?" I asked, striding ahead into the sitting room so I could hide the wineglass.

"A few developments." She sat down, shrugged off her jacket and laid it across her knees, and took a notebook and some papers from her bag. With a brief smile, she signalled she was ready to talk.

"I'll fetch Gareth. He's ringing his client to explain he won't be at work today."

"Right. What does he do?"

"Bespoke kitchens. He's a carpenter."

As I approached the study, he ended his call and whipped round with a blank stare. His breath smelled of whisky, and the sour sweat of a sleepless night clung to his clothes.

"Gareth, you haven't showered!"

"Nor have you."

"I didn't spend all night necking Scotch, did I?" I lowered my voice. "Go up and clean your teeth at least. Please."

He screwed his face into a scowl, but he stalked past me and went upstairs. I lingered in the study looking at all the equipment on standby: blue lights on the router hub, red under the computer screen, yellow on the printer. A metaphor for our lives – so connected, yet so cut off from Ellie. I heard the shower blast into life for a few seconds. When Gareth came down, with his hair damp and slicked back, he was wearing a clean blue shirt. I nodded approval, but he wouldn't catch my eye.

"Sorry," I said to DS Tranter, after he'd introduced himself. "Neither of us slept last night."

She came straight to the point. "We have news. The CCTV footage has been viewed, and Ellie was seen going into the station at around four-thirty yesterday, as your colleague said.

The camera showed her paying for her ticket with a card, so we're checking booking office records to find out where she went."

"She wouldn't have needed a card to buy a ticket to Rhiwbina. I gave her enough cash."

"Young people rarely use cash these days."

That was true. Plastic or a phone app was part of their DNA.

"While we wait, I'll go over some points from my colleagues' fact-find yesterday."

Gareth and I sighed, the first thing we'd done in unison since this nightmare began. "Must we repeat everything we told PC Jenkins? I don't think I could bear it."

Her mobile rang. "I'll take this in the hall." She got to her feet and strode out of the room.

"Ellie did catch a train," she told us when she returned. "But not the local one to Rhiwbina. She bought a ticket to London. A single."

25

LAURA

"London!" My hands trembled, and I clasped them together as DS Tranter's cool grey eyes watched us absorb this news.

"Think of it as a positive." She slipped her phone into a pocket and picked up a silver pen. "She wasn't snatched off the street and bundled into a car. She's made a positive decision. No one was coercing her. Most teenage runaways turn up within a few days."

Runaway – that word again.

"Why would she go to London?" Ellie's life seemed so uncomplicated: academic achievements, a hectic social life, the summer to look forward to. My stomach churned. "If you think she'll turn up, why are you going to such lengths to find her?"

DS Tranter tilted her head to one side. "Some cases we classify as 'absent' rather than 'missing' – which means 'not in the place they were expected to be'. It's common among young people in care. Ellie's not in that position, but she's vulnerable because of her age."

"What happens now?"

"Officers are visiting Llewellyn High this morning to talk to staff and students. Did Ellie have problems at school?" She held her pen discreetly poised above her notebook.

Sensing my personal and professional life were on a collision course, I swallowed – my colleagues being questioned about my missing daughter, seeing my life falling apart...

"I teach at Llewellyn. And no. Ellie wasn't being bullied."

She gave a tight smile. "Even so, parents are often the last to know."

Gareth's look of sympathy felt manufactured. Was he secretly gloating, convinced this was my fault for giving Ellie too much freedom?

"Should I go into school?" I asked.

"No. It's best you stay here. Ellie might ring. As she doesn't have her mobile she might remember the landline number. Can you think of any reasons Ellie might suddenly go to London without telling you?"

"No!" Gareth spoke through gritted teeth. She gave him a sharp look, as if his answer was too quick.

Weariness washed over me, turning my memory into a jigsaw with pieces missing.

"We have to rule out her leaving the train somewhere along the route," DS Tranter went on, "though it only stops at three stations. There are cameras on the train and at Paddington. Once we're certain she went to London, the Met will be involved. Have a think about anyone she knows there: friends, relatives, or places you might have stayed on family trips."

"Okay. That makes sense."

"Make a separate list of her friends. And their numbers, if you have them. Later on I'll be taking your statements."

"Haven't we given those already? To PC Jenkins?"

"No those were an initial fact-find to kick off the search. Have you got paper?"

It felt like we were in kindergarten and she was our teacher, setting us a mindless task to keep us quiet while she got on with her important work.

"I've plenty in the study."

DS Tranter followed me out and along the hall to the room we used as an office. "I'll park myself here for a bit and make some calls." Without waiting for my answer she lifted a pile of books off my desk and put them on the floor while I collected a bundle of A4 paper and went out, leaving the door open. Two minutes later her phone rang, and I heard her get up and close it.

"Are you okay?" Gareth asked. "I'll make a hot drink. Shall I make one for her?"

I shook my head. "She's on a call. Wait till she finishes."

We sat side by side on the sofa, keeping our knees from touching, sipping tea and making lists of Ellie's friends, and a separate one of people we knew in London.

"This is pointless." I flung down my pen and leaned back. My mobile vibrated, and I scanned the missed calls and messages that had come in without me hearing. None was from an unknown, or London, number; all were attached to colleagues' names. Mindlessly, I tapped on the most recent one – from Val, who was on break.

"What news of Ellie?" she asked, but without waiting for my reply began filling me in on happenings at school. *Bryn said he was dragged from his bed at 3am by a police officer...* She made it sound as if a Gestapo-style search of the school was in progress, with lockers opened and interrogations conducted in the secretary's office.

"Have they found anything?" I asked, desperate for any glimmer of hope.

"Only that Ellie's locker was empty."

"That's hardly surprising, is it? Her exams are over. She's left school. For now."

"Where d'you think she is?" Val was obviously pumping me for gossip to feed the staffroom grapevine.

Bleakness descended like fog. "I have to go. Tell the others not to ring me, please. I'm keeping all our lines open for Ellie."

Gareth had stopped writing. He brandished his list of names. "What am I meant to do with this?"

"Give it to me." I scanned his list with six names written on it. "Who's Kevin Brewer?"

"My mate from uni. He lives in London. Camberwell, I think."

"Has Ellie ever met him?"

"I don't think so." He got up, rubbing his stiff knees. Gareth was a year off forty, but bending and kneeling were integral to his work, and decades playing rugby had taken its toll. "I'm going stir-crazy cooped up in here." He went back to his pacing and headed outside. I guessed he was heading for the garage where he kept his tools and materials. A few minutes later the whirr of a lathe starting up. Occupying his hands would help him. I wished I had a similar hobby, but I'm no crafter. I don't knit or sew; I read, write, think – and over-analyse.

DS Tranter stayed closeted in our study. She must have had a strong bladder, because I didn't hear her coming out to use the cloakroom. Our lists of names lay on the coffee table while I scanned news headlines on my tablet and sensed how dyslexia must feel. Words turned slippery, taunting me. Nothing made sense.

When she came to find me, I was staring mindlessly at the contents of the fridge – eggs, cheese and ham. I'd lost touch with what meals might be due and whether I ought to be cooking one.

"We have the CCTV from the train," she told me, leaning against the draining board but evidently not noticing it was wet.

A damp stain seeped into her crisp white shirt. I didn't mention it.

"Tell me." I was hyperventilating for lack of news, and couldn't wait to call Gareth.

"When the footage was matched and viewed, there were some inconsistencies." She glanced down at a hand scrawled note. "You said Ellie didn't take her phone with her?"

"That's right. I found it in her room and gave it to PC Jenkins."

She paused long enough for my anxiety to come creeping back. "Ellie was seen using a mobile on the train, so she must have had a second one."

My hand went to my mouth and I gasped.

"It sounds as if she left hers behind deliberately, so her location couldn't be tracked. When she arrived at Paddington station, CCTV footage shows her making a call."

Paddington, the bustling London terminus for trains from South Wales, rolled through my mind like a cinema screen. I knew from experience it could be difficult to find the person you were meeting. Was someone waiting for Ellie?

"Ellie's train arrived in London at around 6.45," she told me. I shivered – that was when I was snatching my mid-evening tea break at school, thinking my daughter was at Mum's. "She entered the underground station alone, but more investigation will be needed to find out which line she took."

"Your shirt," I said. It had soaked up water like a sponge. I tore off some paper towel and handed it to her. It was easier to focus on that.

"Thanks." She blotted her shirt and moved away from the sink. "Prepare yourself, Laura. This won't be quick. Think of how many young runaways the Met have to deal with, arriving in London from all over the country, and the amount of work to track her in crowds. I have to get back now, but I'll keep you updated. Try to stay calm. We could be waiting some time."

26

LAURA

After DS Tranter left, I went out to the garage and stood in the doorway watching Gareth measure up a length of beading. His head was bowed in concentration, his hands caressing the cheap pine as if it were a precious rainforest specimen. He must have sensed I was there but carried on with his task. I envied his focus. When he'd finished, he turned to me, his eyebrows lifted in a question.

"Ellie arrived in London and was seen using a phone," I told him. My chest felt tight. "Maybe she kept an old one?"

"Sounds like a burner phone. Come here." He held out his arms and I went to him and rested my head on his shoulder, feeling the rhythmic beat of his heart. Mine felt less steady.

I sniffed. "I don't know why I'm crying. She's not actually missing, is she? I mean, she's made a plan and gone somewhere. But she hasn't told us."

He nodded. "If she's gone to such lengths to cover her tracks, it sounds like she doesn't want us to find her."

"What d'you think will happen next?" A small part of me was hoping the next phone message would be Ellie, contrite, saying it was all a mistake. That she was on her way home.

I peeled myself out of the comfort of Gareth's arms. "I must ring Mum." After my panicked call the night before I'd half-expected her to phone, but as far as she knew this was a normal day – a school day – and I'd be at work.

"Watch what you say about Ellie - don't upset her."

"Of course!" I snapped, and my irritation returned. My mother was one of Gareth's greatest fans – practically his cheerleader. When he gave up Law to retrain in carpentry, she understood immediately – unlike me. Mum was his first client, and he built a stunning handmade kitchen for her. He'd offered to work for the cost of the materials but she'd insisted on paying for his labour. Pictures of Mum's kitchen featured in his first brochure, because back then marketing material was mostly in print form and he had no website. It was – still is – a stunning kitchen, and Gareth's business took off fast, with clients from the posher suburbs and across the Vale of Glamorgan.

I dawdled inside, but every time I picked up the phone to call Mum I hesitated, telling myself I ought to keep all the phonelines free for Ellie to ring. When I finally called, it was almost nine o'clock.

"But where is she?" Mum repeated, though I'd explained three times over. "She didn't come here."

Did she think I was accusing her? Finally, it sank in. I'd played down the police involvement, making it sound as casual as if we'd reported our car stolen and the police were keeping a vague look-out.

So I shouldn't have been surprised when, early Saturday morning, while I was taking my first shaky sip of coffee after a second sleepless night, Mum appeared on my doorstep and deposited her overnight bag in the hall. "I'd have come yesterday," she said, pursing her lips in reproach, "but you rang so late. You know I don't like driving in the dark."

I kissed her soft, creased cheek, picked up her bag and carried it up to the guest room. While I laid out towels, I tried to remember if I'd washed the sheets since her last visit. Why did it matter? Downstairs, I heard her moving around, embarking on her mission to keep us fed and supplied with hot drinks.

The smell of toast wafted up towards me and she called out, "Breakfast." My legs felt heavy as I clumped down the stairs. Mum had found an old embroidered tablecloth in a drawer and laid it on the pine kitchen table, as if civilised manners could transform this into a normal day. "Here you go." She slid a plate of toast towards me.

"Sorry, I just can't."

"I can." Gareth let the door bang behind him as he came in from his workshop. He can't have heard Mum arrive, but he'd presumably detected the scent of toast and followed it. When he saw her his pleasure was evident.

"Angharad – just the woman I needed to see." He hugged her. "That new hairstyle suits you." I couldn't see any change – maybe it was an inch or two shorter – but he was trying his best. He nibbled at a piece of toast and ate half before giving up, while I updated Mum on the search for Ellie and watched her smile fade like the flickering that foreshadows a power cut. If I'd known her joy in life would be forever frozen in that moment, I don't think I could have borne it.

Later I went next door to ask the Nixons if they'd noticed anyone coming to the house on Thursday, and discovered the police had already tapped up the neighbours.

"What did they want to know?" I asked, feeling my cheeks redden.

"Nothing much. When we'd last seen Ellie. How she seemed."

Why would the police question our neighbours? I remembered some high-profile cases of parents abducting or hiding their own child, and my heart bumped inside my chest. Surely the police didn't suspect we were involved in Ellie's disappearance?

"Did you notice if anyone visited Ellie on Thursday while I was at work?"

Mr Nixon shook his head. "We've not seen her for a while, have we Babs?" His frail wife had crept into the hall and hovered, her hands plucking at a paper tissue. Her face was set in a stone lion expression, and I guessed she was losing her memory. When Ellie was small the Nixons doted on her, delivering chocolatey gifts each Christmas and Easter. Once I caught Ellie red-handed as she trotted up their path to post a drawing with the date of her birthday scrawled on it through their letterbox.

"I hope she's all right. Let us know when they find her." Mr Nixon closed the door and I trudged back home.

"Any calls?" I asked Mum.

"Nothing, darling."

Fuming, I rang DS Tranter's number but my call went unanswered. "How can they leave us dangling like this?"

Mum took my hand and tried to soothe me.

I pulled away. Out of a corner of my eye I noticed Gareth sneaking down the hall – presumably heading for the rugby club bar. "How can you think of socialising?" I yelled.

He stopped but didn't turn to face me. "They'll be doing all they can. They'll tell us when there's news."

"Then stay home and wait with me!"

He pivoted round. "What the fuck can I do here? If I'm out, I can ask around. Perhaps someone's heard from her."

"Like who?"

"Your teacher colleagues for a start – some of them drink at the club. Have you spoken to them?"

I hung my head. I hadn't rung colleagues; it was too humiliating. I let him go. After the door slammed I rang around Ellie's friends again, and learned some had already been interviewed by the police. I sensed a reluctance to speak to me. Conversations were shut down faster than I could get my questions out.

I rang her friend Megan. "Have you heard from Ellie?" I asked, trying to sound calm but coming across inappropriately upbeat.

"Megan's out," said her mother. How could I have mistaken their voices? In my current state, easily.

"Please ask her to ring me when she gets back?"

"She's told the police everything she knows."

"It would help me so much to talk to her."

"Listen, Laura. I'm sorry about the worry you're going through, but Ellie and Megan aren't friends any more, are they? So how would she know?" She rang off.

Why were these women lying to me and falsifying my daughter's image? Megan and Ellie were in the school netball team, and shared a room at training camps and when they travelled to North Wales for inter-county championships. Now Ellie was being treated as a non-person. Did other parents feel she was tainted and not want a connection attaching to their families? Those stories you hear about communities rallying round in a crisis: don't believe them.

I wasn't in the best frame of mind, but someone had to challenge the insipid non-cooperation in the hunt for Ellie.

"I'm going out," I called to Mum, picking up my car keys. I slammed the door behind me and drove round to the home of Ellie's friend Rosie.

27

LAURA

It wasn't only local friends who were ghosting us. DS Tranter wasn't in touch on Saturday, and by Sunday she seemed to have dropped off the radar. She had warned me that it wouldn't be quick to track Ellie, and would involve viewing multiple CCTV cameras across Paddington and the tube.

Gareth, Mum and I sat outside in sweltering sunshine that seemed to be mocking my mood. I stared at the lawn; the grass was four inches long, but no one could be bothered to get up and fetch the mower from the shed. At midday we switched from coffee to beer, and by mid-afternoon all of us – Mum included – were swigging wine. The endless circular *Where in London could she be?* conversation loop was exhausting, so I fetched my tablet and we took turns choosing music on Spotify.

My phone finally rang on Monday morning and I raced to answer it: Ellie? DS Tranter? But no. The person who was desperate to speak to me was Val. After thirty seconds asking about Ellie, she launched into her own problems.

"Laura, are you coming in? It's Armageddon here. Jess's

daughter has a vomiting bug and she's gone to collect her from nursery, and Bryn's stuck in Kent with his mother who's in hospital with a suspected heart attack. I'm holding the fort on my own."

Part of my brain clicked into work gear. Perhaps there was something I could do apart from this limbo of waiting. "Well, I suppose I could."

Mum looked up from the Sudoku in the Saturday newspaper she'd brought with her, and shook her head as I ran around the house searching for my school laptop. I found it on top of a pile of books, underneath a chair where DS Tranter had stashed it when she commandeered our study. As I packed my work bag, I burst into tears.

"Laura. Stop." Mum put her arms around me to comfort me while I sobbed. Her hair smelled of chemicals, so Gareth was right – she had been to the hairdresser and had it coloured before her birthday.

"I must go into work," I wailed. "There's only Val in."

"Nonsense. You need to stay here." Mum hugged me tight as I wept for my missing child.

"Where is she, Mum? Why did she leave?"

Mum shook her head. "I wish I knew, darling, but she'll be back soon. Isn't that what the police said?"

What the hell were the police doing to trace her? A sickening image formed in my mind of the investigation team assembled at the station, drawing lots to decide whose turn it was to be the bearer of bad news. When the doorbell clanged just minutes later, my heart was racing.

"Don't answer it," I said to Mum.

"I think it's the police. I'll go."

I dropped my laptop bag onto a chair and traipsed down the hall behind Mum, who answered the door and introduced herself because I was tongue-tied. "I'm Angharad Lister, Laura's mum."

DS Tranter nodded and they shook hands. Her eyes fell on my lank hair and creased t-shirt. "We've been working flat-out over the weekend. The Met are on the case, too."

"Can I make you a cup of tea?" asked Mum, reciting her familiar mantra.

"No thanks. Is your husband around, Laura?" I'd given up telling people he's my partner, not my husband. After all, he's Ellie's dad.

"I'll fetch him." Mum padded outside in her slippers.

When Gareth joined us, we stood in the kitchen in a semi-circle, waiting for her to speak. I couldn't say anything because of a lump in my throat.

"I'll leave you to it," said Mum and took herself off upstairs.

DS Tranter coughed and cleared her throat. "Actually I'll have a glass of water if I may."

"Sure." I filled a glass, but my hand was shaking so much I spilled some as I set it down in front of her.

She took a sip and wiped her mouth discreetly with the back of her hand.

"We've had some luck with the CCTV. The cameras picked up the distinctive logo on Ellie's hoodie, and she was seen leaving the underground at Oxford Circus and going into Top Shop. When she came out of the store she was carrying a large bag with the store's branding, but no backpack – maybe she put it inside the new bag. Cameras picked her up as she strolled along the north side of Oxford Street and disappeared into a department store. John Lewis."

Something told me I should be confused about this. "What time was that?"

"Around eight-thirty."

"And the shops were still open?"

"Yes. Ellie arrived in London around seven, but Oxford Street shops stay open until nine o'clock."

Hearing Ellie was doing normal things like shopping calmed my worst fears. And then came the body-blow.

"After that the cameras lose her," DS Tranter said in a flat voice. "We've no sighting of her leaving John Lewis, so we're guessing she left by one of the rear doors leading onto Cavendish Square. We're working on the theory that she went into the department store's cloakroom and changed into clothes she'd bought in Top Shop. Perhaps she did something to alter her hair, or changed into a different hoodie."

Gareth leaned across me. "Surely you have facial recognition cameras?" His face reddened, but he blustered on, as if he knew about technology. It turned out he didn't.

"I'm sorry, Mr Barton, but no. Not if we don't have stored characteristics. But the Met's on the case, and we're considering a reconstruction of her walk along Oxford Street to see if it jogs any memories. It would help if we knew where she might be heading in London."

And then it came to me. How could I have forgotten?

"Gareth?" I said, and his head jerked up, as if I was calling him back from a faraway place. "Remember those photos Ellie showed us on her phone on Thursday morning?"

"What photos?"

My hands clenched. "You must remember. On her social media. It was a photo of Hubert Petit, and his friends, posing by the fountain in Trafalgar Square. Ellie told us Hubert had recently arrived in London…"

28

LAURA

The temperature of the kitchen dropped several degrees as DS Tranter's eyes narrowed.

"What's this about?" She glared at me as if I'd purposely withheld key information. "Who is Hubert Petit?"

I cleared my throat, and incoherent words tumbled out as I explained about Hubert.

"You have Ellie's phone. Your team will have seen the photos." It sounded a feeble excuse. I darted sideways glances at Gareth, willing him to chip in and support me, but his face looked wooden as if my words weren't getting through.

"We need your co-operation to signpost what's relevant. Where were the French teenagers staying?" She waited, notebook open, pen poised.

I stared down at the pine table but it offered no inspiration. "I don't know. She didn't tell us." Why hadn't I paid attention when Ellie told us about Hubert? It obviously hadn't registered with Gareth either. Amnesia was written all over his face – or else he was a better actor than me.

"This could be vital," she said, tapping her pen on the table.

"Are you sure it was Thursday morning when Ellie showed you the photo?"

Mute with misery, I nodded.

Finally, Gareth caught up. "So Ellie might have travelled to London to meet up with Hubert? And now she's too embarrassed to phone us or come home."

All those hours of racking our brains for the names of long-lost university friends, who lived in London but had never met Ellie, and the obvious explanation was in front of our eyes. I felt a spurt of hope and relief.

"As a matter of interest," DS Tranter interjected, "if Ellie had told you she was going to London to meet Hubert, what would you have said?"

My feeble "Yes" was drowned out by Gareth, rocking forward in his chair and banging his fist on the table. "We'd have said 'No', of course." Gareth scowled. He looked flushed, his face revealing his recent heavy drinking.

"How about you, Laura?"

I revised my reply. "Gareth's right. I wouldn't have let her go to London on her own, but I'd have invited him here."

"Do you think Ellie realised that? Might she have thought you'd stop her seeing him, and decided to go anyway?"

What could I say? A few days earlier I'd have sworn that would never happen, that Ellie would always confide in me. Now I couldn't be sure.

"Where is this boy?" asked Gareth, rising from his seat.

"That's what we need to find out," said DS Tranter, warning us of the raft of procedures she'd have to go through to get permission to question a group of French teenagers. Hubert was only seventeen, but seeing as he'd been kept down a year in school his friends were likely to be younger. "From your school, right, Laura?"

We went to my study and phoned the Head. I had to listen intently to hear what he was saying. I think he was telling the DS he'd need to take advice about protocol from the local education authority, but then I was distracted by the sound of the front door closing.

"All this is wasting time," she said, jingling her car keys. "We'll go into school and hurry things along."

DS Tranter had told me she'd recently transferred to South Wales from the Thames Valley police force, so I tried to explain that headteachers in Wales have less autonomy than in England because we haven't adopted the academy system. She wasn't listening. She went out to her car and waited for me to follow.

I ran through the house looking for Gareth to update him, but he wasn't upstairs or in his man-shed. "Where's Gareth?" I asked Mum.

"I think he's popped out."

I sighed. What was he up to now? We were operating in separate hemispheres. Only once had he taken me in his arms and offered comfort. On Saturday night, after he supposedly went to the rugby club, I suspected he didn't come home. Was he walking the streets searching for Ellie? Or drinking in some late-night city-centre bar?

DS Tranter focused her eyes straight ahead as she drove, and when I glanced at her profile her mouth was set in a grim line. I warned her there was no left turn at the end of the next street due to roadworks, but she seemed not to hear me, so we were diverted along the sea front. Sun beat down on the pebble beach where a group of youngsters about Ellie's age were playing ball games. Elderly couples were strolling along the promenade, and near the entrance to the Victorian pier a young mum was sharing her takeaway fish and chips with a child in a pushchair. The sea sparkled, and the view across the Bristol

Channel to the nature reserve islands of Flat Holm and Steep Holm made me unbearably sad. I turned my face inland to the terrace of shops and cafés, painted in blue, yellow and shocking pink. My hands wouldn't stay still, so I fiddled with my wallet and phone.

We drove in through the school gates. All the visitor spaces were full, so I pointed out the empty parking space reserved for me as head of Modern Languages. DS Tranter wanted to meet with the Head in private, but asked me to wait outside his office in case she needed to call me in. Unable to face the staff room and my colleagues' concern and pity, I lurked in the corridor, inhaling the smell of disinfectant and floor polish. A classroom door banged, and Val stepped into the corridor. She strode towards me, a surge of high-pitched Year Seven voices following in her wake.

"Laura, you've come. Thank goodness. What news of Ellie?"

"Nothing yet. And sorry, but I'm not here to teach. I'm with her." I pointed towards the Head's office where DS Tranter's back was just visible through the etched glass door panel.

She shrugged. "You're still helping with enquiries, then? I've found cover. It's been tough, but Jess should be back tomorrow. Bryn's mother's at death's door, so he'll be off for a while."

"I'm really sorry," I said. "There's nothing I can do at the moment. I have to focus on Ellie."

"What's up with her, anyway?" Val narrowed her eyes. "Was something going on at home?"

I grabbed her arm and dragged her closer so I could hiss in her ear. "Don't say that. Things are difficult enough…"

She reddened. "I'm only repeating what others have been saying." She pulled free of my grasp and gave me a hard stare. "Right – I must get back. Someone has to work."

Wow, that was really unsympathetic. I already felt like an imposter in my own workplace. Why was I even here? DS Tranter didn't need me for her meeting with the Head, and I had nothing to offer my colleagues or students.

"Did you get what you needed?" I asked, when the DS emerged from the office. She made a gesture that could have been Yes or No and swatted my questions away. She was redrawing the boundaries between us, and I sensed the cautious sharing of information was about to dry up. I wondered if the Head had mentioned Gareth and the nightclub incident. Did she think our family was dysfunctional? Or was she punishing me for not mentioning Hubert sooner?

As we drove away from the school a motorcyclist pulled out from a side road in front of her car. She stamped on the brake, so my head whipped forward and I winced as my neck jolted back.

"Sorry," she said, but it felt as if she'd done it on purpose. She dropped me outside my house and drove off.

Mum must have been watching from the window, because she opened the door before I inserted my key. "I don't know how to tell you this, Laura."

My heart lifted. "Is there news? Has Ellie been in touch?"

She shook her head. "Gareth's gone to London."

"Wh-aat!" I flung my keys and handbag down on the floor. "Why?"

She clasped her hands in front of her, almost as if she were praying. "He said the police weren't fit to do their job, and he charged off to find her himself."

After the humiliation at school and DS Tranter giving me the silent treatment, I almost understood how he felt. Inertia was killing us.

"Gareth said to message him as soon as you have Hubert's London address."

"Oh, Mum. This is a nightmare." I followed her into the

kitchen, where she bustled into essential tea-making duties. "Tell me again. Exactly what Gareth said about London."

Mum hooked the teabag out of a mug expertly, but slopped it on the way to the bin.

"Remember he went out early this morning? He came back soon after you and the detective had left, with a box of flyers printed with Ellie's photo. He's planning to hand them out at Paddington and Oxford Street and other places where she's been spotted."

"Why didn't you stop him?" I shouted. Mum's lower lip trembled. "Sorry. I didn't mean to snap." This wasn't Mum's fault. Why must Gareth make bad situations worse? And what would the police say?

Mum sniffed and blew her nose on a sheet of paper towel. She stayed on the far side of the kitchen table, as if she needed to keep a barrier between us, while I dug around in my bag for my mobile and tapped on Gareth's number. It rang out.

"What are you doing?" I yelled into his voicemail. "Call me as soon as you get this."

Half an hour later he did.

"Where are you?"

"Membury Services in Wiltshire. Have you got that London address for Hubert yet?"

"No I haven't. DS Tranter was livid – hardly spoke to me. She thinks we've been withholding information."

"Call her up. Say we insist. Or, better still, ring Hubert's family in France and ask them."

Why hadn't that occurred to me? It would be a massive breach of protocol, but worth it if it helped find Ellie. DS Tranter would have to jump through bureaucratic hoops to get Hubert's London address, but I still had my organiser's master copy of the spreadsheet with all the addresses and phone numbers of the French exchange host families.

"I'll get it for you," I promised Gareth. It would be easy to spin a story to Hubert's parents that Ellie had heard he was in London, was going there on a day trip and wanted to contact him. If I acted fast, Gareth might reach Hubert before DS Tranter's team had the address. And our nightmare would be over.

29

LAURA

Clouds have blocked the sun and turned the sky gunmetal grey. My face feels tight and my eyes itch as I sip water and realise a whole afternoon and half the evening have slipped away, and Bill has listened without prompting or interrupting. On the table in front of us are the remains of a snack of cheese, bread, hummus and tomatoes. I don't remember going indoors to get food, but I suppose I must have done, and my stomach feels acid so I must have eaten something – probably the olives. Judging by the plate, Bill must have finished the oat biscuits and reduced the slab of Comte cheese to a sliver. Paper napkins have blown around the garden, and two are caught on the Acer, like ragged blossoms.

"Did Gareth find Ellie with the French lad?" asks Bill. The wind has tousled his hair; he looks younger.

I shake my head, because what comes next is too painful. Bill doesn't press me, but stands up to lean across and hug me, but his thigh knocks against the table and it tips up. The plate, with the last piece of Comte cheese he was too polite to eat, slides to the ground and smashes.

"Sorry." He bends to pick up the shards of pottery.

"It doesn't matter. It wasn't special." I give him my hand, and when he's back to standing I bury my head against his shoulder, inhaling his musky scent that owes nothing to shower gels or body sprays.

"You're shivering," he says. "Let's go inside."

"Yes. Good idea. I've got cramp." I'd been sitting with one leg tucked under me, and my right foot has gone to sleep. I prop it on the chair while I flex my ankle and massage my foot, then a creaking noise makes me glance up as the upstairs sash window slides open. A leg appears through the open window, followed by Callum's body and, when he turns, his grinning face. I feel a surge of irritation. He gives me an innocent stare, daring me to challenge his squatting rights on my roof. But when he notices Bill his expression changes, and he purses his lips as if to give a knowing whistle.

"Hey Laura – you've got company, I see."

"Honestly, Callum!" I glare at him.

But Bill says, "Hey, mate," in a calm voice, and raises his hand in a casual wave before shifting his attention back to me.

"Have a nice night," Callum says as we go inside out of range of his prying eyes, but something inside me has shifted. It's as if Callum has seen right through me, and called me back from a temporary place of safety to the reality of my life.

When Bill takes my hand my whole body tingles, and I feel a connection I never thought I'd experience again. Last night, when Bill and I made love, I forgot the canker in my life. But telling him about my past has brought the grief and rage back to the surface, and I realise it's not just Callum's intrusion that has pressed some kind of reset button inside me. I don't regret a moment of my short time with Bill, but how can I let it continue? It wouldn't be fair. I'm emotionally scarred, not a whole person. If Bill gets close to me, I'll damage him. The only way to protect him is to push him away.

I snap on the light and tell him, "I think it's time for you to leave." I try to say it in a calm tone, but the yellowish glare of the kitchen light falls on his face like a spotlight and he looks stunned. He flinches and takes a step back as if I've slapped him, bumping into the fridge door and triggering the humming part of its cycle.

"How can I leave? It's impossible." Bill's voice reflects the hurt I read in his eyes.

My stomach cramps from the acidity of the olives. I swallow, trying to stop the bitterness rising in my throat as I repeat, "You must go tonight. I'm back at work tomorrow." That's not strictly true. Tomorrow's Wednesday, the final day of my leave, but I need a day alone to decompress before picking up the threads of my monastic existence.

Standing in the kitchen staring at each other is agonising, so I busy myself with pulling clean office clothes out of the washing machine. I bundle them in my arms and go to the spare room where I keep the ironing board. The bed is stripped of linen to remove all traces of Miriana's stay, and the soulless room echoes my mood. As I bend to plug in the iron, I double-check under the bed that she left nothing behind. I'm still crouching down with my backside in the air when Bill opens the door, and I wince and cover my awkwardness by picking up laundry from the wicker basket.

I don't mean to shout at him, but even when I try to explain it comes out all wrong.

"Go home, Bill. It's not fair to drag you into my messed-up life." I'm racked with guilt, as if I've exploited him by inviting him into my bed for a mercy shag. He's a decent man, so perhaps he thought we were on the verge of a new relationship. Telling him my pathetic story was a kind of emotional abuse.

But he might as well hear the ending before he leaves. I'm no Scheherazade, and I don't do cliffhangers.

Bill hasn't tried to touch me since coming into the room, but he tries to catch my gaze. I won't let him and fix my eyes on the floor.

"You asked if Gareth found Hubert in London and if Ellie was there?"

He holds his hand up in front of him. "Don't say any more if you don't want to."

I do want to, because once he knows, he'll understand and have no choice but to go away and leave me alone.

"Getting the address from Hubert's father was easy," I say. "He was working from home, and we had a friendly chat. I didn't tell him he'd soon be getting a call from the police asking for the same information. Once I had Hubert's London address I messaged Gareth, and he went straight to the hostel in Islington. Later that evening Gareth phoned to tell me he'd confirmed Hubert was staying there, but he and his friends were out for the evening. Gareth said he'd showed Ellie's photo to the hostel manager, who couldn't recall seeing her. He was waiting outside the hostel for Hubert to return."

My breathing feels laboured, and the whole of my chest fills with air but no oxygen as I'm taken back to that night, sitting on my sofa, landline in one hand, mobile in the other. Waiting.

"I heard nothing from Gareth that night, and by next morning it didn't matter."

"What do you mean?" Bill darts a glance at me and shifts from one foot to the other.

"Next morning DS Tranter arrived at my door and told me..." I pause to choke back a sob. It's been three years, and still I struggle to force the words out. "...a young woman had fallen in front of a rush-hour underground train at Oxford Circus Station."

Bill's eyes widen in shock. "The police thought it might be Ellie?"

I nod. "It was Ellie. They knew Gareth was in London, searching for her. But he didn't expect to be called in to identify her body."

30

LAURA

The hours of waiting for Ellie's return had seemed endless, but they were a mere nanosecond in the eternal limbo my life became afterwards. The moment I learned my daughter was dead, I refused to stir up the murky waters full of unanswered questions and guilt. Ellie was gone. End of. Nothing else mattered; nothing could bring her back.

Don't get me wrong, the fallout continued for months: more questions, an ongoing investigation, an inquest – and, during that time, Gareth and I were in the media spotlight and hung out to dry. The tabloid press branded me an ice queen. The public wanted rawness, tears, a hysterical performance for the camera, but I refused to engage with the grief-porn stereotype. People in our area, who already had me down as a bad mother, decided I was unnatural. But I didn't care. The only way I could cope with the anguish and face the bleak future was to slam the door on the past.

Not Gareth. He was like a vulture scavenging on roadkill, picking over every detail. He claimed the investigation was incompetent. The word on the street was that family conflict had driven Ellie to run away to London, and one sub-text implied suicide. Others said she didn't know the London transport system and stood too close to the edge of the crowded platform, losing her balance as a train raced into the station.

After an investigation, the coroner didn't give one of the short-form verdicts we expected, such as accident or misadventure, but produced a narrative verdict detailing overcrowding on the station. A few passengers who came forward described being caught in an unusual crowd surge, and said it was hard to keep their balance. One witness mentioned a man wearing a dark hoodie, acting oddly, and described him running forward, flapping his arms and setting off a crowd chain reaction like a Mexican wave.

It turned out some of the cameras on the platform were faulty, so the witness's statement couldn't be corroborated and no man in a dark hoodie was ever traced. But Gareth clung to this idea because he needed answers. Ellie had left no message to tell us why she'd gone to London, condemning us to a lifetime of questions and if-onlys. Gareth needed someone to blame. He became fixated on the 'man in black', and, in his own shambolic way, began investigations.

There wasn't much Gareth could do to track down a stranger with a possible learning difficulty who might have sparked the crowd reaction which flung our daughter onto the tracks, so Gareth became convinced the clue to Ellie's death was linked to the manner of her leaving. "She didn't leave on a whim," he insisted, citing the evidence of her covering her tracks by leaving her mobile behind. "It must have been planned." For a man who'd originally trained in Law, his interrogation skills weren't subtle. He antagonised and intimidated everyone he spoke to, especially Ellie's friends. If they didn't answer his calls, or their parents banned them from talking to him, he'd lie in wait outside their houses. As his obsession grew, I made up my mind to leave him – and Wales.

That was when Gareth found a new focus for his anger: me.

Bill clearly wasn't expecting to hear Ellie's life ended under a train. I hadn't prepared him for a scenario so violent and final. His mouth gapes open, and I watch him wrestle with not saying the wrong thing. He says nothing. I remember telling him emphatically I hadn't seen Ellie since saying goodbye to her outside the staff room, but I hadn't told him she'd died. It seems his mind created an alternative ending. Perhaps he assumed Ellie had had a teenage strop and taken off to the other side of the world. Or maybe he thought she'd run away from home and not made contact with us but was still out there somewhere, waiting to be found?

To give him credit, Bill doesn't try hollow words of comfort – there are no words – but holds out his arms. When I don't go to him, he stutters my name, his voice cracking with emotion.

I shake my head. "It's no good, Bill. You must leave. Please."

Changing the subject gives him back his voice, because it spares him from having to mention Ellie. "I get that you need space, Laura. But don't let's break up before we've even started."

"Sorry, but there's no point."

His eyes lock onto mine but I look away, hoping he didn't notice my turmoil.

"We have a connection, Laura. I feel it and so must you. Let me come back at the weekend. I can work from anywhere."

My heart beats a little faster. He talked about photographing open-air swimming pools for a feature. Some of the best-known are right here in South London. He could be hanging around for weeks, nurturing false hope.

"The truth is, I'm not ready to be with someone. I might

never be, so I'd only hurt you." It sounds brutal and pathetic, and I hate myself for saying it.

"I understand your pain – don't push me away. Let me help you."

I shake my head, take a deep breath and go for the jugular. "Why don't you contact Amy? I'm sure she'll be happy to see you."

Bitchiness does the trick. He glares at me with confusion in his eyes.

"Right, I'm off. I see that's what you want." He stalks off and collects his canvas bag of camera equipment.

When he comes out of the sitting room with the bag slung over his shoulder, he's tight-lipped. I'm hurting inside, but I can't let him see. I watch him stride along the hall without looking back. My front door slams, the stained-glass panel rattles, and another player in the messy melodrama that is my life leaves the stage.

31

LAURA

THURSDAY

My office welcomes me back with a purposeful hum: a symphony of aircon, a buzz of computers on standby. I log in to check our workflow system, but my password's refused. A pop-up message tells me to fill in the IT helpdesk's form, but I can't because it's behind the password barrier. I dial the helpdesk number and study my rouge-noir varnished fingernails. What possessed me to paint them yesterday? I never add colour to my appearance, and now my hand looks like a phantom limb.

While I'm on hold, my colleague Marlene arrives and says "Hi" but doesn't stop by my desk to ask about my holiday. Why would she? I'm a monosyllabic bitch who only ever talks about work. Minutes later Dana comes in, hangs her jacket over the back of her chair, a proxy for her presence, and she and Marlene head down to the café in the atrium for coffee, bagels and a chat.

"Hey, Laura. Glad you're back." At least Harry, my boss, is pleased to see me. There's a bounce in his step as he approaches my workstation and plumps down on my visitor chair. "Good break?" His eyes are cornflower blue. I've never noticed, but since my holiday the world seems to have changed from black and white as if my senses have reawakened.

"Very good, thanks. I went to West Wales."

"Is that where your family's from?"

"No. They're in Cardiff. I visited my mum, but the holiday was more outdoorsy – water sports and stuff." I don't say I opted out of the paddle-boarding, but surprise myself by adding, "I went in my – um – campervan." I'm blushing because that's more personal information than I've shared in two years of working here.

At the mention of campervans, Harry's face brightens. "I've always wanted one, but Alison says we should wait till I retire."

"It wasn't all old people. The group I was with were aged thirty to early forties. Anyway – what's been going on here? I can't log into the system."

"Grab us both a coffee and come into my office. I'll update you."

I could go down to the sandwich bar for better coffee, but I decide to make it in the screened-off alcove in our open plan office. While I wait for the kettle to boil, I read the wall posters. Next week there's a bake-off fund raiser in aid of Help for Heroes – perhaps I'll make a chocolate walnut cake. What's come over me? I don't join in.

Harry's office is glass-fronted like an aquarium. We can be seen but not heard. I hand over his scalding cardboard cup. "My password's disabled, so I couldn't log in and get up to speed."

"It's routine for a forensic audit," Harry explains. I learn that the auditors swooped while I was away, but found no evidence of me cracking the systems and squirrelling away millions in a numbered offshore bank account.

"You passed with flying colours." He grins, delighted that his model employee, who produces a high volume of quality work, isn't a fraudster, and assigns me a batch of new projects to fit alongside my daily work routine. I return to my desk to find my password has miraculously been reset.

All day I focus solidly on work with no lunch break, but at 5.30 I hitch my bag over my shoulder and head for the exit. The few remaining colleagues turn their swivel chairs to watch with surprise, because I have a reputation for staying until the overhead lights dim and I have to switch on a lamp to cast a pool of lighting over my solitary workstation.

The rush-hour air is thick with dust and fumes, and I dodge around motorcycle couriers and get stranded on a traffic island. A cacophony of taxi horns blares as I run to the opposite pavement, where a *Big Issue* seller yells at me. Homeless people are on my mind, so I buy his magazine. Passers-by hurry past, staring at their mobiles but seeming to have evolved a sixth sense that stops them cannoning into one another. I don't do social media, so I take long strides and look up at gleaming glass and steel towers of the city of London, often rewarded by glimpses of ancient stone churches tucked into spaces between them.

I force myself to travel home by underground instead of my usual mainline train. When I see the red circular sign with the name *Oxford Circus*, I shudder and squeeze my eyes shut. The train jolts and I'm flung against a man carrying a folding bike in an enormous bag. "You all right, love?" he asks.

I nod, but I'm not all right. I've watched films where ghosts haunt underground stations and kick drink cans along the platform trying to make contact with the world of the living. Do I really expect to hear Ellie's voice whispering *"Don't worry, Mum. I'm okay"*? This isn't even the right platform. When she fell she was waiting for a northbound Bakerloo Line train, and I'm travelling south on the Victoria Line. If I'd hoped to sense her spirit, I'm disappointed. Ellie isn't here. She's not anywhere.

I still feel numb when I leave the underground at Brixton and catch the bus outside the station for the last few miles. The final stretch of my journey is on foot, alongside the soothing greenery of the Common. Was it only two days ago I walked this route with Bill? Being with him felt so safe, so normal, but I seem determined to sabotage anything good or hopeful in my life. I turn into my street and approach my house, noticing with annoyance someone has dumped one of those charity sacks of old clothes on my front doorstep.

As I draw closer it moves, and I see it's not a plastic sack but a small figure, crouching in my porch. It's Miriana.

My heart gives a flip of relief and I pick up my pace.

32

LAURA

As I reach the gate, Miriana scrambles to her feet. She's still wearing the cut-offs I gave her, and she looks rumpled but not dirty. Where's she been for the past four days? And why has she come back?

"Hello, Laura." Miriana keeps her eyes fixed on the path and pokes at the moss growing in between the tiles with her sandal. "I'm sorry. I didn't mean to worry you. Can we talk?" Her voice tails off.

My thoughts are in turmoil. If I invite her in, I'll be back where I started, wondering how to get rid of her. But as I reach into my bag for my key, I hear myself saying, "You'd better come in then." Ever since I told her to leave, I've been fretting to know she's all right. She waits meekly behind me while I tap in the alarm code.

I know she'd prefer coffee, so I make tea. While I wait for it to brew, I unlock the back door and tell her, "You know the routine. Get the chair cushions out of the wicker chest." Entertaining unexpected guests in my courtyard garden is becoming a ritual.

Carrying the tray of tea, I pause on the doorstep to glance

up at a plane on the flight path to Heathrow Airport and watch its vapour trail dissolving from arrow-straight into a smudged line. When I refocus on the garden, Miriana is speaking.

"What are you up to?" I hear her say, which seems an abrupt tone to take with me. Then I realise she's not talking to me – she's staring up at my flat roof, chatting to Callum. I remind myself there are worse neighbours than Callum. One day last winter, when I was putting the bin out, my door slammed and Callum helped me get back into my flat. His entry method was a bit unorthodox, but saved me the cost and hassle of calling a locksmith. After that we agreed to be keyholders for each other in case of emergencies, and I had a spare set cut for him.

Callum grins, and the gap between his front teeth makes him look younger. I'd always assumed he was in his mid-thirties. He looks beyond Miriana, sees me watching, and says, "I'm getting to know your lovely new friend. Maria, isn't it?"

Neither Miriana, nor I, correct him.

"You have a lot of new friends, Laura. Or is she your lodger? I'd choose her over that bloke who was here the other day – she's far better looking."

I blush. "For God's sake, Callum! No, she's not my lodger."

"Lighten up. I'm joking." He scrambles back across the roof, opens his window and calls down to Miriana, "See you around."

She's still grinning up at Callum's closing window when I set our mugs of tea down on the metal table.

"Callum's not a bad bloke, but he's way too old for you."

"I dunno," she says. "I thought he was nice."

I sigh. Miriana needs to put men out of her mind and sort out her own life. "So, where've you been staying?"

She sips her tea and makes a face. Perhaps she thought it was coffee. "I didn't stay anywhere. I moved around. One night I rode the night bus out to Essex and slept on a bench. In the morning I got on the first bus and watched a yellow sunrise over the Isle of Dogs! It was beautiful – just like Penarth."

It's not a comparison I'd make. A long time ago, when I sometimes went out for an early morning run in Penarth, I'd see the sun rise over the Bristol Channel and watch ripples of yellow and orange light dancing on the dark surface of the water.

Miriana leans towards me, a smile relaxing her face. "I have news. I've found a job in a café."

"Congratulations. Where?"

"Not far from here – Wandsworth Common. I can get there by bus, so maybe I could be your lodger, like Callum said."

Bloody Callum. "Sorry, Miriana. I'm not looking for a lodger."

Miriana's lower lip trembles and her voice is shaking as she says, "I could pay rent from my wages. But if it's 'no' I'll go away again."

Why does she think I'd want her money? This whole situation feels out of control, but something inside me has shifted. Stiff, moody Laura has stepped back into the shadows, and a more impulsive woman has taken her place. It's that woman who speaks now.

"All right," I say. "You can stay, but just for this week, while you get settled in your job. Perhaps someone in the café will have a spare room in their flat."

"Thank you." She leaps to her feet and hugs me. I don't pull away. Three days ago being hugged would have made me taut and anxious, but thanks to Bill I can now cope with a human touch. "I gave the café this address and said you'd give me a character reference."

"A reference! I hardly know you." How breathtakingly presumptuous. But I'm beginning to realise Miriana doesn't understand boundaries.

She shrugs and puts me in my place. "I told them you were a friend of my mother's. You have a daughter of around my age, don't you?"

Tears well in my eyes and I can't trust myself to speak, so I go indoors and make a cheese omelette and toast for supper. It's still warm in the garden, so I take the food outside and we eat in silence. The scent of honeysuckle drifts across from the trellis on top of my neighbour's wall. Miriana eats without pausing between mouthfuls. When she's finished, she tells me she's spoken to Jamie.

"Liam won't be looking for me."

"How can you be so confident?"

She reaches for another slice of toast. "Liam breached his parole conditions and is back inside for a long stay. When he gets out he won't remember me."

"How was Jamie? Will you go back to him?"

"Him? No way. He has a baby now, but I think he's already left that girlfriend."

"Sounds like you had a lucky escape. It's best you steer clear of him." It's almost dark, and invisible flying creatures are biting my arms. I think about fetching insect repellent or lighting anti-mosquito candles, but decide to move back indoors. "What clothes do you need for your job?"

"Black trousers, white top."

"I'll see what I've got." I leave Miriana washing up in the kitchen to go and sort through my wardrobe. I find a pair of black trousers, slightly too large, but she can wear a belt. White tops are more elusive. I unfold a t-shirt and hold it up; it looks grey from being thrown in the washing machine with darker colours. The only other white top is a high-necked blouse with a lace ruffle collar, but it looks frumpy. I hear footsteps, look round and see Miriana standing behind me.

"Please don't come into my room without knocking."

"Sorry. I was hoping you'd have a picture," she says.

"What do you mean?" I point at a cheap framed print of Monet's *Waterlilies* on the wall. "Like this one?"

She shakes her head. "No. Of your family. I've seen Ellie's photo, but what about her father? Don't you have a picture of him?"

I shake my head. When I left Wales I put everything from my past life behind me, especially Gareth. My mum warned me I'd regret making a bonfire of family photos and deleting everything from my phone, but she was wrong. Not once have I wanted to look at them. I'm glad they're gone.

"Why do you want to see his photo?"

"His name's Gareth, isn't it?" Miriana is tiny, scarcely five foot one, but the way she's standing, hands on hips, she seems to tower over me.

Did I tell Miriana his name? Perhaps I did, but I don't remember. I nod. "What's that got to do with you?"

Miriana shifts her weight from one foot to the other. "While I was away from here, riding the night buses, I was too scared to sleep. So my thoughts went in circles, trying to figure out why I'm here. And then it all fitted together."

She pauses for breath, and her next words tumble out in a rush. "I've worked it out. It's not me who isn't safe – it's you. I must stay here to watch over you."

A wave of exhaustion engulfs me, though today was my shortest working day ever. "You're not making sense, Miriana. Why wouldn't I be safe?"

"Someone's looking for you, Laura. I was sent to find you – and get your address."

"For heck's sake. Your blasted drug-dealer mates? Why would they be looking for me? I don't do drugs!"

She touches my hand lightly. I snatch it away.

"Not them. The man in Wales."

"What man?" To calm my dizziness I reach for the tumbler of water standing on my bedside cabinet and take a gulp. It tastes dusty.

"It was him – Gareth – who sent me." Her voice drops to a whisper. "He told me to find out your address and give it to him. I'm supposed to stay with you, but he didn't explain why. When I was riding that night bus, it came to me – perhaps I'm his gift to you, just like a daughter."

33

LAURA

Why would Gareth send a young girl, with a passing resemblance to Ellie, to track me down and move in with me? My legs feel shaky, and I lean against a chest of drawers for support. The whole idea seems deranged. Yet haven't my actions been equally demented – hiding from him, and cutting Mum out of my life because I thought she'd tell him where to find me? It seems my instinct not to trust her was right. She knew the campsite I was heading for, and noted down the registration number of my campervan. My own mother has betrayed me.

But how could I expect her to act differently, when I never told her the truth about the night I barricaded myself in the bathroom, with blood pouring from my broken nose, listening to the rhythmic pounding of Gareth's fist on the locked door...?

It was nine months after Ellie's death before I summoned the courage to tell Gareth I was leaving him. Investigations had formed the backdrop to our existence, but the inquest was over and we were living separate lives of cold misery in our once warm and busy family home.

It was early spring; daffodils were in full bloom in the window box and clouds shape-shifted in the sky when I told him: "I'm leaving Wales. I've decided to move to London." It was rare for us to eat together, but we were both sitting at the kitchen table.

Gareth twiddled a teaspoon and nodded. "Uh-huh." He didn't ask any questions, nor did he seem interested in my plans. Maybe he assumed I'd applied for a teaching job, but I knew I'd never work with teenagers again.

"I've had the house valued and it's going on the market next week."

His deafness and lack of interest vanished. "You're selling our house?" He lifted his head, and I stared at the puffy red face of a stranger whose t-shirt was cutting into the flesh around his swollen neck. The alcohol stink on his breath had become familiar, but lately even his sweat smelt different, as if it were tainted with toxins excreted from his pores.

"**My** house," I pointed out, knowing it sounded brutal and would antagonise him. I'd owned the house before Gareth and I started living together, using money my dad had left me for the deposit. Because we'd never married I didn't get round to putting a share of the house into Gareth's name, though he paid half of the mortgage. Now arrears were building up. Gareth hadn't worked for months and I was off sick from school. I was still on half-pay, but I knew that would soon end. I was incapable of returning to Llewellyn High, where everyone had known Ellie, and the process to dismiss me was kicking in. There was still a decent chunk of equity in the house, but mortgage arrears would soon swallow it.

"I'll give you a share," I said, but a small part of me, the mean part, couldn't bear to make it fifty per cent. I decided to give Gareth forty per cent, and keep sixty for myself to start over in London.

The property market was buoyant, and the house soon attracted a queue of interested buyers. I kept Gareth updated on discussions with the estate agent, but didn't involve him in the selling process – or tell him I'd gone for the lowest asking price in the range the agent suggested. I wanted rid of this hated house and my bitter memories.

"It'll take ages to sell," Gareth informed me regularly.

"Why do you say that? Is that what your rugby club mates are telling you?"

He glared at me with pure animosity.

"All the same, you might want to think about where you'll live," I warned him. "There's one potential buyer, who wants to move within six weeks."

The spider-veins on Gareth's cheeks became more inflamed. He didn't want to face reality. But I should have been more sensitive, knowing he wouldn't be able to borrow money after not working for so long. I'd destroyed what remained of his self-esteem.

A couple of days later I told him I'd accepted the cash buyer's offer. Now Ellie was gone, the ties that bound me to Gareth had snapped. We'd have drifted apart anyway, perhaps when she left for university. I didn't expect our split to be civilised, but I wasn't prepared for it to spill over into violence.

The morning after Gareth attacked me, I unlocked the bathroom door at first light and crept out of the house. All night I'd been terrified he'd kick the door in, but as I tiptoed down the stairs, I heard his gravelly snores and guessed he'd passed out in an alcoholic stupor. I drove myself to A&E at the hospital, where a doctor examined my broken nose and told me that as I could breathe through it I didn't need surgery, and it would heal naturally. The bone did mend, but now my nose is crooked.

When I look in the mirror, a stranger with a shifty expression stares back at me.

I was terrified of going back to the house, so I went and sat on a bench on the promenade gazing out to sea, where clouds, brimming with unshed rain, were gathering. The air was chilly and I thought of buying a coffee, but what if one of my former students was working in the café and saw my purple, swollen face? I went home and found Gareth awake, sober, and full of remorse.

When he saw me, he hid his face behind his hands and wept.

"I'm sorry – I don't know what came over me. I didn't mean... I'll do anything."

"It's a bit late for that. Just get out of here and don't come back." I could have threatened to make a Domestic Violence report to the police. At the hospital they'd pressed me quite hard to explain how I'd been injured, and I came up with a lame excuse of falling down steps on a night out with girlfriends. But I didn't need to threaten Gareth – my smashed-up face spoke for me. He bowed his head and went upstairs to pack a bag.

For the next fortnight I lay low, and used the time to clear the house of all reminders of my past life and happier times. The fireplace in the sitting room hadn't been used for years but I pressed it into service, plus every evening I lit a bonfire in the garden after I thought the neighbours would be in bed. Unfortunately, the Nixons weren't. Babs Nixon appeared in the garden in a white nightdress, pointing over the fence at my fire and wailing. Her husband came outside, his face contorted with rage, and shouted at me about the smoke before hooking his arm through his wife's and leading her back indoors. Knowing I'd soon be gone, I ignored him and carried on feeding Ellie's school reports and swimming certificates to the flames.

I avoided saying Gareth had hit me, and waited a while

before visiting Mum with a made-up a story about a fainting fit and a fall to explain my fractured nose.

"What did the doctor say?" she asked. "Did he test you for – you know – epilepsy?"

"No, Mum. It's not that."

How easily she swallowed it. Perhaps I'd secretly hoped she'd realise the truth, but Gareth had got to her first. Conveniently omitting to mention he'd hit me, he poisoned her mind with lies about my unreasonable behaviour and – the final indignity – evicting him from our home.

"Laura, please don't do this," Mum begged, and later raged at me. "You're irrational. It's grief that's driving you. You'll regret it."

I pretended to listen. But two weeks later, with the money from the house sale safely in my bank account, I rented a storage unit in Gareth's name, using one of the credit cards he'd left behind when he hurriedly moved out, and had all our furniture transported there. I transferred forty per cent of the proceeds of the house sale to Gareth's bank account, emailed him the paperwork for the storage unit, and left for London.

34

LAURA

In all the years we'd lived together, bringing up our daughter, Gareth had never threatened or hurt me. For years, our little family unit of three had been close and happy. We were both proud of our lively, talented daughter. Gareth taught her to sail, and always volunteered to drive her and her friends on hundred-mile round trips to compete in school sports championships, while I was the one who bagged tickets for Ellie and her mates to see their favourite boy band or YouTube celebrity.

Why was I so determined to keep my new address secret from Gareth? Was I really frightened he'd turn up and attack me? Domestic Violence sickens me, and I could never forgive or forget, but over time I came to understand this single flare-up was due to the fallout from Ellie's disappearance. Gareth had doted on his daughter, but in the eyes of the world he was potentially an abuser, and on that fateful night when he attacked me, he'd embodied the role.

Miriana's claim that Gareth was the man she'd been living with shook me to the core.

"You're talking rubbish!" I say, still clutching the off-white t-shirt, blouse and black trousers. For a moment I can't think why, then I remember and thrust them into her arms. "Try these. They might be too big, but they'll see you through till you can afford to buy some in your own size."

She holds the frumpy lace blouse, and her eyes glow. "I love this one."

"It's yours." I flump down on my bed and press my hand to my aching brow. "Come and sit here and explain. Are you saying the man you were living with was called Gareth?"

She nods. "He told me he was Gareth, but I was never quite sure. He seemed to have other names."

Of course it can't be him. Gareth's a common name in Wales, and he hated having the same one as Welsh sporting legends: Gareth Bale, Gareth Thomas, Gareth Davies. It made him feel inadequate. Despite his achievements as a Law graduate, and later a craftsman carpenter, all he'd ever really wanted was to play rugby for Wales but he didn't make the grade.

My mobile beeps. Bill's name pops up on the screen and sets my heart racing. The way I behaved was so brutal, I never expected to hear from him again. Now I realise I was rash. Perhaps there's still a chance, but after Miriana's bombshell I can't gather my thoughts, so I let the call ring out and tap a quick message.

> I'm sorry for how I acted. Can't speak now. I'll ring soon. I promise. x

He messages straight back.

> Don't leave it too long. I need to hear your voice. xx

Bill's forgiven me! I can hardly believe it, and I don't deserve it, but knowing he's at the end of the phone makes me feel cared-for and oddly safe.

When my phone rang Miriana tactfully left the room, and now she returns with two mugs of coffee. I wouldn't normally drink it after ten o'clock, but I sense this is going to be a late one.

"Tell me everything," I say. "I need to understand why you think this man might be Gareth."

35

MIRIANA

SEVEN MONTHS EARLIER

Miriana stepped off the bus into the raw chill of a December afternoon. It was three days after Christmas and schools hadn't yet restarted. The coach journey from London had taken three hours, and she remembered the bus crossing a bridge, but after that she must have dozed, because she woke with a jolt when it came to a stop. The man in the aisle seat next to her leaned over her to pull his rucksack off the overhead rack. "Can I get something down for you?" he asked, shouting because he was wearing headphones.

Miriana shook her head. Everything she had was in the backpack she was cradling on her lap. She hadn't let go of it for a second, not even to place it on the floor under her feet.

As the remaining passengers left the bus, the driver called out to her. "All right, love? This is as far as we go."

She dawdled along the aisle towards the exit, noticing the driver's face was creased but kindly. Perhaps he could help her. From her pocket she took out a paper with a scribbled address that seemed to be written in a foreign language: *Heol Something, Pillgwenlly*. So many consonants, she had no idea how to pronounce it. "Do you know where I'll find this street?"

The driver's friendly face took on a shuttered expression. "Sorry, love. I don't live around here. I'm from Tonypandy."

"All right." Miriana shivered as the frosty outside air stung her face. The dropping-off place was a bus shelter on a busy main road, and all the other passengers had melted away into the growing darkness. On the opposite side of the road were some bus stands, with three coaches waiting and a few passengers milling around. She needed the toilet badly. She crossed the road and looked around.

"You all right, love?" asked an elderly woman. Miriana explained she was looking for a cloakroom and the woman gave her directions. The toilet block floor was flooded and stank of urine, so she tiptoed around the edge, holding her breath. When she left the cubicle, a skinny woman with staring eyes and wild grey hair accosted her. "Got any money?"

"No."

The woman trapped her in a corner. "I don't believe you." She pawed at Miriana with a scrawny hand.

"Get off me," Miriana snatched her arm free and elbowed the woman, knocking her off balance so she slid down onto the soaking floor and sat in a crumpled heap, shouting obscenities. Miriana fled. In the street outside, she spotted a noticeboard with a faded street map under glass. An arrow pointing to a red circle read *YOU ARE HERE*, but the surrounding street names were too faint to make out. Keeping an eye on the cloakroom door in case the crazy woman broke out and attacked her, she noticed some areas in block capitals in a darker typeface and one was that place – Pill-something. She calculated it was about a mile away, orientated herself, and set off to walk along a road so wide it was almost a motorway inside a town. One side of the road was lined with trees and glass-fronted office blocks. Beyond that was a river. Her feet ached in the flat, thin-soled shoes. There were no people around but the traffic was brutal, and she had no smartphone with a map, only a cheap Pay-As-You-Go. The desolation of this place reminded her of Croydon. The cold burnt her face, and her lips felt sore and cracked.

Somewhere she'd need to turn right, so she took a risk and chose the next road. As she rounded the corner she almost cannoned into a gang of young lads on chopper bikes.

"Do you know a place called Pill-something?" she asked. The boys gaped at her and one mocked her accent. She jutted out her chin and strode on, but they followed, calling her names. *SLAG* was one; the others were worse. Miriana picked up her pace. Ahead of her was a road that seemed to be blocked to traffic. As she stepped over a barrier one of the lads lifted his bike, as if to pursue her, but the tallest one, who seemed to be the leader, signalled to him not to bother.

Miriana put her head down and wound her blue and white woollen scarf twice around her neck. Jamie's mum Frankie had knitted it for her for Christmas, with a matching bobble hat she hadn't brought with her. Miriana's eyes filled with tears. Frankie had been so kind, taking her in. She was shrewd enough to see the dark heart of her elder son Liam, but she forgave and prayed for him.

One Sunday, soon after Liam was released from prison, Miriana had offered to go with Frankie to church. "I'm really a Catholic," Frankie had explained, "but I can't be doing with confession." She gave a raucous laugh. "For me, it would take too long."

"So what church do you go to now?" Miriana had asked.

"I try them all out for a few weeks. If the folk are snooty or if they don't have biscuits with the coffee afterwards, I move on to the next one. We're United Reformed just now. How do I look?" She was wearing a mauve silk dress and purple jacket like a guest at a posh wedding.

"You look lovely."

"Thanks, sweetie." Frankie finished applying her lipstick and sucked in her lips. Miriana wondered whether to mention the red stain on Frankie's top teeth, but the front door banged and Liam came in, face flushed as if he'd been running.

"Smarten up, son, and come to church with us," said Frankie. "We can thank the Lord for giving you a second chance."

Liam's smile could melt the hardest heart. "Sure, Ma. The one in Wyndham Way, is it? I'll make a couple of business calls and I'll be with you."

Miriana hadn't been brought up in any religious tradition, but was expecting a grand building like the domed cathedral with a whispering gallery she'd once visited on a school trip. But Frankie's church was a simple brick building with whitewashed walls and polished wooden chairs in rows. Congregation members poured in until the church was packed and young men in dark suits brought out extra seats from a cupboard. The service was dull, and Miriana struggled not to yawn. She was sitting next to Frankie, with Jamie on her other side and Liam next to him at the end of the row. About half an hour in, Liam got up. She heard his trainers scuffing along the centre aisle, and swivelled round to watch. He stopped in the porch to talk with a couple of lads of roughly his age, and they exchanged something then left the building and the door clanged shut.

Twenty minutes later, while the congregation were on their feet singing, Liam slid back into his place, reeking of cigarettes. He elbowed his brother in the ribs and passed him some small plastic bags which Jamie crammed into his pocket.

Later, when they left the church and women in cardigans were setting out coffee cups, Frankie held onto Miriana's arm and viewed the biscuit selection. "Not worth it," she pronounced. By then Jamie had slipped away from their family party. When Miriana got outside she scanned the street and spotted him up ahead, turning a corner. She followed, but couldn't catch him up until Jamie stopped in front of a house where two young boys were kicking a football against the wall. In the front garden was a rusting washing machine and a pile of builders' rubble. All the curtains in the house, upstairs and down, were drawn, and Jamie had his finger on the doorbell. She called his name. He spun round and scowled at her, flapping his hands to shoo her away. Miriana felt cold inside with a pain that was almost physical. She put her head down and trudged home.

That night Jamie didn't come home for supper. She helped Frankie cook and serve the meal, but felt uneasy. Her relationship with Jamie was unravelling. She had no appetite, pleaded an upset stomach and went to the tiny room where she and Jamie shared a single bed. To make the bed seem larger they each had separate pillows, so their heads, if not their bodies, had breathing space. Jamie slept on the outside and grumbled every time his pillow slipped onto the floor. After they'd had sex, a mechanical ritual, repeated each night and most mornings, he'd turn his back on her and stretch so his long limbs filled the bed and Miriana's tiny body was crushed up against the wall.

She was lying on the bed, staring at a crack in the ceiling, when she heard a heavy tread outside. The door opened, but it wasn't Jamie, it was Liam. He didn't ask if he could come in, so she sat upright and waited for him to speak. Since he'd come out of prison Liam had been sleeping on the sitting room sofa. The top half of the bunk beds he and Jamie had used as children had broken, and was propped up on the balcony until someone found the energy to drag it downstairs and dump it by the communal bins. Liam scarcely acknowledged Miriana's presence in the household. Sometimes she overheard arguments between the brothers, and once she'd seen Liam shoving Jamie up against a wall and yelling in his face –

which was odd, because Jamie spent hours lifting weights at the gym and was taller and more muscular than Liam. A common theme of their fights was *You owe me*, but Miriana could never figure out who owed whom or what.

Liam crossed the floor in two paces and stood above her, glaring down. He made a swift grab for her dark blonde hair, twisting it around in one hand as if fashioning a pony tail into a bun. Miriana sat white-faced and silent as a thousand pinpricks of pain shot through her skull.

"You wanna keep staying here with my family, sister?"

She blanked her expression and stared back at him.

"It's time to earn your keep." Still holding her hair bunched in his hand, he leaned so close to her she could feel his breath, hot against her ear, and smell the garlic she'd recently chopped for supper.

"Sure. I'm looking for a job." She prised her hair free and shook it out. Her skull ached, inside and out. She'd made forays into the town centre, handing out her CV in shops, but none of the potential employers had called her back.

"Look no further," said Liam. "From now on, you work for me." He tweaked her hair again, though less roughly. Within a family this would be sibling horseplay, barely even a threat, but she wasn't family and had nowhere to go.

It started small. Liam would drop her off around the corner from the school she'd so recently attended, and drive away. She suspected he was watching her from a distance as she waited, leaning against the wall of a fried chicken shop, waiting for lads of around thirteen to approach her. They'd give her their names, but not real ones – names like Scally or Jokester – and she'd hand over a small package. That was it. Liam never asked her to handle money, but he paid her, randomly – a tenner here, a twenty there. She kept her hood pulled down over her face.

What if one of the teachers drove out of the school gates and recognised her? It was humiliating.

Miriana and Jamie never discussed her work, but she guessed he was working for Liam too. He'd been training to be a mechanic, but after a few months he packed it in. Poor Frankie was distraught, but Jamie bought her flowers. "Don't worry, Ma. I'm starting a new trade soon. I'll have plenty of money."

Why did Frankie swallow that? To Miriana, Jamie had simply said, "I'll get my flash wheels faster this way than grafting in engine oil and shit."

Miriana asked no questions, and Liam seemed pleased with her work and increased her pay. The occasional tenners became small bundles paid up promptly each Saturday. For the first time Miriana had money of her own, and could head into central Croydon to go shopping. One day, while browsing the rails in Primark, she bumped into Holly, a school friend.

"Hey, Miriana. What you doing now?"

"This and that. You?"

"At college studying childcare. Let's go for a coffee." She pointed across the road to a smart café and Miriana followed her. Holly chose a table outside. "I'm skint," she grumbled. "The only money I get is from babysitting."

"I'll treat you." Miriana swelled with pride as she queued for their skinny lattes and a chocolate muffin to share.

"What was it you said you do for a job?" Holly sliced the muffin into quarters and took three of the pieces for herself.

"Um. Deliveries."

"Like pizzas?"

"Not really. More like gifts." Her answer seemed to satisfy Holly. "In your college, do they run a course for animal care?"

"Yeah," said Holly, taking an e-cigarette out of her bag. "I think so."

Miriana wondered: Could she go to college, too? Maybe it wasn't too late. But first she'd have to get away from Liam.

Liam was rarely at home, and when he was Miriana kept out of his way. One evening when Jamie was out driving his mum to the supermarket (he had a provisional driving licence and Frankie was, theoretically, supervising his driving practice, though she'd confessed to Miriana she hadn't driven more than a handful of times in the fifteen years since her own test), Liam came into her room.

"Sister, it's time you were moving on to better things," he said. "How's about some travel?"

And that was how she found herself in Wales with packages to deliver to an unpronounceable address she was tramping the streets of Newport to find. Half an hour after dodging the lads on bikes she was back at the spot where she'd bumped into them, and her eyes stung with tears of frustration. She sensed she was in the right area but must have walked in a circle. She'd been wrong in thinking it was like Croydon – this area was way more desolate, and the few people she passed were hunched against the frosty wind with faces bleached by street lighting. She turned into a street where there were shops, and a woman in a hijab was fixing a metal shutter on the front window of her grocery store.

"Do you know this street?" Miriana asked, holding out the paper Liam had given her with the scribbled address.

The woman did, and when she spoke her voice had a friendly lilt. "Yes, love. Take the next right turn. It's only two minutes away."

Miriana thanked her and headed off. Number 36 was a terraced house with a front door that opened right onto the street. Miriana jabbed her finger on the doorbell but it was broken, so she hammered with her fist on the glass panel, waited, then knocked again.

She heard dragging footsteps and a young man, with old man's eyes, came to the door. He was wearing grey tracksuit bottoms and a white t-shirt with brown stains. She noticed his arms and averted her eyes.

"Are you Tinker?" she asked, blushing at the ridiculously childish name.

"Yep. That's me. And you must be Angel. Come inside, my darling."

Miriana shuddered. Behind her the dark street had an air of suppressed menace, and her hands were so cold she couldn't wiggle her fingers, but inside the house smelled of rubbish bins and vomit. This job Liam had sent her to do was overwhelming. He didn't want her simply to deliver the stuff to Tinker – her mission was to befriend him and move in. How the hell did Liam think she could stay in a place like this even for one night?

Studying Tinker's glazed eyes and shambling walk, she realised the befriending part would be easy. He seemed like a young child in an old man's body. But recalling Liam's briefing on her mission, hot and cold sweats washed over her.

"Tinker's house could be a hub for our business," he'd told her. "And you're the Angel who'll set it up. Move in with him for a few weeks. If he wants sex, let him have it."

She'd put her hand over her mouth, but couldn't disguise the horror in her eyes.

Liam's lips had curled into a snarl. "What's up, sister? Don't play the innocent with me."

Where was Jamie? Why didn't he come home and stop this? She'd held her breath, expecting Liam to grab her hair as he'd done on other occasions, but instead he'd reached into his pocket and produced a knife. He'd laid the blade flat across his left palm and, with a casual movement of his wrist, angled it to nick his own thumb. Blood had flowed, then seeped, from the wound. "See that? What a beauty!"

She'd stepped back. He'd pinned her against the wall and rubbed his bloodied hand across her face and mouth so she'd gagged on the metallic taste, spat and twisted, but his grip had held her firm. "I mean it. If old Tinker takes a fancy to you, let him."

Miriana had bitten down hard on Liam's hand.

"Ouch." He'd snatched it away. "You fucking tease." He'd lunged at her and pressed his body against hers as the front door had slammed, announcing Jamie and Frankie's return.

"Stop it!" she'd screamed.

Liam had put the knife in his pocket and slouched away, delivering his final threat from the doorway. "Mess this up and you're dead."

36

MIRIANA

Inside Tinker's house, locks were busted and windows were covered with sheets of newspaper, painted black. Pale-complexioned strangers drifted between rooms. Tinker pushed open the door to the front room, where an elderly-looking man, most likely younger than Miriana's father, lay on a stained mattress, moaning.

"I told you to eff off out of here," Tinker yelled. The man raised his head on a neck too fragile to support it, looked at them anxiously, then slumped back down.

Tinker slammed the door and turned to Miriana. "See what I have to put up with, Angel?" He led her along a hallway where an icy draught blew in through a broken window at the top of the stairs. "Here's the kitchen. Fix us a coffee. Mine's two sugars." He slunk away, and his uneven footsteps clumped up the uncarpeted stairs.

In the cubbyhole that passed for a kitchen was a microwave and a lethal-looking gas ring. The light was dim as she peered into cupboards looking for coffee and mugs, and a voice called out to her. A man had followed her into the room and was crouching on the floor. She stepped back, almost tripping over him, but he clearly wanted her attention and told her his name was Mickey.

"Take a look at this, love," Mickey said. She turned and saw he was pointing at his bandaged leg. With a rush of shock, she realised it had been amputated above the knee. "It's my own fault, sweetness," he said. "The docs in A&E warned me, but I couldn't ditch them pesky substances. My circulation went to pot, then I got gangrene, or was it sepsis? Or are they the same? Doctors tried to save my knee but it was too far gone. Let me show you." He began unwinding the swaddled bandages. "Ever so clean and neat it is."

Feeling nauseous, Miriana shrank back against the door frame. "Don't, please." She held up her hand as Mickey worked at the bandages, his tongue poking out from between his lips with the effort of unwrapping.

Abandoning her mission to make coffee, she fled, cannoning into Tinker, who had come back downstairs to look for her.

"Not hassling you, is he?"

Miriana shook her head and followed Tinker up the stairs to his room. Compared with what she'd seen of the rest of the house, Tinker's space was minimalist calm, with two futon mattresses spread on the floor, and candles – one with a Christmassy smell – glowing on a low table made of beaten copper.

"Now let's take a look at what you've brought me, Angel."

Miriana swung her backpack off her shoulders and knelt on the floor as she unzipped it and extracted the merchandise Liam had sent.

"Here you go." She passed him a dozen small packages and watched him tease one open, his fingers oddly nimble as he took care not to spill the contents. He spread out his booty on the table and opened another couple of bags, sniffing and licking the contents before pronouncing his satisfaction.

"How about a little something for ourselves." He reached for a battered black tin and took off the lid.

So he wasn't going to smoke the new supplies she'd brought him as a freebie from Liam. Miriana wondered why – Liam's stuff was safe, not cut with powdered glass and other shit, but it made no difference to her. "I don't."

"Whaddya mean you don't?" Tinker lit up. The distinctive chemical smell like burning plastic caught the back of her throat and she sneezed into the crook of her elbow. Tinker was gazing at her in awe as if she really was an angel, but he didn't press her. She accepted a beer from his cool box and sipped it slowly while he smoked. Tinker's thought processes seemed ponderous, and she expected his speech to slow further, but it seemed to animate him. He became chatty.

"You're gonna like it here in this house abroad," he told her. So Liam must have told him she was moving in. Tinker's words suggested he must have been part of an advance party sent to take up residence. Liam had taught her the lingo, and she knew a 'house abroad' was a trap house outside London. So who was the actual owner of this place? Probably the sick old man she'd seen lying on the mattress in the downstairs room...

"Don't tell your man, but I've found a great spot for hiding the cash. I'm stacking, y'see, though I shouldn't be keeping over a thousand in the house." Tinker winked, and she realised he was trying to impress her. In the candlelight his face looked distorted, monstrous.

Soon after, he passed out and lay on his back on the futon mattress, mouth open and snoring. Through the thin walls she could hear people moving around. Her throat felt parched, so she risked another kitchen run hoping Mickey would have gone elsewhere.

He had. An olive-skinned man had taken his place and was waiting for the kettle to boil. "I hope you're not looking for food," he grumbled. "Tinker's accused us of stealing so he ripped off the cupboard doors. But there's never any food. We have booze, we have fags. And other stuff. What's to worry?"

"Just water for me," said Miriana. Where were the glasses? But nothing made of glass would survive in this place. She found a plastic beaker with something mouldy congealing inside and tipped it out. There was no hot water or washing-up liquid, but she found the remnants of a bar of soap and took some boiled water from the kettle to scrub it.

"You're Angel, aren't you?" said the man.

"I guess so."

She could feel his eyes watching her. It was impossible to get the tumbler clean, so she stuck her head under the cold tap and took some gulps of water. Other people wandered past and stared in, but no one bothered her. They must assume she was under Tinker's protection. People assumed it was his house, though she now knew otherwise. She wondered if any of them knew Liam. It was a supply chain, Liam had told her, and names were neither known nor needed.

Wiping her mouth with the back of her hand, Miriana rehearsed her instructions in her head: stay in this house with Tinker; get to know his friends; find out who their local suppliers are. So was she also meant to be spying on Tinker? She knew Liam's next step would be to entice customers with freebies and gradually divert their business from local dealers. At some point, further down the track, after Miriana had identified all the key players, Liam and his heavies would come steaming down from Croydon and claim the territory.

Miriana left the kitchen and clattered up the stairs, noticing a second flight leading to an attic floor but lacking energy to explore. She returned to Tinker's room, where he was still lying on his back with his mouth hanging open. She flung herself down on the second futon. It was damp.

"Eurgh!" She sprang up again. On the floor was a folded-up sleeping bag, stained but dry. She unzipped it and wriggled inside, fully dressed, and lay on the hard floorboards. Car headlights from outside shone through the gaps where newspaper didn't cover the windows, and painted an eerie glow across the ceiling. She lay tense and watchful. Tinker stirred and got up. He stumbled around in the gloom and left the room. Further along the landing a door banged and she heard someone pissing into the toilet. He shuffled back along the landing and a floorboard creaked as he entered the room. She squeezed her eyelids shut. She sensed he was standing over her.

"Angel," he murmured in a high-pitched drawl.

As he lunged, Miriana tucked up her knees inside the sleeping bag and rolled sideways out of his path. He landed on the floor and yelped. Pulse racing, she heard his laboured breathing as he approached her, on all fours, like a prowling dog.

"No." She braced her hands against his chest and pushed him back. "Get off me." In the sallow glow, she could see his open mouth and the moist pinkness of his dangling tongue. He'd removed his t-shirt and trackie bottoms and was clad only in boxer shorts. His legs were twig-thin. He collapsed onto the fetid mattress and dragged her towards him. Didn't he notice it was wet and smelled of piss? She tried to stand but he grabbed her leg, his grip surprisingly strong. Miriana was trapped, with only the sleeping bag to protect her. Tinker curled his disgusting body around her and wriggled and writhed as if having a fit. When the tempo and volume of his breathing changed and he moaned, she realised, sick with disgust, he was pleasuring himself like an animal. When he'd finished, he patted her and tried to kiss her.

"You're lovely, Angel." He laughed, crawled back to his own mattress and flopped down.

Miriana shuddered. This was beyond disgusting. It was bad

enough standing outside schools with small packages pimped up to look like birthday gifts. She wanted nothing to do with these people. She ought to pity them, because with Liam involved some of them were going to get hurt, but she'd have no more part in it. From now on, she would look out for herself.

Tinker's snores rumbled around the room as Miriana lay still, waiting for this house, full of whistling sighs and groans, to fall silent. The street door banged, and footsteps thundered up the stairs. Miriana crept out of her sleeping bag, padded across to the bay window and peeled back a corner of the newspaper covering the glass. She peered out at the street and saw a police officer, on foot patrol, stop opposite and look across. Had he been tailing whoever had just come into the house? What if there was a raid? Would she be arrested? Heart hammering, she watched the officer making notes. He put his notebook away and took out a phone, or perhaps a radio, and spoke into it. Moments later a patrol car cruised into the street, with no blue light or warning siren, and stopped to pick up the uniformed officer. The car parked up for a few minutes, then drove away.

Miriana's hands wouldn't stop shaking. She found her shoes, retrieved her backpack and slung it over one shoulder. On an instinct, she rolled up the sleeping bag and stuffed it under her arm. She tiptoed down the stairs and let herself out into the night.

In the distance a siren wailed. She ran until she rounded the corner, then slowed to a walking pace so as not to draw attention. If Tinker's house was under surveillance, a police patrol car might come screeching back to carry out a raid. By staying close to the buildings, she calculated she could dodge into a doorway if she needed to hide. Like a silent shadow, she edged along deserted streets back towards the main road, where she picked up a sign for the station.

At the mouth of an underpass she paused, swaying with

exhaustion and indecision. Small heaps of glass on the ground suggested lights on the approach to the tunnel had been purposely smashed; the dark heart of the underpass seemed unfathomable. What if someone was lying in wait in the underbelly of the main road? For several minutes she watched and waited, but not a single car drove past, so she climbed over a barrier and ran across several lanes of major road. As she clambered up a grassy embankment on the other side her chest was burning, but she could see a bright light ahead. That must be the bus station. She'd find a place, out of the wind, hunker down and catch the first bus out in the morning.

But where would she go? Croydon was the obvious place. She'd never lived anywhere else, had hardly ever travelled, except on school trips to the theatre in London and once to Chessington, where she and her classmates were made to stare at caged wild creatures but forbidden to visit the theme park. Returning to Croydon and a vengeful Liam would be impossible – he'd been working for weeks on this plan to expand his territory. She was his emissary – his angel – and she'd bottled it...

She hadn't had to collect any money from Tinker. She'd assumed that delivery was a sweetener to build loyalty, as Liam had told her: "They'll pay me back in shedloads." But if Tinker was already part of Liam's crew, what did that mean exactly? She had the money Liam had called 'subsistence allowance' – around fifty pounds to cover food for up to four weeks and her return bus journey. Liam had told her not to return to Croydon for at least a fortnight, and she was meant to phone him every day and report back on her research: who was living at the house, local dealers, volumes and prices.

She crossed another road and headed towards the beam of light, but when she arrived it looked unfamiliar. Then it struck her – she'd walked to the railway station, not the bus station. Ice had settled on the windscreens of parked cars and the ground was slick with damp frost. She hunched her shoulders and looked for somewhere to wait out the rest of the night. She paced, turned, and retraced her steps as a swirl of snowflakes fluttered in the air. Next to the station entrance were some wide steps and a metal handrail leading to an office called *Swyddfa Eiddo Coll*. She squinted to make out the English translation – *Lost Property Office*. An overhanging porch offered some shelter from the next flurry of sleet.

She put the sleeping bag down on the top step and sat on it, the frozen concrete biting through her jeans. She rooted around inside her backpack for the wallet containing five ten-pound notes, then tipped everything out onto the sleeping bag and organised it into piles. Her phone was there, and a small washbag with toothbrush, comb and lipstick, underwear and two changes of clothes. But no wallet. She emptied her pockets: sweet wrappers, tissues, her outbound bus ticket. She shuffled everything again. Still no wallet. Someone at the house must have stolen it. Her money was gone.

37

MIRIANA

Miriana's eyes felt sticky and hard to open. She rubbed them with the back of her hand, and blinked in the yellow-grey light. The snow hadn't settled, but frost had thickened to ice and her sleeping bag was soaked through. She patted her jeans – so damp she wondered if she'd wet herself; her shivering body was playing tricks with her brain. On the floor beside her someone had left a half litre of milk in a plastic carton that hadn't been there when she lay down. Someone had come and stood over her while she slept. Yet this stranger had done her a kindness. Perhaps it was the sensation of another person close by that had woken her? She stared along the empty street and heard the sigh of electricity cables and the distant rattle of an approaching train.

Miriana stood up and peeled the sleeping bag away from her body. She moved around and stamped her feet to get some feeling back into her numb legs, wondering if you could die of hypothermia in one night? How could she move on from here? She didn't even have the bloody bus fare, but she wasn't going to shoplift or mug someone for money. That only left begging.

She inspected the carton of milk, noticing the top was

sealed. So whoever left it didn't intend to poison her. She opened it and took a long gulp, suddenly aware she was no longer alone. A train had arrived, and decanted grey-faced men and women who were leaving the station and weaving past Miriana's hiding place. One younger man had a laptop bag slung across his shoulder and was unlocking a bike from the racks. She tried to get his attention, but he swung his leg over the crossbar and wobbled as he rode away, the heavy bag dragging him to one side. There were men wearing paint-spattered jeans, and women dressed in the sort of clothes her mother had worn for early-morning cleaning jobs.

As the final stragglers approached, Miriana cupped her palm, cleared her throat and mimicked the whine she'd heard down-and-outs using in Croydon. "Hungry and homeless."

No one stopped. One man said, "Sorry, love," without turning his head to look at her.

She watched them scatter, some heading into the town centre, others striding towards the main road. Before the next train arrived, she must get organised. The sleeping bag smelled of alcohol and vomit, but not piss. She shook it out and it flapped like washing on a line. She folded it and draped it over the handrail outside the Lost Property Office. The sleeping bag wasn't lost – it was stolen. She, Miriana, was the one who was lost.

Standing in one spot was making her teeth chatter. She needed to move to dry off, so walked briskly through a car park and found herself in a street of yellowish stone buildings and shuttered shops. In a paved plaza she came upon a cluster of statues fashioned from metal. One had a vengeful look and sharp wings pointing skywards. That's me, she thought. An angry angel.

When the shops and cafes opened she'd find a cloakroom to get cleaned up, but first she needed money for a coffee. She wondered briefly about looking for a job, but what if Tinker or one of his henchmen found her? Newport wasn't safe. She must move on. Besides, who would employ her in these filthy clothes?

As she hurried back towards the station, a crowd surged out of the entrance and scattered. Drat. She was out of position and had missed a whole trainload. As she scurried back to her place by the entrance, a young mum with a baby in a pushchair met her gaze and held it for a moment.

"Homeless and hungry," muttered Miriana.

The woman hesitated but continued past, digging her hand in the pocket of her fur-trimmed parka. Seconds later she wheeled the buggy round, retraced her steps and dropped two coins into Miriana's cupped palm.

"Thank you."

The woman nodded, adjusted the rain cover over her sleeping baby, and walked on.

Two pounds! Miriana stared at the coins as if they were riches. If she stayed focused and kept on her pitch, she'd soon gather enough for a coffee and a coach fare. The station was a symbol of hope. She glanced across at the taxi rank where a man was waiting, with two massive sports bags at his feet. Miriana couldn't remember seeing any taxis arriving or departing the rank. The man noticed her looking and caught her eye. Embarrassed, she dropped her gaze and studied the cracks in the pavement, but when she looked up the man was strolling towards her, carrying a bag in each hand.

"Are you all right?" he asked.

She nodded, noticing he was smartly dressed. "I've lost my wallet," she said eagerly. "And I'm trying to get my bus fare back to London. Can you spare a couple of quid?"

"Sure," he said, just like that in a matter-of-fact tone. He took out a slim leather wallet, removed a ten-pound note and handed it to her.

She felt scared to touch it. It was too much. A couple of coins, maybe, but not a tenner. Begging was degrading. She needed to work harder for it.

He flapped the note at her. "Go on. Take it."

"Thank you." Overcoming her embarrassment, she took it from his hand.

"Are you sure you're okay?" the man asked, running his gaze over her damp clothes.

She shrugged. "Yes."

"You look like you could do with a hot drink. And a sandwich." He swung his sports bags, one in each hand. "Come on. I'll buy you a coffee."

Miriana shrank back, shaking her head. Yet he looked a safe person – the sports bags were like a badge of respectability. He had brown hair with lighter patches, and smelled of some kind of clean, spicy man-spray. He wasn't a boy, but she was hopeless at guessing the age of anyone above twenty-five – perhaps early thirties?

"I would like a cup of tea," she mumbled. She'd have preferred coffee, but guessed tea would be cheaper.

"Then follow me."

Miriana trailed one pace behind the man as he crossed the road and turned into a side street close to the shopping centre. They passed a café – the kind her father had told her was called a greasy spoon – where the windows were partly steamed-up, but she could see people inside dressed in work overalls. She'd feel comfortable in there in her grimy clothes. An aroma of frying bacon reminded her she hadn't eaten for over twenty-four hours, but her rescuer strode on until they reached a café with sleek windows and a wood and chrome interior.

"Sit there," he said, pointing to a round table, flanked by a sofa and two armchairs covered in a striped velvety fabric. She hesitated to sit on it in her wet jeans, but the man dumped his sports bags down on the sofa even though she could see there was dirt on them.

"You wanted tea? Is English breakfast okay, or do you want mint or Earl Grey?"

"No, that first one is fine." How many different teas were there? Her parents and Jamie's mum always had the same kind. PG Tips. Not that her parents drank it; her mum always drank Turkish coffee which she made in a long-handled copper pot on a burner, but she kept tea for visitors. Thinking of her mother made Miriana feel sad.

The man joined a short queue to place the order and brought their hot drinks over to the table with a sandwich on a plate. He didn't have food himself. "I got tomato and mozzarella, in case you're a vegetarian."

She nodded, unable to find words to thank this kind stranger. She fished the tea bag out of the mug and dangled it over the handle where brown liquid dripped into the saucer while she poured in a trickle of milk. The first gulp burnt her mouth. She put the cup down and took a bite of the sandwich. The chilled mozzarella soothed her tongue, and the sweetness of the tomato was the most delicious food she'd tasted for weeks.

"I'm sorry for interrupting your day. You were waiting for a taxi, weren't you? I hope you won't be late?"

The man stirred sugar into his coffee and pointed the end of his spoon at the sports bags.

"I'm delivering these to the local rugby club. They're running a taster day for under-elevens and needed some extra equipment." He glanced at the silver metal watch on his wrist. "The session doesn't start until nine-thirty. No rush."

"It's the school holidays?"

"Exactly. Are you a student?"

Miriana blushed and took another sip of tea. "No. I left."

"I see. What do you do now?"

Shame prickled her face and body. What was she doing? If she said she was a courier, he'd ask more questions. She could get up and walk out of this café right now. "I'm still looking for work. In a shop or a café, but I haven't had much luck."

"Do you live around here?"

Miriana shook her head. She'd already told him she was trying to collect money for her bus fare back to London, but he'd obviously forgotten. In the muggy warmth of the café she was finding it hard to breathe. She watched a woman make her way to the back of the café and realised there must be a toilet where she could wash her face and get cleaned up, but what if her jeans hadn't dried out? Would she leave a damp patch on the velour seat? Her face grew hot with shame, and the tears she'd been holding back slid down her cheeks.

"Hey." The man spoke in a quiet voice. "I didn't mean to upset you." He strolled across to the rack that held sugars and cutlery, poured a glass of water and handed it to her with a pile of paper napkins. "Take these."

"Thank you," she sniffed, dabbing her face while he turned his head, tactfully, to look out of the window. She sipped the water. There were ice cubes in the glass, and it soothed her throat better than the tea.

"I sense you're in some kind of trouble," he said. "Am I right?"

"Maybe."

"Do you have somewhere to live?"

"No. But I should go back to London."

"Is London where you're from?" He scrutinised her face. "There must be a reason why you've left and travelled to south Wales?"

"Perhaps London isn't the best place for me."

"Listen. If you're looking for a place to stay, there's a spare room in my flat you can have for a while."

Miriana's head jerked up in agitation and she gaped at him. It was time to get away.

The man laughed. "Don't look so worried. There's no catch. I have a spare room and I rent it out to help me pay the mortgage, but my last tenant recently left so I'm advertising for a new lodger. See." He picked his phone up from the table and swiped the screen. With a tap of his index finger, he brought up a website. "Here it is. It's on spareroomdotcom."

Miriana looked. It was a tiny room and everything in it was white: the walls, door, wardrobe and ceiling, a single bed, a painted chest of drawers. It was so beautiful. He swiped again and brought up more pictures. One was a view over the sea. Although the water was grey and the sky blanketed with clouds, it had a brooding calmness.

"That's the view from the window. I took it last week so it looks a bit misty, but in spring it's stunning."

"Wow." She handed back his phone. "It looks awesome. Thanks, but it's impossible. I couldn't afford it."

"There are plenty of jobs in the area," he said. "Even in winter it's busy with walkers, and people come for the sailing, so cafés are always looking for workers. When you find a job you can pay me rent."

A picture of a different kind of life shaped itself in Miriana's mind. There really was a room, after all – it was advertised on a letting website, so it wasn't as if the man was some kind of stalker. He'd been going about his business, waiting for a taxi, and when he noticed she was in distress he'd taken pity on her. No one could be more threatening than Liam or Tinker, so why not opt for his rented room? If it didn't work out, she could move.

"I'd like to look at it," she said. "Is it around here?"

He shook his head. "It's not in Newport. It's just outside

Cardiff, in a seaside town called Penarth – a short train journey away."

"But what about your rugby?"

He glanced at the bags and shrugged. "Christmas is a tough time for me – I've no family – so I volunteered to deliver this gift from my rugby club to theirs. I guess they could come and collect the stuff from me." He took out his phone and tapped a number. "Hey, how's it going, mate? That's right. It's me. I've brought the kit to Newport, but something's come up. I can't drop it off at the club."

He pressed the phone to his ear and listened. "Yes. ... No. I'm all right, thanks, but I need to head straight back. Can you get one of the lads to drive into town and pick it up from me, outside the station? ... Ten minutes? Cheers."

Miriana listened in on the one-sided conversation. When he'd ended the call, he turned to her. "Do you think you can find your way back to the station?"

She nodded.

"Good. Use the cloakroom here to get yourself cleaned up. Take your time. I'll go on ahead to hand over this kit and wait for you outside the station."

"Okay. Thank you." She hesitated, took a deep breath and asked the question she needed to ask. "Why do you want to help me?"

The man glanced away. When he turned back, there was a look in his eyes like pain, or sadness. "You remind me of someone. What's your name, by the way?"

"Miriana."

"That's unusual. A pretty name."

"What's yours?" she asked.

For the barest fraction of a second, he seemed to hesitate. "Gareth," he said.

38

LAURA

Miriana stops talking and her eyes briefly meet mine before she averts her gaze. Through my bedroom window, I see the pale globe of an over-sized moon but no stars. We're sitting side by side on my double bed; Miriana has one leg bent beneath her and her other foot on the floor, while I'm leaning against the headboard with my legs stretched out. My back is aching. As is my head. The past few days have been full of stories. Miriana's life history; me pouring out to Bill my grief at Ellie's death – and somewhere along the way lines have become crossed, as if Miriana's story has become entangled with my own. Who is Scheherazade? Is it Miriana, or me?

"I don't believe you." It feels like the only thing I can say, because a cold dread weighs on my chest. "What possessed you to go off and live with some stranger?"

But, the voice inside me nags, what if it was Gareth? Why else would she be here?

Miriana shrugs. "We were living together in Penarth, but not in the way you think. I had my own room and worked in a café. I had a small life and it suited me. He was often out. I think he went to his rugby club most evenings and weekends, but if he was home, one of us cooked and we watched films together. We never went anywhere together outside of his flat – not once in all the months I stayed there." She must have caught the expression in my eyes. "And no, we didn't have sex, if that's what you're thinking."

That's something, I suppose. "Then what did he want with you?"

She tosses back her hair. "I worked. I paid rent. Perhaps he was lonely?"

"This is serious, Miriana. When you climbed into my campervan and hid, you told me you were scared this man would be looking for you. Did he threaten you?"

"No. I told you." She stands up and rubs her calf. We've been sitting so long she must have cramp. "He was kind to me. He bought me books and talked to me about going to college, because he knew I wanted to work with animals. But how could I? I don't even know my status in this country. Am I allowed to stay? If I go to college, will they send me back to Albania like my parents?"

Something is wrong with Miriana's reasoning. If she's genuinely concerned about her immigration status, it would make no difference whether she works in a shop and pays tax and National Insurance or studies at college. I'm exhausted, and my patience is parchment-thin.

"I'm struggling to understand you. First you tell me you're scared of this man..." I won't say the name 'Gareth' because it sticks in my throat. "Then you say he was kind to you. What am I supposed to think?"

The only light in the room comes from the moon and a lamp on my bedside cabinet which has a black shade, so I can't make out her expression, but she lifts her hands in a helpless gesture and lets them drop. "It's complicated. Everything between us was calm, until, some days ago, his mood changed."

A sudden mood change, acting out of character – that's exactly what I experienced. It's hard to cling to the hope this was some other Gareth. I've never wanted to know anything about his life after I left, though my mother has tried to fill me in – and I remember her telling me he'd bought a flat with a sea view, which checks out with what Miriana's saying. Didn't Mum also tell me Gareth had been back involved in rugby for a year or so? After Ellie died, he developed a kind of paranoia and believed even the rugby club crowd had turned against him, but time has passed. It makes sense he'd have picked up the important threads of his life.

"What colour is this man Gareth's hair?" I ask.

"Mostly brown with lighter bits." Fifty per cent of men in the country would match that description, and Gareth's dark brown hair developed fair highlights when he was outdoors in the sun.

"His height?"

"Quite tall."

"Six foot? Or taller?"

"I'm not sure."

For the first time, I regret not keeping any family photographs on my phone or in hard copy. I could show one to Miriana and settle this once and for all, but cremating our photos was the only way I could annihilate the past and face the future. I know other bereaved parents find comfort in preserving their child's bedroom, keeping the bed covered with soft toys, not even washing the sheets – but I needed exorcism, not a shrine. I understand now that nothing I did was rational. I was deeply traumatised and on medication from my doctor. Everyone told me counselling would help, but I'd refused. As for Gareth's frame of mind – even before I left him his behaviour was verging on psychotic. He had delusions and fixed ideas about Ellie's death not being an accident. Even so, would he use such an unorthodox method to send Miriana to find me?

My mind is chattering and full of questions. I can't live with this uncertainty but I'm not sure if I can trust her, so I say nothing. I must know the truth. Even if I have to step outside the protective barricade I've erected around my life, and return to Wales to confront him.

39

MIRIANA

Miriana longs for Laura to stop asking questions – she's running out of answers. It's gone two in the morning and both of them are exhausted, but Miriana focuses hard on keeping her eyes open and staying awake because she mustn't let her guard slip, or say the wrong thing. She notices Laura's head slide down onto her pillow and sees her eyelids are closing. Soon she'll drift off to sleep. Miriana watches for a while but Laura doesn't stir, so she gathers up the black trousers and frilly blouse and takes them into the spare room where she hangs them up in the empty wardrobe. There are no sheets on the bed and the duvet has no cover, but Miriana doesn't mind. She's slept in many worse places. She kicks off her shoes and slips underneath the covers, fully dressed. Breaking her promise to Gareth is a worry. He's been very clear she mustn't tell Laura he sent her, and he's coached her through all the stages of what to do. But now she's blurted it out.

When she found Laura, her mission was to befriend her and find out her London address. "Use your initiative," Gareth had told her. "She's a caring person. Let her think you need her help." Stowing away in the campervan had been Miriana's idea, and she was proud of herself for thinking of such a clever scheme. After that silly mistake when Laura overheard her talking to Gareth on the phone, she was gradually winning back Laura's confidence. She'd hardly begun the second part of the mission Gareth had outlined for her...

Thinking about it makes her shudder, and she pushes it out of her mind. She can feel her allegiance wavering between Gareth and Laura. Sure, Gareth rescued her from a desperate situation and he's been kind to her, giving her a place to stay though she could only afford a small rent from her wages at the café. Miriana longs to tell Laura the truth about Gareth, but she doesn't want to hurt her because Gareth was once Laura's partner – why else would he send Miriana to find her? Laura could solve it by showing her a family photo and she could tell her "Yes – it's him" or "No – it's not", but Laura is being evasive on purpose. Perhaps she doesn't want to know the truth? Miriana doesn't believe Laura would have thrown away all the pictures and memories of her entire life – even Miriana's own father wouldn't have done that.

The things she hasn't told Laura weigh heavy on her mind. It's true that she's a lodger in Gareth's flat, and that they live detached lives but when he isn't out they often eat together and chat. Gareth talks to her about rugby and the series they watch together on Netflix, but never about his work. She doesn't even know what kind of work he does. During the months she's lived in Penarth, Miriana has made friends with other waitresses and the owner of the Green Kitchen café, but when they invite her to go out with them she always says no. She isn't seeking friends. It's enough to do her shifts, eat, and watch TV. She's found a safe place where she can keep her head down.

When Miriana told Laura that Gareth was kind to her, she didn't say her own feelings towards him were confused. Sometimes she wakes at night in her narrow single bed in her own room, and through half-closed eyelids sees him standing in the doorway gazing at her. Once he approached the bed and bent to kiss her – a peck on the cheek, the kind a family friend might give a child. Her body stiffened, she snapped awake and challenged him because she could read in his eyes that he wanted more. It's true, as she's told Laura, that he's never had sex with her, but that's because he's promised he won't touch her unless she's willing.

Gareth said he wants her to come to him when she's ready. But she isn't sure when that might be. If ever.

40

LAURA

FRIDAY

When I wake up on Friday morning I'm still dressed in yesterday's clothes and can't keep my eyes open. How many hours did I sleep? Three? A shower helps. Miriana must have heard me, because when I go into the kitchen she's there with the kettle already boiled.

"What are your plans for today?" I ask. "I don't have a spare front door key to give you but I'll get one cut during my lunch break." In fact I do have a set, but after the incident when I locked myself out, I asked Callum upstairs to hold onto them for me. That was before he started driving me crazy by using my roof as a sun terrace. If Miriana is going to stay here for a week and go to work, I'll have to decide whether to give her keys and whether to tell her the burglar alarm code.

"Don't worry, Laura. I'm not going anywhere today. I'm starting at the café on Saturday."

I haven't had a phone call asking for a reference, but perhaps cafés around here aren't picky. And she has experience from her waitressing job in Penarth.

Talking to Miriana has delayed me, but when I reach my office and touch my pass on the automatic barrier I realise I'm still earlier than the rest of the team, so my first task is to pick up the phone and ring Mum.

"Laura!" The delight in her voice fades to reproach. "I was hoping you'd call in on your way home from holiday."

Holiday? I'd almost forgotten. So much has happened, but I'm the one who should reproach her. "Mum, after my visit last week, did you ring Gareth and tell him where I was going?"

There's a long pause. While I wait for her to speak, I guess her answer.

"I might have done." Her tone is light but defensive. She doesn't think she's done anything wrong, but she's worried because she's been found out.

"Did you happen to mention," I ask, through gritted teeth, "which campsite I was heading for?"

"I'm sorry, Laura. It just slipped out. Gareth was thrilled to hear I'd seen you. Did he... come down and visit you?"

"Mu-um!" My groan is audible. I rake my free hand through my hair. I didn't have time to dry it properly this morning, and tousling it won't improve my look. "You shouldn't have done that."

Her voice is still in my ear. "I didn't mean to say which campsite. Perhaps I did."

If only she knew the chain of events she set in motion when she noted down my registration number and Gareth – allegedly – despatched Miriana to track me down. Even if she didn't, my red campervan would have been easy to find.

"It's time Gareth and I had a talk," I tell Mum, knowing this will set her off hoping and praying we'll get back together. "Give me his number. Unless he doesn't want me to know it."

"That secrecy nonsense was all down to you, Laura. Gareth's always wanted to see you. When I spoke to him that evening after you called in on me, he said he had some important new information about Ellie. That's why I told him you were in Wales..."

I groan. So he's still pursuing hopeless conspiracy theories. Mum goes off to find his number. I picture her putting the handset beside the phone cradle in the hall, even though it's the hands-free kind she could carry with her. When she opens the sitting room door, the theme tune of a morning news programme blares out.

"Here it is." Again she sounds breathless, and I let go of my anger and vow to visit her soon. She reads out his mobile number and it sounds familiar, because unlike me Gareth must have kept his original number.

"When will you call him?" Mum asks.

"I don't know, but don't get your hopes up. We're not getting back together. Ever. There's something I need to clear up with him."

After ending the call, I sit with my chin propped on my hand, staring at my blank computer screen. I can't tackle Gareth about Miriana on the phone. If I'm going to question him about why he's taken in a homeless teenager, I need to see his eyes. Does Gareth realise Miriana's now scared of him, I wonder, and is too frightened to go back?

I think of everything Miriana's been through – first her parents abandoning her, then Jamie, Liam, and Tinker – and my chest constricts. How dare Gareth join this queue of men who've exploited a vulnerable girl?

I force myself to wait until lunchtime to make the call, because I remember Gareth always took a break to eat his sandwiches between 12.30 and 1. I take a punt he follows the same routine, and I'm right because he answers immediately.

"Hello," I say, keeping my voice bland and non-committal as if this was a routine phone call. But my stomach isn't fooled and twists into a knot.

The catch in Gareth's voice is audible. "You've rung." He pauses before adding, "Thank you."

"I need to talk to you," I tell him, but he's talking too and not listening.

"Did your mum tell you I've got news? It's about Ellie. I think we're close to a breakthrough."

Irritation surges inside me – why should I listen to more of his wild theories? Is he still pursuing his amateur detective role? Or has he truly flipped? Perhaps he'll try to convince me our daughter was abducted by aliens.

"I can't discuss it on the phone," he says. "It's too important. We need to meet."

I take a deep breath. "It sounds like we both have things to discuss," I reply. Tomorrow's Saturday, so why delay? "I'll drive down to Cardiff and meet you. Tomorrow?"

"Will you come to my flat?"

I hesitate. If I go to his flat, I could check out the room with the white furniture and sea view where she's supposedly living, but do I want to face Gareth indoors? A public place would be better. The thought of returning to Penarth engulfs me in a wave of misery, and stirs up memories of a life interrupted, a daughter who never grew up, and everything we'll never understand about why Ellie ran away and ended up under a train.

"Not your flat," I say. "And not Penarth. Neutral ground."

"I'm so sorry about that day, Laura," he says. "I don't know what came over me. You selling the house, not consulting me, then leaving... It felt so brutal. I've said it over and over, but I'm truly sorry."

"I've tried to forgive, but it's hard." I can't forget, because I'm reminded every time I see my crooked nose in the mirror.

I make a quick calculation. I'll be driving to Wales in my campervan, so multistorey car parks in the centre of Cardiff are out. Even if there's enough headroom for the van to enter, I'd never be able to manoeuvre into those small spaces. What if Gareth turns aggressive when I challenge him about Miriana? Our meeting place needs to be somewhere with a large car park and plenty of other people around. Somewhere like the sprawling grounds of the National Folk Museum.

"St Fagans," I say. "I'll meet you in the main car park at midday tomorrow. Text or ring me when you arrive."

I end the call and glance at the empty seats in the office around me. It's still lunchtime, and I need to run out and get a key cut for Miriana. My life has been empty for so long, and now it's brimming with other people's needs.

As I walk the last few paces home, jingling the new set of keys in my hand, I foolishly imagine Miriana's delight for this gesture of trust from a woman who scarcely knows her. I open the front door and step into my hall. Silence.

"Miriana?" I call, checking the sitting room – it's empty – and tap softly on the guest room door. I glance inside. Miriana must have gone out. I hear a banging sound, and notice the door to the garden has blown open. Of course – she'll be outside, sunbathing. My garden's tiny, but she's not sitting at the table, so maybe she's laid out a rug on the ground in the sunny spot behind the potted Acer.

I hear a ripple of laughter: Miriana's soft giggle and the deeper rumble of a male voice, and wrench my gaze upwards to my flat roof. I was right about Miriana sunbathing. She's sitting with her legs dangling over the edge of the roof, flaunting a black bra in place of a bikini top, and swigging beer from a bottle. And Callum is bending over her, massaging sun cream onto her bare shoulders with his large hands.

41

LAURA

SATURDAY

For the second time in as many weeks, I prepare my campervan for the drive to South Wales. So much has happened that I've not yet unloaded the van since the holiday, and the bed, with its black and white striped duvet cover, is still assembled.

"I'll be gone all day," I tell Miriana, handing her the spare set of keys. I held them back yesterday because I was silently fuming over her rendezvous with Callum on my roof. "When you go out, double-lock the door but don't bother setting the alarm." I've decided not to tell her the code. I've also not told her I'm off to Wales to talk to Gareth. I don't want her phoning him, and I gather from what she's said that she wasn't meant to tell me about their connection. "What time are you starting work at the café?"

"I'm just doing a lunchtime shift today." She's already dressed in her work clothes, and the frilly white blouse looks surprisingly un-frumpy on her. "I think it's like a trial."

"Well good luck with it." I hesitate, wondering if she'll take my next piece of advice the wrong way. "Take it easy with Callum, yeah? He can be a bit... unpredictable."

What do I really mean? That he's a couple of decades too

old for her? That walking in on their little tryst last night took me aback? At least I restrained myself by holding my tongue when I saw them. It's not my place to tell her what to do and who to see.

"Oh, him upstairs!" She yawns, not bothering to put a hand over her mouth. "Don't stress. He's going away this weekend. Brighton, I think. When you get back, I'll cook dinner for us both." She opens the fridge door and rummages. "Good, you have pizza."

She follows me to the door to wave me off. At least I won't have to worry about Callum and Miriana frolicking together in my house while I'm away. Instead I think about Bill and how good it will be to hear his voice. I'll definitely message or ring him today. I crawl through South London traffic and join the motorway at Kew. My van is running smoothly, so I risk driving above sixty-five miles an hour and soon I'm speeding through Berkshire into Wiltshire and passing the junctions for Bath, then Bristol, before crossing the bridge into Wales.

I'm half an hour early turning into the car park of the National Folk Museum at St Fagans. I've always loved this place, set in a hundred acres of parkland, and often brought Ellie here for picnics when she was young. We both loved the original buildings, transported from all over Wales and reconstructed to showcase history, and my heart is heavy with memories. Ellie loved the old stone farm houses, especially the ones where animals and people lived side by side and children slept on straw mattresses inside a sort-of cupboard. My favourites were the old school house and a terrace of identical cottages, each decorated and furnished to show how domestic life evolved between 1805 and 1985.

Ellie's footprints are everywhere, but I can't picture Gareth here with us at all. Then, as now, he'd have been in his usual weekend place – the rugby club. I park on the end of a row, lean my head on the steering wheel and let memories of my daughter flood back. I don't fight or block them.

In my van I have teabags and week-old milk, so I could make tea for Gareth and talk to him here, but meeting in a public place would be better. I'll go on ahead into the café and text him to meet me there. I lock the van and make my way through the entrance into the grounds and on to the restaurant, where I settle at a quiet table. First I message Gareth to say where I am then I remember my promise to contact Bill. I can't ring him now because Gareth might show up at any moment so I dash off a quick text.

> Hi – sorry I haven't called yet. I'm in Wales.
> Family stuff. Ring you this evening. I promise.
> L x

I put my phone away, but two minutes later I take it out again to see if there's a reply. Sunlight glints off the café windows, turning my screen into a dark mirror. I squint as I scroll. There isn't a message, but anyway I was the one who said I'd contact him. Yet I'm ridiculously disappointed. As I stash my phone in my bag, I sense someone standing beside the table and glance up into the face of a stranger.

Gareth's dark brown hair has lighter patches – just as Miriana described – but now they're grey, not gold; his once-angular jaw is slack from the weight he's shed, and his eyes have the hollowed-out look that settled in them after Ellie died.

I inhale sharply and my chest tightens. Gareth stares – he must be noticing my crooked nose. He flinches and looks away briefly, but the misery etched on his face absorbs some of my bitterness and I have an odd compulsion to embrace him. Not in an amorous way. but as if meeting a long-lost friend who needs cheering up. We don't hug.

Gareth holds out his hand, stiffly, and we shake like strangers.

"Coffee?" He shifts his feet and mumbles.

"I'll get them," I say and join the queue. Since I arrived, the clock has ticked on to lunchtime and customers are hesitating between soup and the all-day breakfast while staff act as if a snail emoji is tattooed on their foreheads. After two years in London, it's hard to adjust. I grit my teeth and will them to hurry up.

"Here you go." I bang an Americano down in front of Gareth. He always used to drink his coffee black, but for all I know he might now prefer macchiatos or lattes.

"How've you been?" he asks.

"So-so." I fish out the tea bag and skip pleasantries. "I need to talk to you about—"

Gareth interrupts me. "Yes, I know – but I need to tell **you** about some developments."

We gape at each other. I'm no mind-reader, but he must know what I'm here to discuss.

"Okay. You go first," I concede.

He clears his throat. When he speaks, it's not Miriana he wants to talk about. It's Ellie.

42

LAURA

Gareth shifts in his chair and stirs his coffee. "I think we're close to a breakthrough. Rosie's ready to share what she knows about Ellie leaving."

Rosie? Ellie? My head is spinning. "Well, I'm here to talk about Miriana!" I've made this journey of a hundred and fifty miles to find out why he's scooped up a young woman from the street and taken her into his home. What was he planning to do? Adopt her?

Gareth's dark brown eyes narrow, almost as if Miriana's name hasn't registered. He looks at me as if I'm the one who's not quite with it, and continues. "I'd given up hope, but now I think we're close to finding out why Ellie ran away."

My body tenses. He's still trapped in his old conspiracy theories. I'll have to let him have his say, but it's an effort to recalibrate my thoughts. "We already know what happened to Ellie."

"Yes, but we don't know why! Why did she go to London? Where did she stay and who did she meet?" He's practically shouting, and a woman at the next table glances across as if our conversation's more interesting than her companion's wittering small talk. I signal to Gareth to lower his voice.

"After you left – and I don't blame you – I lost the business. The cocktail of meds I was on did nothing to numb the pain. It was a year before I could work again, but I steeled myself to go back to the rugby club. There was compassion and camaraderie. The lads gave me space to breathe. Not like those bastards at your church—"

"What do you mean, **my** church?" I was never religious. My only connection with the church was taking Ellie to Sunday School, and running a French class in the church hall.

"You know what I mean." He raises his cup, and I see his hand is trembling. "You were always down at that church, turning people against me."

"For heck's sake, Gareth. That's not true. I rented the hall for my French classes. It was nothing to do with the church." A memory of Gareth going crazy and chucking a brick through the church hall window, while a meeting was discussing safety of children and teenagers, comes to me. On that day, our local newspaper had splashed Ellie's photo across the front page with the headline WHY DID SHE RUN? and a smaller picture of Gareth and me underneath. The inference was clear: no one had been found culpable, so her parents must be to blame.

Twitter exploded. Vile trolls, who knew nothing about our family, spread filthy lies and conspiracy theories. By then we had a family liaison officer keeping us updated on the investigation, and she advised me to come off social media. I did, and I've never gone back.

I straighten my shoulders, pulling myself back into the moment. "You were saying?"

"The whole world had turned against me," says Gareth, "but not the lads at the club. It helped that there were some new members – Oliver from your school..."

"I'm sure Oliver was always a member," I point out. "He was a Games teacher, so he belonged to the cricket and football clubs, and the sailing club too."

"Yes, but he encouraged staff and students from school to join, including Ellie's friend Adam."

"Adam?" I can't help asking. His mother Jen and I were friends in our baby group days, and she used to bring Adam round for play dates. Fresh grief unbalances me: Adam must have finished school a year ago. His life is moving on, but Ellie's ended before she even learned her GCSE results. "What's Adam doing now?"

"He deferred his place at Leeds University to work for a year and save money. Drinking at the rugby club is cheaper than in town. Calls it his gap year staycation." Gareth gives a hollow laugh. "Not that he talked to me much until recently. Things are better now, but most of the time, only two people have been there for me."

"Who were they?"

"Your mum," Gareth says in a solemn voice, and I bow my head thinking of them consoling each other for a double loss – first Ellie, then me – "and your former colleague, Bryn. Did you know he's head of Modern Languages now?"

I shake my head. "So Bryn's got my old job! Good for him. Since I left I've had no contact with anyone."

"It took time for Ellie's friends to get used to me being there. Adam was the first to speak to me. A couple of weeks ago I was drinking late and most people had left, but Adam came and sat beside me. He'd had quite a bit to drink, so I was bracing myself for him to say something abusive. He was het-up and emotional, and wanted to talk about Ellie. He said she wasn't being bullied at school – he was sure of that – and none of his mates bought the rumour about her being abused at home."

I shudder, because this is hard to listen to.

"Adam told me Ellie had been distant with her mates for months. She kept breaking up with friends, letting them down over nights out, not responding to messages—"

I leap to my dead daughter's defence. "Ellie was revising hard for her exams. And she did go out with friends. Clubbing with Zara—"

Gareth holds up a hand to silence me. "Adam said her behaviour started to change while she was on the French exchange, staying with Hubert."

"We noticed that," I admit. "After she got home, she was forever closeted in her room, chatting to him online."

"Perhaps it was the taste of freedom while she was there? Even worse, her friends suspected she was using."

"Using what?"

"Err, drugs, substances."

"Never!" I stare at him in horror. "That can't be right? Ellie's mood swings were hormones and exam stress."

He nods. "Adam said they dismissed that theory and decided Ellie was seeing someone, who wasn't local or from school, so they guessed she'd met him at Phantasia. Rosie spotted her walking on the cliff path at Southerndown, hand in hand with a tall, dark-haired bloke, but she was too far away to see them clearly. Later someone else saw her in town, but she was with a shorter, fair-haired guy."

My heart thuds painfully inside my ribcage. "Are they suggesting our daughter was some kind of slapper with a different man every week? Did they tell the police about these men while the search was on?"

Gareth lowers his head, avoiding my gaze. "According to Adam, Rosie thinks she knows who the mystery man was. But after your, um, visit to her house, before her police interview, she decided there must be truth in the rumour Ellie was having problems at home."

I shuddered at the memory I'd suppressed for so long. "Why didn't she tell the police?"

"Maybe she didn't want to get involved." Gareth's voice trails off, and he turns his head so I can't read his expression. Does he think that I'm to blame?

"I see." I feel a deserved sting of humiliation, guilt and failure. In the early days of the investigation, when Ellie was missing but still alive, my actions might have led to a major clue going unreported.

43

LAURA

THREE YEARS EARLIER

Ellie had been missing for three days, and over the weekend we'd heard nothing from the police. Mum, Gareth and I passed the day in shared silent misery. I remember Mum, sitting straight-backed on a garden chair, yet somehow falling into a doze, and Gareth mumbling he was going out, so I was left alone to dwell on frightening scenarios.

Why were the police working so slowly? Did they even have leads? Surely some of Ellie's friends must have known her plans – no sixteen-year-old would disappear to London without telling someone. Ever since the Thursday evening I'd been phoning Ellie's so-called friends, but according to their over-protective parents they were always out. Why wouldn't they speak to me? Were their parents scared their own children would be influenced by Ellie going to London?

Leaving Mum dozing in her chair, I slunk indoors and put in a call to Rosie's house. Her father answered, and I could hear Rosie's voice in the background, refusing to come to the phone. When he rang off I was steaming mad, so I rammed my bare feet into sandals and picked up my car keys.

The front door of Rosie's house was painted olive green. In the minutes between jabbing my finger on the bell and waiting, I came to loathe that colour and swore I'd never use it again. Rosie's mother, Karen, opened the door. Although it wasn't late, her smile vanished when she saw me.

"Laura. What do you want?" The overhead hall light bleached colour from her face making her skin appear waxy.

What a dumb question. I felt like slapping her. Ignorant cow. I wanted my daughter to come home.

"Where's Rosie?" I stuck my foot into the frame so she couldn't close the door in my face.

"She's up in her room. I'll see if—"

But before Karen could see, or say, anything, I pushed past her and headed for the staircase.

"Laura..." she called, but didn't try to stop me. Perhaps she'd seen the devastation in my eyes, or noticed my hunched shoulders and lank unwashed hair. "I suppose it won't do any harm." She went to the foot of the stairs and called up to say I was on my way, but I was already opening Rosie's door, without knocking.

Rosie wouldn't have heard her mother calling because she was sprawled on her bed, wearing earphones and watching a film on her tablet. The fact she was doing something so teenaged, so normal, while my daughter was god knows where, infuriated me. A draught from the door alerted her and she gaped at me, furrowing her brow, as I crossed the room in two paces.

I took a deep breath and raised my hands. "Can I talk to you?"

Rosie pulled out the earpieces, leaving the wires dangling around her neck. "What d'you want?" When she looked at me, her eyes had a guarded expression.

"Tell me what Ellie was planning," I pleaded. "Why's she gone to London? She must have told you."

Rosie gave an ugly-sounding laugh. "Ellie tells me nothing. We've hardly spoken for like, six months. Ask her yourself." Her hand covered her mouth as if to take the words back, but she didn't say sorry.

"I – don't – believe – you." A toxic mix of rage and panic surged through me. My brain clouded. I clenched my fists.

"Suit yourself." Rosie's chin jerked up, but a mascara smudge under her eyes suggested she'd been crying. She stuck an earpiece back in her right ear, twisted her face away from me and stared at the wall.

As I grabbed for her shoulder to force her to turn round, my hand became tangled between her ponytail and earphone wires. I tightened my grip, and suddenly I was tugging her hair, shaking her and yelling. "She must have told you something."

"Ouch, get off me, you're crazy." Rosie squirmed away and hit out, so when I snatched my hand away I was left holding a clump of her hair. Her breathing altered, and she gulped out a brief sob followed by a chilling scream.

Footsteps pounded up the stairs, and seconds later Karen burst into the room. "What's going on?" she demanded, gathering her sobbing daughter into her arms.

"She attacked me," wailed Rosie. "She's crazy."

"Wh-aat!" Karen's shrill voice slid higher up the soprano scale.

I stared in horror at my hand holding the pale strands of Rosie's hair. Did I really attack her? "I just wanted Rosie to tell me—"

"Why would I tell you anything? After what you and your sick family did to Ellie." Rosie burst into noisy sobs that sounded fake to me.

"Get out, Laura," said Karen, in a frosty tone.

"S-sorry." Mortified, I caught my breath, turned and ran from the room. I trudged down the stairs, out to the street and my waiting car.

A cup rattling against a saucer summons me back, and I glance across the table to see Gareth watching me with an anxious expression.

"Threatening Rosie was a mistake," he says.

"I didn't threaten... it was a misunderstanding. I told you that at the time!"

He shakes his head slowly. "It wasn't your fault. The police didn't ask Ellie's friends the right questions. They weren't persistent. I've always believed someone else was involved. Someone who lured Ellie to London."

My head hurts. "Ellie's dead. It makes no difference." Searching for a reason is Gareth's mission, not mine. "Besides, she did have a reason for going. To see Hubert, even though he denied it and swore he hadn't met her. She probably turned up at his hostel and he sent her away, and she was too embarrassed and ashamed to come home."

"Yes, I've thought of that. I never quite believed Hubert's story, until Adam told me Rosie has information she's never mentioned about some bloke Ellie was seeing. What if she was involved with some low-life she met at Phantasia night club? Perhaps someone older, who came down from London for business and turned her head? Mightn't he have suggested a post-exams adventure? Ellie would have known her uptight father wouldn't let her to go to London."

"Why doesn't Rosie just tell the police about this man?"

"Adam and I talked it over with a couple of my mates at the rugby club. He thinks Rosie's worried she might be in trouble for not mentioning it at the time in her police interview."

"Fair point. So why raise it now?"

Gareth's eyes took on a faraway look. "It's been three years, Laura. Three years tomorrow."

I flinch, because it isn't at the front of my mind. I don't observe anniversaries, and I've forced myself to forget the terrible ones. "Ellie's friends are young men and women now. They've matured. Rosie's already completed the first year of a nursing degree."

"So what did your friends say about pursuing this?"

"They said to leave it alone. They know I've been through hell, and don't want me set up for more disappointment. I promised them I wouldn't do anything until I'd discussed it with you, because we'd need to talk to Rosie together and we both have baggage there. If you could reach out to her..."

I shut my eyes, not sure if I can bear to confront the memories I've blocked. Talking to Rosie will stir nightmares, and pin images of Ellie's death back inside my inner eye. I'll never be able to fall asleep without seeing a repeat loop of my daughter falling underneath the train.

"I know that the man in the hoodie, who set off the crowd surge, was never found," I say to Gareth. "But that was just terrible timing. An accident. All the investigators cared about was directing London Underground to act on overcrowding to prevent future tragedies. As if Ellie was a poster girl for public transport safety."

The inquest returned a narrative verdict, not a straightforward finding of accidental death, and the coroner said the reason for Ellie being in London and on the platform at that time was unknown.

Gareth's eyes meet mine. "I've always thought the police lost interest in why she left and stopped investigating because they expected there'd be an accident verdict – they only had to mark time and wait for the inquest."

The more I think about it, the clearer it becomes. My meltdown in Rosie's bedroom had sealed our reputation and forfeited any claim to sympathy. Karen would have made sure everyone heard that it wasn't only Gareth who was angry and aggressive – clearly everyone wanted to believe I was an abusive mother. Why wouldn't Ellie run away from a home like ours?

44

LAURA

SATURDAY

Gareth takes a swig of coffee. It must be stone-cold by now, but it's warm in here and his face looks flushed. All around us knives and forks scrape across plates, and the smell of frying chips taints the air. The self-service queue is snaking out of the door.

"What makes you think Rosie would talk to us now? I mean, why would she talk to me after what happened?" My mind feels sharper, as if I've woken from a long sleep.

"Rosie's at university in Cardiff. Adam's confident she wants to talk to us, but we'll need him as a go-between. I was thinking you could write her a short note."

"An apology, you mean?"

He nods, sheepishly.

"I'll do it. I still think Rosie should talk to the police if she has information."

"They'll think I put her up to it," says Gareth. "The police have me down as some kind of nutter with PTSD."

"How long have you known about this?"

"A couple of weeks. I promised the lads I wouldn't do anything until I'd discussed it with you, and they knew it wouldn't be easy for me to get hold of you. I reckoned the police would be more likely to listen if you're on board."

"I'll write the apology," I promise. "Then we'll see. You've surprised me, I admit, because I came here to discuss something entirely different."

I need to know what possessed him to send a vulnerable teenager to track me down. I remind myself that every time he'd tried to reach out to me, via Mum, I'd blanked him. Perhaps this was his last shot at getting my attention.

I take a deep breath. "I need to ask you about Miriana, the girl you sent to find me."

The newly-slack skin under Gareth's jaw gives his face a hang-dog look. "What girl?"

Up to now we've been having a civilised conversation. Why is he being so obtuse?

"Don't be ridiculous. Miriana: the homeless teenager you took pity on and scooped up off the street in Newport. Who did you think you were? Professor Henry Higgins rescuing Eliza Doolittle? Or was it because Miriana looks a bit like Ellie?"

Gareth gapes with genuine puzzlement. "Who's Miriana?"

Lunchtime at the folk museum café is over and it's time for afternoon tea. The staff couldn't keep up with the rush and trays have run out, so customers are awkwardly balancing plates of scones and tubs of jam and cream while they search for a seat. Every vacant table is piled high with dirty plates or stained with ketchup and spilled baby food. An elderly woman in a smart belted raincoat, a strange choice for a summer day, is looking pointedly at our empty coffee cups. I ignore her.

A headache pulses inside my skull as I stare at Gareth. "Are you saying you *didn't* send Miriana to find me on the campsite in Tenby?"

"Honestly, Laura, I've no idea who you're talking about. But no, I didn't send anyone to find you." He scratches his left hand

and I notice a scaliness around the knuckles – his eczema must have come back.

"You're lying! Mum told you I was heading to Sand Dunes campsite and gave you my registration, so you sent Miriana to stalk me. That's what she told me."

Gareth scratches behind his ear – perhaps there's eczema there too? My own face itches, and it's a huge effort not to mirror his body language and join in with the scratching.

"Your mum might have told me where you were going, but honestly, I didn't send anyone. I'd have come myself, if I thought you'd speak to me."

Amid the clatter of knives and hubbub of the restaurant, I'm stunned into silence. The events of the last ten days have been surreal. Surely they were orchestrated by Gareth.

"I always hoped your mum would persuade you to see me, and it seems she did, because you phoned me yesterday."

In the stuffy air of the crowded café, my face feels hot. Why would Miriana lie to me? And if Gareth didn't send her, how does she know so much about us?

"Swear to me, Gareth, you don't know a girl called Miriana? Because she knows you. She told me you found her, begging outside Newport railway station when you were delivering rugby kit for a holiday training camp, and because she reminded you of Ellie, you took pity on her and gave her a place to stay."

He shakes his head. "No. I live alone in a flat in Penarth – always have done since you left – and I rent a lock-up unit for my carpentry workshop because I don't have a garage."

Grief and loss have left Gareth looking older than his years, but through the mask, I glimpse the man I once loved. Although I can't forgive him for lashing out at me, it was because he was broken: a devastated father, robbed of words and reviled by the community. When I rejected him, the only emotion he had left was anger.

"Who is this girl?" he asks. His hands lie still on the table now and he listens with renewed interest.

"Her name's Miriana. Her parents originally came here from the Balkans before she was born, but a year ago their permission to remain was withdrawn. She can't have been much more than sixteen at the time, but she stayed on alone. She told me she'd been renting a room from you, and you sent her to track me down in Tenby and find out my London address." I grip the edge of the table until my knuckles turn white. "She said you told her to move in with me!" It sounds ludicrous, and when I flick my eyes up to meet his, he looks troubled.

"Jeez, Laura. I don't like the sound of that ... You're saying a stranger has moved into your house?"

"Yes." A tingling sensation creeps along my spine. This is beyond curious – it's downright terrifying. If Gareth didn't send her, why did Miriana worm her way into my life? If she's lied about Gareth, she's probably lied about her parents and Liam and Jamie, and everything else she's told me. Most unsettling of all, I've left her alone in my house with her own set of keys. What is she doing in my absence?

"Do you think someone's planted her there?" Gareth asks.

"Who the hell would do that? I thought **you** had! She played mind games with me. Told me she was scared of you because you were sometimes angry."

"Which fitted in with what you thought."

"But she was definitely living in Penarth. She knows the area, and she worked at the Green Kitchen. She described it to me. Think, Gareth. Didn't you ever see her around town?"

"If I'd seen a girl who looked like Ellie, I'd remember."

What if there's a link of a different kind? Could there be a predator in our small seaside town, one who has a preference for teenage girls with dark-blonde hair?

45

LAURA

Gareth and I are talking in muted voices, but our conversation is going in circles. He wants to set up a meeting with Rosie so we can convince her to talk to the police, but I'm snatched back to the present, a feeling of unease building in my stomach.

"Sorry, Gareth, I can't stay any longer. I have to go." I grab my bag from where it's hanging on the back of my chair and put my phone away in the zipped compartment. "I must find out what Miriana's up to."

"Did you tell her you were meeting me?"

"I didn't."

"That's probably a good thing. Be careful. You don't know what her game is, and there might be other people involved. Can you call ahead and ask a friend to go to your house with you? Or flag your concerns with the police?"

I think of Bill, and remember my promise to ring him this evening. I'll do it as soon as I get back – as soon as I've had the showdown with Miriana. Will he give me another chance?

"I'll be fine," I tell Gareth, "but thanks for your advice. I might knock on my neighbour Callum's door before I go in."

"And you'll write that card for Rosie?"

"Give me a break! Yes – I'll do it." Doesn't Gareth understand I have new worries? My chair makes an angry scraping noise on the hard floor as I stand up.

Gareth walks with me to the car park, and when I speed ahead of him he breaks into a half-jog and catches up easily. It's clear he's back in training and his fitness has returned. I'm glad about that. When we reach my campervan I see a flicker of admiration in his eyes, and know he'll want a guided tour, but I don't have time. I jingle my keys and turn towards him.

"Let me come with you to London," he says. "Tomorrow is Ellie's... um..." he gropes for words, "three years. I don't like to think of you going back alone to a stranger in your house. How old is this girl anyway?"

My thoughts are in turmoil, but I'm touched by his spontaneous kindness because it feels like more than I deserve. Moral support would be comforting, but this is a separate chapter; Gareth's not part of my London life, and Miriana's my problem. It's down to me to get rid of her once and for all.

"She claims she's eighteen, but she looks younger, and she's tiny – five-feet-nothing. It won't be a problem." I take off my lightweight jacket, ball it up and chuck it onto the passenger seat. "Thanks for offering. I'll be fine."

To my surprise, Gareth holds out his arms and I let him hug me while each of us contemplates the three long years separating us from Ellie. Knowing we've made our peace is a kind of comfort. We'll go our separate ways as two damaged people, who once shared a beloved daughter. I climb into the driver's seat, wind down the window and lean out to wave.

"Take care," he says. "Keep my number in your phone and ring if you need me."

I nod, start the engine, and my campervan glides slowly out of the parking space.

Motorway traffic is heavy for a Saturday evening, and it's a stop-start journey, rarely accelerating above fifty. Warning signs tell me the speed limit ahead is going down to forty, then thirty miles an hour. I stop, start, crawl forward and halt again. A red warning light on my dashboard control panel flickers, goes out, and returns ten minutes later but this time it stays on. I smell hot dust and realise my elderly van is overheating. As the queue is stationary, I switch off the engine to let it cool down.

The standstill lasts ten minutes. I open my window and smell fish on the air. Blue lights of a police patrol car speed along the hard shoulder, and traffic crawls forward in single file, past the lorry that's shed its load of salmon across two carriageways. Fish corpses carpet the road like the bloody aftermath of a battle. Most of the tiny bodies are whole, with staring eyes, but others have spilt their innards on impact. It's an upsetting sight, but I tell myself the fish were dead already, the lorry's rear door lock must have failed and they slithered out on a bed of ice. After the stress of the day, this gore on the road leaves me close to tears. My warning light's still on, so I urge my van to keep going to the next motorway services at Reading.

I pull off the motorway and fill up with fuel, then curse myself for wasting money because I'm going to sell the campervan, aren't I? This might be my last trip. In the petrol station shop I buy coolant but I can't figure out how to open the bonnet. A roadside rescue patrol man takes pity on me, even though I'm not a paid-up member of his organisation. In minutes he's found the right catch and topped up the radiator.

"Why not sign up for membership," he grins, handing me a leaflet. "I might not be around next time."

I thank him, and he gives a mock salute as he moves away. The dead fish and my close brush with a breakdown have left me feeling shaky, so I park the van and crawl into my living quarters for a break. I could make myself a coffee, but though I have water and a kettle, the gas bottle is turned off into travelling position and it feels like too much effort to switch it on. I sip water instead, lie down on the bed and shut my eyes. Just for a few minutes...

When I squint at my phone, more than an hour has passed. Have I really been asleep so long? I've a list of missed calls and messages, and one is from Bill! My heart leaps, and I fire off a text:

> I'm on the road heading back from Wales. I'll call you later. x

Miriana has been phoning me too – six missed calls. Her most recent voicemail is just a few minutes old, so it must have been this message that woke me. I press the phone to my ear and listen.

"Laura, where are you? I thought you'd be back hours ago." The message rambles on but her voice grows faint and trails off.

It's none of her business where I've been. I've caught her out in her clumsy lie. I play the voicemail again. This time I listen carefully and her next words after "I thought you'd be back hours ago" drive a chill through me.

"Hurry up, please. Gareth's here, waiting for you. And he's getting angry."

46

LAURA

Miriana's infantile fantasies are messing with my head. I've spent the whole afternoon with Gareth, who denied all knowledge of her existence. His shock when I told him about her seemed genuine, and we said goodbye in a civilised, friendly manner. So how can Gareth be in London?

Is it possible he was so worried about me confronting a strange girl alone that he made a snap decision to drive to London? Did he wonder why Miriana had claimed to be living with him in Penarth, and decide he needed to find out what was going on? In that case he might well be angry when confronting her. And what about the logistics? It's true I was driving slowly, and my break here at the motorway services has lasted ninety minutes. I suppose it's feasible he could have reached south London by now, but it makes no sense.

A familiar creep of fear returns. All afternoon Gareth acted normally, but what if the things he was telling me about Rosie were a ploy? Miriana wasn't meant to tell me about Gareth, so perhaps when I challenged him it caught him off-guard and now he's raced ahead of me to London – to do what? Take her back with him?

No point in ringing her. If I press on I'll be home in just over an hour, but a traffic jam after I've left the motorway costs me another twenty minutes and my anxiety skyrockets. To distract my thoughts, I turn the radio up to full volume and let the chirpy voice of the presenter draw me in. He's at some kind of music festival for families, interviewing a mum who's adopted a group of three siblings. The presenter's careful not to give their real names, and I listen to the mum describing the harrowing time settling the younger children. It's hard to believe she's sharing so much personal stuff, telling the world the eldest can't come to terms with his birth mother's rejection and regularly runs away to search for her. My heart breaks for this woman, who's offering unconditional love for a child, who keeps running back to a mother who doesn't know how to nurture him. Tears slide down my cheeks. If I don't stop crying, my eyes will be too blurry to see the road ahead. I think of Miriana, left to fend for herself, and the troubled life she's fallen into, moving from one exploitative man to another. And what about Ellie? Was it my fault for letting her go out clubbing at weekends where she met a man from London and embarked on an adventure that led to her death?

As I turn into my street, the setting sun is painting patterns across rooftops, and attic windows glow as if on fire. As usual there's no parking space large enough for my van, so I turn the corner and find one in the next road. It's not yet dark, but there are lights on in my flat. That surprises me, because Miriana's super-careful with electricity and follows me around, switching lights off.

As I step into the hall, a TV theme tune blares out to greet me. It sounds tinny, so must be coming from the small portable set in my kitchen, not from the sitting room. I recognise the tune and clap my hands over my ears because it's *Casualty* – a programme I can't bear to watch, because ambulance sirens trigger images of violent death.

"Miriana, where are you? Switch that off," I shout as I sprint along the hall past the closed sitting room door to mute the programme. I put down my handbag, drop my campervan's keys on the kitchen counter and head for the bathroom. After hours on the road I need the loo urgently.

As I'm washing my hands, my phone pings with a message from a number I don't recognise. I tap on it automatically. Gareth! But Miriana's last voicemail said he was in my house, so why's he texting me? Either someone's mistaken or I'm being gaslighted. I glance at the message – something about him having spoken to Adam who's heard Rosie is ready to talk to us. I can't deal with this now.

In the mirror my eyes have black smudges underneath, and I dampen a corner of a towel and scrub away the mascara. I take a deep breath and unlock the bathroom door.

"Miriana," I call, turning the handle of the sitting room door. From the direction of the kitchen, I hear a clunk as if the door to the garden has blown shut. Is she outside? I'm sure that door wasn't open when I dropped my keys on the counter. I hear a footstep behind me and, as I turn round, something heavy strikes the back of my head. There's a searing pain. I cry out and collapse forward. Everything goes dark.

47

LAURA

Rough fabric is scratching my cheek. I shift my head fractionally, and pain burns my skull. When I open my eyes everything looks foggy, and I'm lying, face down, on my sitting room carpet with a heavy weight pressing on my calves. My legs feel as if something's grinding them into the floor. In panic, I slide my right hand to touch the base of my skull. My hair feels stiff and sticky.

"Laura." A muffled female voice speaks from somewhere above me.

"Uh?" I try to lift my head, but my neck feels ready to snap, so I slide both hands forward, take my weight on my palms and slowly raise my head in a cobra position. The room is dark, but some light leaks through a gap in the curtains and falls on Miriana, outlined in a dark silhouette, sitting in an upright chair. The pain in my head undoes me. I groan, close my eyes and fight against the pull of unconsciousness.

"Help me," I mumble, struggling to stop my eyes from closing. "Something hit my head. I can't move." Oh god – am I paralysed from the waist down? Shivery waves of heat and cold wash over me as I summon every ounce of strength and try to move my right leg. It won't budge. In desperation I focus on my feet and manage to wriggle my toes. Maybe I will walk again.

Miriana is muttering something, but I can't make out her words or see her face, only her outline.

"I can't hear you. Come here. Help me get up."

More light bleeds in from outside. If I turn my neck to the right I can see Miriana without triggering that stabbing pain. She seems to be fidgeting, and she's moving oddly, as if she and the chair have melded into a single body. Why doesn't she help me? Her words are strange banshee sounds: oos and aarghs, as if she's been dragged into Babel and lost language. A splinter of moonlight falls on her face. With a wince, I drop my head because I see why she can't speak. Her mouth is covered with thick silver tape.

My heart races. Someone has broken in, tied up Miriana, and now he's attacked me. He must have been ransacking my home when I returned, not that there's much to steal. I keep a small amount of hidden cash as a kind of running-away fund, not that I expect to use it – I'd only be running away from myself. If I offer cash to the intruder, will he leave without harming us? With a massive effort, I kick my feet back and upwards. It hurts like hell, but the weight pressing down on my legs lessens and I hear a thud like boots hitting the floor. Both my legs feel numb and my feet tingle with pins and needles, so I brace my arms to push up onto my elbows. Every slight movement takes seconds. I'm resting to gather strength when someone steps over me, missing my fingers by inches. A man – tall and bulky, wearing dark clothes – but I can only see his back view as he steps towards Miriana and rips the tape off her mouth. Before I catch a glimpse of his face, he strides across to the door and says, in a voice that scrapes my memory, "I'll leave you ladies to have a little chat."

The door slams. A key turns in the lock.

"What? Who?" I splutter, rolling onto my side so I can struggle to a sitting position, drag oxygen into my lungs and wait for Miriana to explain. She stays mute. If I try to stand I'll keel over, so I slide towards her on my bottom, propelling myself with my arms. That's when I see why she can't move.

Miriana's hands are pulled behind the chair and taped at the wrists; her ankles are bound to the legs of the chair.

"What's going on?" With my fingernails, I pick at the tough tape around her ankles, feeling for an end I can work with. This product is strong and designed for mending leaking pipes. I know because it comes from the cupboard under my kitchen sink. Miriana acts as if she's dazed. Her head lolling sideways.

"Who's that man?" I ask, my hands sticky from the tape but not making much progress. I need a pair of scissors, but even if I could stand, how can I get to my kitchen when the intruder is outside the door?

Miriana's eyes roll and she runs her tongue over her dry lips. "You know who he is," she croaks. "It's Gareth."

48

LAURA

Whether Gareth's car could have raced my campervan down the motorway becomes irrelevant, because this man isn't Gareth. His voice is familiar, but I can't place it – the pain in my head is throbbing. My efforts to free Miriana are feeble, but she seems detached, as if she's drifted off to some other place.

 The intruder must have had his ear pressed against the door, waiting to hear what Miriana will say, but she's incapable of saying much. He must have grown tired of waiting, because the door creaks open and his large body fills the doorframe. He's grown a beard, and it makes him look much older. When he joined Llewellyn School he was a slim twenty-nine-year-old, but he's bulked up, and his arms and upper body are muscular like someone who's spent the past few years lifting weights – and playing rugby. Although I can't see much detail of his face I'm guessing the bloom has rubbed off, and the extra weight, though it's mainly muscle, has added years to his age. He can't be much older than thirty-two. I stare at him until my eyes burn and I have to blink. I reach for the edge of Miriana's chair to pull myself up, but my numb legs go into spasm. I reach for the window sill and drag myself up, tweaking the curtain to let in more moonlight.

"I don't know what the hell you're doing here," I yell, "but get that tape off Miriana – and explain yourself."

Bryn laughs. His voice is a deep bass and echoes around my small sitting room, triggering a memory. Soon after Bryn arrived at Llewellyn School the music master went off on sick leave for cancer surgery, and Bryn took over rehearsing the school choir for the Christmas concert. I remember he sang a solo – I think it was *Myfanwy*, usually a choral piece from the songbook of Welsh male voice choirs – and stunned the audience with the purity and resonance of his voice. Congratulations followed his performance of the sentimental ballad that tugs my nation's heartstrings. Now that same voice, rumbling around my sitting room, seems to come from somewhere deep in the earth. Like Hades.

"And why would I do that?" Bryn walks behind Miriana's chair and taps his fingers on the binding around her wrists. "When I took the trouble to make it nice and tight?"

"For fuck's sake, Bryn." Pins and needles shoot along my right leg and I clutch the windowsill for support. Some feeling is returning to my legs, and I realise that while I was briefly concussed and lying on the floor Bryn must have been sitting on the sofa with his feet pressing down hard on my calves.

"Haven't you two had a catch-up yet?" he asks, with a sneer. "Better hurry up. We don't have much time."

"What the hell's that supposed to mean?"

He flumps down into an armchair and examines us as if we're laboratory specimens. He's enjoying watching us sweat. He's flipped. He's not going to tell me anything.

"Is this the man you were lodging with in Wales?" I ask Miriana.

She nods and mumbles, "Yes."

"He told you his name was Gareth? It's not. It's Bryn."

"Wrong." He cuts in before she can speak. "Brynmor Gareth Jones. That's me. What Welshman of my age doesn't have Gareth in his name somewhere?"

Miriana clears her throat and coughs. "What've I done wrong, Gareth?" she asks, in a wheedling tone. *Don't call him Gareth,* I want to shout. "I did what you asked. 'Find Laura,' you said. I went to the campsite, met some teenagers, blended in. And I found her. You wanted her London address. As soon as I knew it, I gave it to you."

I remember that call now. Miriana's voice mechanically reciting my address, and me thinking she was ringing her drug-dealer associates. I should have forced her out of my campervan and left her behind in that picnic layby. She knew exactly how to manipulate my vulnerability. Was it Bryn who trained her in that? And why is Bryn masquerading as Gareth? Where does he even fit into all of this?'

"You weren't very clever, were you?" Bryn says, with a sneer. Is he talking to me? But no, his target is Miriana. "You had one job," he laughs briefly, "to gain Laura's confidence. Be subtle, I told you. What did you do? Opened your fucking mouth and told her all about me. Who did you think you were? Her reincarnated daughter?"

Bryn prowls across the room and switches on a table lamp set on a low cabinet so it illuminates our faces from beneath. Miriana's and Bryn's faces look eerie – all head, no body.

Bryn's eyes narrow, and he glares at Miriana. "You never intended to come back to me, did you? After all I've done for you. You decided to hitch your future to Laura. You'll suffer for that."

"Stop it, Bryn," I yell. Now there's some light in the room, I feel less threatened. If I can force him to look at me, perhaps I can talk him down. "Whatever's between you and Miriana has nothing to do with me. You've already got my job – head of Modern Languages. What else can you possibly want from me?"

"Now there's a question." He gives an ugly laugh. "What could I want indeed?"

Miriana remains silent, staring at the floor, but now she raises her head and says, "It's about—"

But before she can finish her sentence Bryn's on his feet, his back to me and blocking my view of her. Horrified, I watch as he raises his arm and strikes Miriana across the face.

She and I cry out in unison.

"Shut it," he says, glowering at each of us in turn.

"Stop this madness," I yell. "Leave Miriana alone and get the fuck out of my house. You've got two minutes or I'm..." I cast around for ideas. Can I move fast enough to unlock the catch and open the window? I could shout up to Callum. Tell him to call the police.

Bryn notices the direction of my gaze. "Not so fast." His hand drops on top of mine and traps it flat on the sill. "Him upstairs is away. Shame. Didn't you know?"

My shoulders droop. I did – Miriana told me this morning.

"Stay quiet, both of you." Bryn grips my upper arm, forces me to pivot and marches me the few paces to my sofa, then shoves me with such force that my feet fly from under me, my knees buckle and I thump down on the seat. If I'd hit the floor my lower back would have taken the full force, and it strikes me: we're in big trouble here, Miriana and me. *Think, Laura, think.*

With her ankles bound to the chair and her hands stretched behind her back, it's a struggle for Miriana to stay upright. The weight of her head drags to one side, and that blow must have sent her head spinning. Fear for Miriana's safety pulses inside me, but I stay silent and think. Because talking isn't getting through.

Bryn locks my sitting room door from the inside and pockets the key. He picks up the roll of duct tape and waves it in my face, and I flinch as he takes out a pair of thin blue surgical gloves. Surely he's already left forensic traces all around the flat from his clothing and his shoes, so why is he going to such lengths? There's only one answer to that, and fear creeps up my spine.

"Help!" I yell, followed by the loudest scream I can muster, but my windows are double-glazed units designed to block traffic noise. No one will hear.

Bryn grabs a cushion and presses it over my face. The velvet fabric's inside my mouth. Suffocating.

"I warned you. Laura. You should've kept your mouth shut." He holds the cushion in place with an elbow, leaning his full weight on it while he cuts a long strip of tape. He moves the cushion and presses tape over my mouth.

I can't speak, and it's hard to breathe. It pulls my skin like Elastoplast. I try moistening it with my tongue, but my mouth is so dry. Bryn cuts another length from the roll, longer than the first, grabs my hands, and winds the tape – once, twice, three times – around my wrists.

The future flashes in front of me, and it's terrifyingly brief. Bryn's not worrying about DNA because there's nothing that links me to him. And the reason he isn't hiding his identity from us is clear. We'll never be able to turn him in. For Miriana and me, it ends here.

49

LAURA

"Now we're all sitting comfortably..." says Bryn, settling himself in the junk shop armchair I reupholstered in red and black tartan. His face looks sallow in the dim light from the table lamp. I slide along my leather sofa, so I can see past him to Miriana. "I think you'll like this story, Laura. Once upon a time, there was a beautiful young girl called Ellie."

At the mention of my daughter's name, I leap to my feet, raise my bound hands and shake them helplessly in front of me. I splutter inaudible sounds from behind my gag. How dare he defile my daughter's memory by mentioning her name?

"Ellie was just sixteen years old when she went on a school exchange to Nantes and stayed with the family of a handsome young man called Hubert. Ellie's school friends guessed she was besotted with this French lad, and secretly cheered her on. Ellie was having the time of her life, because, you see, she wasn't a good little girl at all. She was wicked and wild."

Pain stabs my heart, worse than the ache in my head. The cushion he used to cover my mouth is on my lap. What if I rushed at him, pressed it over his nose and mouth? But my bound hands are useless, the imbalance between our physiques is vast, and I wouldn't even have the strength to knock him to the floor. I can't lift my hands to cover my ears.

"In France, Ellie distanced herself from her friends, but they covered for her. She stopped attending morning lessons at the *lycée*. In the afternoons the British students were taken out on trips, and sometimes she turned up for those, though Hubert rarely did. The *lycée* staff weren't surprised. Hubert was seventeen, and had been kept down a year for fighting and truancy; they were glad not to have his disruptive influence. Hubert's parents didn't care either: his father worked in Paris and often stayed away; his mother was a nurse, who worked nights and slept all day. So Hubert and Ellie were free to do pretty much as they pleased."

I'm fuming. Hubert and his irresponsible parents should have been looking after Ellie. My daughter came back from that trip a different person, but she was at that stage, like any teenager, where she wanted to keep her life private. Throughout that winter and spring she was trying on new groups of friends looking for the best fit.

"Something happened to Ellie while she was on that school exchange," Bryn says. "She fell in love."

A vision of Ellie and Hubert, making out in his teenage bedroom while his mother slept off the rigours of a night shift, makes me feel a bit sick and let down, but I remind myself she was over sixteen. It's normal for teenagers to experiment.

"It's not what you think," Bryn says. I can't see his face properly, but there's a hint of gloating in his tone. "It wasn't the handsome Hubert who won Ellie's heart, though he was willing to participate in her subterfuge. Ellie was already in love."

A sensation of dread lodges in my chest. What's he talking about? I scan my memory for the Llewellyn High boys who went on the exchange trip. There weren't many, because fewer boys than girls took French. Adam was one of them. I'd always thought he had a thing for Ellie, but she never seemed interested in him.

"Can't you guess?" Bryn is practically bouncing on the seat of my armchair. How much more humiliation does he plan to inflict on me? Miriana's eyes are closed, and I hope she's drifted off to sleep. She doesn't need to hear this.

Bryn turns his head and a shaft of moonlight illuminates a gleam in his eyes. He forces me to look at him, and the truth hits me with a sickening realisation. At some visceral level I must have known all along.

50

LAURA

"You were all so naïve," Bryn says. "Ellie was already in love with her French teacher. Why d'you think she didn't want you on the trip, spying on her? She wanted to be with me."

I bow my head as a single tear rolls down my cheek.

"This teacher," he continues, leaning forward in the armchair and manspreading, "was a young man too. Just a decade or so older than her. He was leading the trip, but had politely declined the *lycée*'s invitation to host him at the home of one of their teachers. He'd spent his university year abroad in Nantes, and planned to stay with a friend at his flat in the city centre. Except that his university friend was away teaching in Morocco..." Bryn watches me flinch. "I had his flat all to myself, but I wasn't alone – Ellie was there with me. And we didn't spend our time playing chess."

A cocktail of pain, emotional not physical, threatens to undo me, but I can't let him see. Another voice in my head – my former self, Laura the teacher – wants to understand how the hell he could pull off such a stunt. Leading a French exchange is onerous and exhausting. What quirk of fate led to Ellie being hosted by a lad who was a serial truant, with absent parents?

The gag prevents me from speaking, so Bryn seems to guess what my questions would be.

"Nothing was random, if that's what you're thinking. Another university friend of mine teaches at the *lycée* and told me about Hubert's family. Hubert hadn't planned to take part in the exchange, but my friend told him it would be a week of few lessons and afternoons out, and there was a rather lovely girl needing a host family. My expectations were low – an occasional tryst with my 'virgin' girlfriend – but fate was kind."

I glare at him.

"Don't look at me like that. You must have known I wasn't the first."

Tears roll down my face and settle on top of the tape covering my mouth.

"It was too easy. In the mornings the students worked on projects, supervised by local teachers and didn't need me, but with Ellie being a no-show in the mornings, my colleagues were worried. So I invented a role for myself to go out and visit, not only Ellie, but all the host families and do random checks. The others couldn't do it, could they, because they were Games teachers with limited French. I reported back that Ellie was unwell and resting. I didn't make any visits. Ellie and I stayed together at my friend's flat."

Each poisonous twist reveals my former colleague is a monster. Perhaps he always was. While he's looking at Miriana I manoeuvre my knee in between my bound wrists and work it around, trying to loosen the tape. If I could make the gap big enough to free my hands...

Bryn's voice drags me back to his hideous story. "It was serious between me and Ellie, and our affair continued when we got home. Did she tell you she was going out clubbing? Staying with a friend?" He laughs so hard I swear a fleck of his spittle hits my hand. "She was with me."

Through my gag, I gasp. When Gareth made that ill-judged attempt to collect Ellie from Phantasia, she wasn't even there. She was with *him* – and half an hour after my call, she strolled calmly into the house.

"Ellie didn't tell you she wasn't going on to Sixth Form, did she? We were going away to start a new life together. But we lay low from Christmas through to the following spring, stayed inside my flat and never went out. I became a bit of a hermit." He glances at Miriana. "You've seen that side of me, haven't you, Miriana?"

At the mention of her name, Miriana raises her head and opens one eye. Her hair flops across her face and she slumps sideways. I wonder if she's suffered a head injury from his blow? I raise my bound hands, wave towards her. Can't he see she's hurt?

Bryn is taking vicarious pleasure from my misery, and he can't keep his secret in silence; he wants to show how clever he is. "When summer arrived," he says, "we risked some late-evening walks. Never in Penarth, but in Cardiff or down on the coast at Southerndown and Llantwit Major. That was a mistake. Too close to home. A friend of Ellie's from school saw us. She recognised Ellie, but not me. This girl wanted to know about the mystery boyfriend, and when Ellie refused to say, she taunted her. Made her life a misery.

"I panicked. What if they worked out the man was me? I'd lose my job and never work as a teacher again. I might even go to prison. Rumours about Ellie and an older man were circulating in the staffroom. I'm surprised no one told you..."

I hang my head. Indignity upon indignity.

"After her idiot father pulled that stunt at Phantasia nightclub, Ellie became a subject of gossip. Teachers took an interest in the love life of a sixteen-year-old student. She was furious. After we were seen together, pressure on Ellie ramped up, and she came to me in tears. I knew she was in love with me, but worried she'd crack under the stress. That's when I knew we couldn't wait for the summer holidays. We had to run – first to London, then on to France where we planned to start our new life."

But Ellie didn't take her passport, I remind myself. But even for that he has an answer.

"You're probably wondering how Ellie could leave the country," he continues. "She wasn't going to be travelling on her passport, that's for sure. Have you ever watched the vehicle checks on outgoing ferries? Of course you haven't, because back then all the detailed checks happened on the French side – asylum seekers stowing away to get into the UK. Have you ever heard of anyone trying to smuggle themselves out of this country into France?" He narrows his eyes and watches my despair.

"The odds of a customs or immigration check were so low I was confident I could hide Ellie in the back of my vehicle and no one would discover her."

He stands up and stomps across to the sofa to gloat. "Romantic, don't you agree? Ellie thought so.

"That day, everything slotted into place: a parents' evening, Ellie's planned visit to her grandma, and Hubert's arrival in London – the perfect smokescreen. You and the police were supposed to be searching for a French student." He grabs me by the shoulders and shakes me roughly. "Except you, and that dozy Gareth, were slow telling the police about Hubert. That was most unhelpful of you.

"Ellie had a phone I'd given her way back to ring or message me. I told her to leave her own phone behind so she couldn't be tracked, plus it contained clues the police would need to discover Hubert was in London, but not his address. Ellie sent him a *See you soon* message to keep the police busy for a while."

Gareth should be here, I think. Not me. He's the one who wants every detail of Ellie's disappearance. Bryn has laid it out on a plate and is force-feeding it to me, and I can't bear it.

"I'd rented a bedsit in Stockwell, and told Ellie she'd have to stay there for a week until summer term ended but I'd join her at the weekend. It was vital no one made a connection between us. All Ellie had to do was lie low until I got there." Under his breath he mutters angry words and turns his furious eyes on me, her mother.

"She left on Thursday. On Friday after work I told colleagues I was going to Kent to visit my mother, and headed for London. Ellie and I hadn't been apart two days but already she was getting cold feet. She knew the search for her was ramping up and was feeling remorse and guilt. Especially for you – her neglectful, blinkered mother. When I arrived in London, I could see she'd changed. She wanted to go back home. I adored her, and warned her I'd be in trouble if our relationship was discovered. We argued. I'd left her alone with too much time to think. That was all the time it took for her to fall out of love with me."

51

LAURA

THREE YEARS EARLIER

One mid-week evening when Gareth was out, Ellie and I each had a sneaky glass of Prosecco and afterwards Ellie painted my nails before remembering she had homework. I had a stack of marking to get through, but my concentration was shot. I ran my hands through my hair, yawned, and slumped back against the sofa cushions watching her turn the pages of a Shakespeare play. Her lips were moving silently, so I guessed she was memorising quotes for her exam. Her blonde hair, which was naturally dark underneath, was pulled off her face with a clip, and her expression slid between fierce concentration and boredom. She drummed her fingers on the book cover, put it down and reached for her phone, checking apps and screens and tapping out messages, lightning-fast. How could she take in so much information without making her head spin?

"Fancy a hot drink?" I asked, yawning as I wrapped up my marking for the night and set the pile of books aside.

Ellie flinched, as if my voice had pulled her back from some secret place. "Sure." She stretched out her legs so the skin of her knees was visible through the factory-ripped holes in her jeans, and asked, "Have we got chocolate sprinkles?"

"I'll find some."

"Then I'll have a cappuccino."

I rummaged in the kitchen drawer and found a stainless-steel stencil, shaped like a heart, and remembered how she and Gareth bought it and surprised me with coffee in bed one Valentine's Day. Ellie could only have been around seven at the time, but Gareth trusted her to carry the mug while he followed with an orchid in a pot, chocolates and a card. As I shook chocolate on top of her drink, I took extra care so my heart-shaped artwork didn't blur.

"Thanks, Mum." Ellie seemed touched, and gave me a quick hug. It was good to feel close to my daughter again. Since she'd returned from the school trip to France, she'd been secretive and oddly prickly if Gareth or I asked about her plans for the weekend.

It was half-past ten and still no sign of Gareth, though that wasn't unusual, so we sipped our drinks in companionable silence. I was thinking of heading up to bed when Ellie put down her mug and turned towards me, a faint froth stain on her upper lip.

"Mum, if I met someone and I knew it was serious, what would you say?"

Her confessional tone took me off guard. I grinned, so my reply must have sounded glib or clumsy. "I remember when you were young you used to ask me how you'd know when you'd found 'the one.' You used to say *What if there isn't a one?* or *What if there are three, how do you whittle them down?*"

She gave me a blank look and I blundered on. "Do you mean a boyfriend, Ellie? Have you met someone special?" She'd had boyfriends before, gangly lads from school who called at the house and sat tongue-tied if we tried to make conversation while they waited for Ellie to finish doing her make up and come downstairs. Usually they all went out together in a group, but

Ellie had broken away from those friends in recent months. Something in her expression warned me she was disappointed in my response, that I didn't get it. Was she trying to share something deeper – could she mean a girlfriend?

"What if it was someone older than me?" she continued. "But we were so sure we wanted to be together, we decided to make a commitment like getting engaged or married? What would you say?"

"Married!" I felt a spurt of unease. "Ellie – you're only sixteen!"

She glared at me. "You and Dad were really young when you got together. You can't have been more than twenty-three when I was born."

"Your dad and I met at uni, Ellie. When you were born we'd finished our education and were both working."

Ellie wouldn't meet my eyes. Somehow I'd blown it, but I didn't understand how. So I took a breath and asked, "Is it Hubert?"

With a sigh, she clambered to her feet, leaving her coffee half-drunk.

"Forget it, Mum. I'm off to bed now." She bent down and treated me to a rare and rapid kiss, then made her way upstairs.

52

LAURA

Whatever feelings of anger, regret or love Bryn claims to have had for Ellie, nothing will stop him talking. "Our love affair unravelled in that seedy Stockwell bedsit," he says. "We stayed in bed, but when we made love, she was going through the motions."

Shut up, shut up, I want to scream at him. This is too much for a mother to deal with.

"I told school my mother was in hospital in Kent, and stayed in London. The search for Ellie had gone public, and the police were doing a reconstruction of her walk along Oxford Street, so we couldn't leave that room. We phoned for takeaways and I locked the door before I went down to the lobby to collect them. Often I'd get back to find she'd shut herself in the bathroom. I could hear her crying through the door. I'd taken her mobile away and there was no landline connection, but what if she found a way to contact the outside world? Ellie begged me to let her go home. She promised to say she'd had a wobble and taken some time out to get her head straight. But I knew how tough the detectives interviewing her would be. She'd wasted so much police time.

She'd crack under interrogation. I couldn't trust her not to betray me."

He starts pacing the room.

"I adored that girl," he says. "But she took the keys from my pocket while I was in the shower early one morning and was out of the door, striding towards the underground before I was dressed. I guessed she'd be heading for Paddington and the train home to Wales, so I followed her, intending to reason with her. But I knew I couldn't trust her. Once the police discovered I'd seduced her, I'd never work as a teacher again. I might be sent to prison."

He's right. At sixteen, Ellie wasn't under age in the strict legal definition, but the rules for teachers and students are far stricter. He was likely to be charged with sexual activity with a child by a person in a position of trust, and it carried a prison sentence.

"I caught up with her as she stepped onto a northbound Victoria Line train at Stockwell, and watched her from an adjoining carriage. When she got out at Oxford Circus station I lost her, but I knew she'd be changing onto the Bakerloo line. Rush-hour crowds were insane. Platforms were overcrowded and I was pinned back by station staff, who were letting passengers through onto the platform in batches. I spotted Ellie standing too close to the platform edge and called out to warn her, but she didn't hear me so I jumped about and waved to get her attention. When she turned and saw me it must have been a shock. She took a step backwards, tripped and fell in front of the train."

So that was it! I swallowed. The crazy-acting man in the black hoodie was Bryn. Was he really trying to warn her? Or did he, as the witness described, intentionally spark a chain reaction and a crowd surge knowing she would topple? He's had three years to assemble his story – it should be tested in a court of law.

"Think how devastating that was for me. I was in love with her." He bends over me, his stance threatening, his eyes moist with what looks like tears. He did have feelings for Ellie, yet everything about him revolts me.

"If she'd trusted me, our lives would be so different now," he says. "Yours too."

He laughs, and I briefly see him as he sees himself: a master of the universe who's been so clever in covering his tracks but is desperate to tell his version of what happened. He's twisted the truth to frame himself as a tragic hero, let down by a young girl he'd persuaded to fall in love with him. I can see right through him.

In the weeks after Ellie's death the hate campaign against me and Gareth ramped up, and the rumour that she'd run away because she was being abused at home was pounced on by the gutter press. Once the bandwagon was rolling, social media climbed on board, inciting people to pick sides.

Bryn takes a folded page from a newspaper out of the back pocket of his jeans and lays it on the coffee table in front of me, smoothing it out with the flat of his hand. He moves the table lamp closer. "Remember this?"

I recoil in horror at the headline. *TORTURED TEEN TAKES OWN LIFE?*

How did they get away with publishing that? A solicitor told me they were relying on the question mark. The article implied that tragic, gifted Ellie had fled an unhappy home life and run away to London in despair, where she threw herself in front of a rush-hour train. The journalist gave unattributed quotes from 'a friend of the family' who described how Ellie's father was involved in a punch-up at a Cardiff nightclub. The paper later printed an apology, but it was too late because many people believed the storyline they'd been fed.

"Perhaps these news reports weren't wrong," says Bryn. "We must stick to this story, and quash any new rumours about why Ellie ran away before they gain traction."

My stomach churns. What does he mean about stopping new rumours?

And then it comes to me. Why have I been so blind?

Bryn was the person who, supposedly, stuck by Gareth through those terrible years. He was the friend Gareth confided in when he learned that Rosie suspected she knew the identity of the man Ellie was seeing. He'd have known Gareth was reaching out to me so we could talk to Rosie together.

I splutter a muffled version of "You knew!" Did Rosie always suspect Bryn, and not mention it because it seemed unconnected with Ellie leaving for London?

"Exactly. Gareth never could keep his mouth shut. Thanks to the rugby club, he's my new best friend. I tried to warn him that following new leads would mean more disappointment, but he wouldn't listen."

I shoot him a defiant look. One way or another, the truth will finally be told.

"You're going to stop the rumours for me," he says. A shiver runs through me. "Because you, Laura, will make a confession, and Miriana here is going to help us." He strokes her tousled hair until her head jerks and she stares wildly around the room.

"We'll start with a nice snap of you two girls together." Bryn drags me up from the sofa and propels me across the room to stand behind Miriana's chair. He hooks my bound wrists over the chair where they're hidden by Miriana's back, my elbows jutting out at an unnatural angle. He rips the tape from my mouth so my face stings, and orders, "Smile please," firing off a round of camera shots before I can yank my bound arms from behind Miriana's back.

"These will look like selfies taken with a time-delay camera." He pushes the screen close to my face. In the photos, I look startled, but my wrist restraints are hidden, though the ones on Miriana's ankles are not. "Thanks for leaving your camera in the desk drawer, by the way. These are perfect."

Perhaps it's a good idea to have pictures. They could be evidence, whether or not I survive. I move my lips and my voice chooses the wrong time to return. "I look like a predator."

"Exactly."

Miriana tilts her head and looks up at me. Her eyes are glazed and rolling, the pupils dilated. I'm sure she's concussed. Now I have my voice I must use it. I speak calmly, pretending this sick scenario is normal.

"Miriana's not okay. She needs medical attention. Please let me call an ambulance."

"You're joking?" He steers me back to the sofa. "Sit!"

I summon my breath and shout, "Help! Fire!" and wait for repercussions, but it's Miriana who gets them, not me. Bryn pushes her chair. I watch her topple backwards, and wait for the sickening crack of her head on the floor, but inches before it hits the floor he catches it and lowers it to the ground. Miriana groans. Her legs flop outwards at the knees, but her arms and hands are trapped under the chair and crushed by her body weight. Silently I pray she's unconscious and can't feel pain.

"I thought you cared about her? Why are you treating her like this?"

Bryn's eyes are hard as granite. "Miriana's useful. She's been keeping a blog, but she doesn't know it." He reaches into a bag propped beside the armchair, takes out a tablet computer and waves it at me. "Her blog's already been published but she has no followers, so no one's read it yet. Not even Miriana." He laughs out loud. "The blog account is set up in her email address and I've been tapping away for her – telling her story. And here's the best bit. It's a story about you."

I reel away as he pushes it in front of my face and scrolls down a few lines, expanding the print so even in the faint light I make out the gist of it. A crazy woman kidnapped her from a campsite in Wales, smuggled her to London and has been holding her captive in her flat.

"It's a sad story, see? People will love it because it's about a desperate grief-stricken mother, approaching the third anniversary of her daughter's death, who snatches a vulnerable young woman. Why would she do that? To replace her daughter? For comfort? For company? As a do-gooder?"

"Stop it, stop it." I shove the tablet away.

His face is menacing as he bends close and hisses into my ear, "Or is it because she's a sick abuser like her former partner, Gareth?" He settles back into the armchair with the tablet on his lap. "I'll add some more text from Miriana at the top: *If you're reading this, I'm dead.*"

I'm sick and faint and scared, but I almost laugh. This is beyond ridiculous. A schoolboy could make up a better story. "Who's going to believe that?"

"Everyone. Because you are going to corroborate it."

My chest constricts, my heart hammers. "You think I'm going to write a diary?"

"No. Not a diary." Bryn strokes his beard. "A suicide note."

53

LAURA

Miriana is lying on the floor, bound to the chair and not making a sound. I've nothing to lose so I sprint across to crouch beside her. Her eyes are closed. With my wrists still tied I can't cradle her head, and I'm scared to move her. In my teaching career I attended several First Aid courses, so I press my joined hands under her jaw and feel for a pulse. When I lay my face close to her nose I sense a light breath. "Call an ambulance! Please," I beg.

Bryn stares at Miriana as if he's puzzled why she's lying on the floor. He's above me, bending over, and the urge to unbalance him is overwhelming. I get up from my crouched position, head-butt him in the stomach and kick his legs.

He staggers but doesn't fall. I brace myself for a blow, that doesn't come because he's reached into his pocket and produced a knife. I suppress an urge to whimper, and shout, "Shit!"

Bryn laughs. "Yell as much as you like. No one will hear."

"But Miriana," I stutter.

"There's nothing wrong with her. Not yet. Forget her. It's time for you to write your confession."

I shake my head. "No way."

"Everyone believes you and Gareth were abusive parents." The hand holding the knife drops to his side. "Now you've kidnapped another teenage girl. Perhaps you wanted to replace Ellie?" He waggles his finger in the direction of Miriana's prone body melded to the chair. "It doesn't look good, does it? And she's come to harm at your hands, so the plot is even thicker. The world needs to hear the truth in your own words." He pushes a notepad and pen towards me. "Handwritten would be best. I'll dictate."

I brush the pen and paper from his hands, and remember Miriana holding up a handwritten note and refusing to speak when she was hiding in my van. Was it the months of living with Bryn that inspired her note writing?

He picks up the pad and offers it again.

"How can I write?" I show him my bound wrists.

"Ah yes. It seems we have a problem with handwriting." He digs back inside the bag and produces a typed page. "Here's one I made earlier. Typed and saved on your laptop and printed on your very own printer. It was so helpful of you to leave this list lying around."

He shows me a second page headed *Passwords and account numbers*. I groan. How did he get that? Did Miriana find it for him?

"As this confession is in your name, I expect you'd like to know what it says." He reads aloud:

"*My name is Laura Lister and this is my confession. Tomorrow is the third anniversary of my daughter Ellie's death at Oxford Circus underground station. In the days before Ellie died, a police search was underway to find her. I hadn't the slightest inkling why she'd gone missing.*

"*Despite what some newspapers wrote, I never believed Ellie's death was suicide, and after an investigation, the inquest* returned a narrative verdict setting out the facts of the case, with emphasis on overcrowding on the platform.

"In the months of grieving that followed, my partner Gareth Barton and I were unable to comfort each other. I was signed off from my work as a teacher, but Gareth became obsessed with investigating Ellie's death. He searched for clues to see if she'd shared a reason for going missing. At home he became violent."

Bryn fixes his eyes on me and I drop my gaze. "I'm right, aren't I? He did become violent towards you?"

I hunch my shoulders and shake my head.

"You're lying. He told me over a pint that he hit you. You fell and broke your nose. I'll continue:

"Gareth had never been violent towards me before, but he was convinced everyone blamed him for Ellie's death. He claimed it was a conspiracy theory. Then, one night, nine months after her death, he broke down and confessed to me he was responsible. He'd been abusing our daughter for years, and I never knew so I couldn't stop him. I will never, ever forgive myself for failing to protect my daughter.

"Why didn't I tell the police at the time? Probably the grief and shame was too overwhelming. I had to get away. I sold our house – it was in my sole name..."

"Nice touch that, isn't it?" says Bryn. "I mean, how could anyone other than you and Gareth possibly know that? You sure knew how to emasculate a bloke. You left him and moved to London. I've written that in the letter too." He waves it in the air again, but I don't look. I'm too devastated.

"I can't be bothered reading out any more of this tosh. Let me just tell you how it ends.

"I couldn't put it behind me. Now I'm telling the truth because I can't live with the guilt any more. My daughter was being abused by her own father, I never knew, and I did nothing to stop him.

"Here's another good bit:

"I tried to make up for it by helping a young woman called Miriana who I met at a campsite. I realised she was in trouble. I thought I could help her and look after her as if she was my own daughter, but she didn't seem to want my support and that made me angry. It also made me realise nothing would help. What's the point of trying to rebuild a shadow life? I don't want to live any longer without Ellie. On the third anniversary of her death, I will take my own life."

I gasp, but he reads on in a toneless voice:

"I won't be around to see it, but I want this confession to bring her father to justice."

My jaw drops open. Did I hear that right?

"You think anyone will believe that cesspit of lies?" A sinking feeling in my stomach tells me they probably will, if I'm no longer around to tell them otherwise.

"It's a shame I can't persuade you to add in a few touches in your own words." He holds the flat of the knife under my chin while I stay rigid. "But you can sign it. I'll guide your hand."

He clamps the pen into my fist and presses my hand to hover over the letter.

Stuff that. I'm not going to make it easy for him. With an effort, I stab down at the paper and punch a hole in it with the pen. Desperately I move the pen across the paper, scribbling and making crossings out in black ink. Didn't I just hear the pronouncement of my own death?

I hurl the pen at him and bolt for the door. It's locked, and the key is in his pocket. Bryn slings both arms around my waist and drags me back to the sofa. "You **will** sign it."

"I won't." I lean back against the cushion, trembling.

He flips open my laptop, consults my list of passwords and shrugs.

"I don't need your signature. I've found your electronic one and it's just fine." With a swift tap on a few keys, he prints out another copy of the letter with my signature affixed, and shows it to me. I close my eyes as all hope fades.

"I was thinking," he says, "about a little accident on the tube station? So many parents kill themselves when their child dies by suicide. They can't live with the guilt. It would have a nice symmetry."

"You bastard. Ellie didn't take her own life. It was an accident. Or did you murder her?"

Bryn bangs the laptop shut and leaves my confession letter on top of it. He crumples the extra copy into a ball in his fist and drops it strategically on the floor, letting it roll under the coffee table. Another indication of my state of mind for the police to find.

"An underground station isn't practical," he says. "Perhaps pills?" He holds up his left hand to show me what looks like a pack of prescription medicine. The knife is in his other hand. "I think pills. But this isn't the place. Perhaps a small dose to get us started."

I watch him crush some white tablets between two spoons and drop them into a glass of water. He grabs my hair and tips back my head so I feel like I'm being scalped. He pushes the cup to my mouth. It clinks against my teeth but I won't let him dominate me. Ignoring the pain, I writhe from his grasp and roll my head from side to side, regurgitating and spitting until the liquid leaks from my mouth and dribbles onto my clothes, the floor, anywhere but down my throat. He cuts more lengths of duct tape, then binds my ankles and my mouth.

With no option but to swallow, I gag on the last of the dissolved tablets, their bitter taste coating my tongue and the roof of my mouth. I pray they were medicinal, perhaps tranquillisers, as the packet suggested, and not some poisonous concoction.

Bryn towers over me, pointing his knife at my throat. Why doesn't he just stab me and get it over with? Then I realise: the knife is my saviour. He can't just stick a knife in me because it wouldn't fit in with his carefully-crafted suicide scenario. Whatever he's planning, he'll want it to look like I've taken my own life, and that will buy me time.

For the first time, I feel a glimmer of hope.

54

LAURA

Bryn leaves the sitting room door open and walks to the kitchen. I'm too dazed and weak to get out of the room. He's only gone a few seconds, and returns jingling the keys to my campervan. "Time for a little road trip."

I snatch a glance at Miriana. No reaction. My sense of foreboding deepens. Her eyes are closed and her face has a sickly pallor, but that could be due to the dim lamplight. What time is it, anyway? It feels like it should be tomorrow – the anniversary of Ellie's death. Using my chin, I edge back my left sleeve to see my watch. It's hard to believe it's still only half past midnight. Miriana is mumbling in her sleep. She's alive, but she needs medical treatment. Urgently. What's Bryn planning to do with her? It's not hard to figure out his intentions for me now he has my keys. A road accident with a convenient tree, perhaps? I'm not sure how many tablets I swallowed, but my brain feels fuzzy. I need to stay focussed – and alive – if I'm to get help for Miriana.

Bryn manhandles me towards the door. I make my body go limp so he has to stick his hands under my armpits and pull me.

I resist, so he positions my feet on a rug that glides over my polished floorboards and drags me the length of my hallway, dumping me by the front door. He opens it and looks out. "Your campervan. Where the fuck is it?"

I can't speak, and it's hard to point with joined hands. I make a sort-of gesture along the street to the left and curve my hands to indicate it's round the corner.

"Why didn't you park outside? There's a space right there."

There wasn't a space when I arrived back, but I'm in no position to debate. I mumble from behind the tape, but it comes out quieter than a mouse squeak. Inside my head, I'm screaming.

"Damn!"

I guess he'd planned to bundle me a couple of yards into the van after checking for no passers-by, but he can hardly drag me along the street. I lie still, pretending to be more dozy than I feel. Bryn's played his last card, and the clock is ticking. With Miriana lying semi-conscious, does he think she's so badly hurt that she'll slip away? My mission is to stay alive until I can get help to her.

"Make a single sound and I'll kill you here," he says – as if it made any odds to me whether I die in my own hallway or dumped in dense woodland. No one would ever make a connection between me and Bryn, so he'll get off, scot-free. I picture him back in Wales, offering condolences to Gareth when my body is discovered. Soon after that, I'm guessing the police will go to my flat and discover Miriana's body, along with my supposed suicide note, accusing Gareth.

Gareth will turn back into a social pariah and face investigation. Adam and Rosie will suppress their suspicions about the mystery boyfriend. I'll be dead and buried. And my mother... But I can't bear to think of her.

Bryn strides back down the hall. I drag myself closer to the front door, praying someone will walk past. I'm practically on the threshold when his footsteps return. I look up. He's holding my kitchen scissors. What now? He snips through the duct tape he's only just wrapped around my ankles and frees my legs.

"You're going to have to walk," he says, "but no messing about." He screws up the used tape in his hand; it sticks to the blue surgical gloves and he needs two hands to pick it off. The scissors are lying next to me on the floor. While he's distracted, I shuffle my bound hands, inch by inch, grab the scissors and tuck them into my sleeve.

I stand up and lean against the wall to steady myself. From his pocket, Bryn takes a scarf – one of mine from my bedroom drawer. He's obviously ransacked every room in my home. He winds the scarf around my neck, covering my mouth to conceal the gagging tape, pulls it tight and ties it behind my head.

As we step outside, he props me against the porch like a department-store mannequin and pulls the door closed behind us, then drapes his arm around my shoulders and inserts his hand underneath the folds of the scarf so I feel the sharp point of a blade pressing into my throat. We walk. He leans into me, propelling me like a puppet. If a passer-by saw us, they'd think we were a loved-up, drunken couple staggering home.

There are no passers-by. I act compliant on this walk because attempting to break away from him would be futile unless there's someone to help me. When I see the friendly metallic red of my van, gleaming under the street lamp, I start to hyperventilate, but my mind is calm. Will my campervan become my coffin? Bryn opens the rear door and pushes me inside, his muscles straining to lift the dead weight of my body. The mattress breaks my fall and Bryn clambers in after me. I act floppy and malleable and don't let him see the pair of scissors concealed in my sleeve. With my hands still bound, I can't risk a feeble stabbing motion. I'll need to bide my time and wait.

From a nearby road, a police siren wails, growing louder as it heads towards us. I attempt a scream. It sounds like the urban foxes that inhabit our gardens and nearby railway embankments, but it seems to spook Bryn.

"Shut up!" He checks the rear doors are secured, scrambles through to the driver's seat and starts the engine. He's forgotten to bind my legs! Soon, we're pelting along at a speed higher than I'd ever attempt on an urban street. and I'm bouncing on the mattress battling with drowsiness to stay alert and conscious. I can't see out, but pulses of streetlights flicker around the edges of the drawn curtains of the van.

I must have dozed. When I come round I recognise the sound the engine makes when it goes above sixty, and I guess we're on a motorway – but which one? We could be heading south towards Dover or north on the M1. A melodious sound reaches me, and my eyes fill with hot tears. Amid all this loss and horror, Bryn is singing to himself in a rich, pure baritone, and the song he's chosen, *Ar Hyd y Nos,* is the lullaby I used to sing to Ellie in its English translation *All Through the Night.* The grief I've kept bottled inside me for three long years overflows, and I weep for my lost daughter until the mattress is sodden. The tears are more than a release; they're a small triumph, because Bryn has given me my daughter back. I know now she didn't hate or reject us. When she died she was full of regret for her actions and the pain she'd caused. She was on her way home to us.

Lying on my side protects me from the buffeting, but my shoulders ache. My headache roars and my heart is pounding. I urge myself to focus on Miriana. If she dies in my London flat it will give credence to Bryn's story. What if she survives? Does he have such a hold over her she'll say whatever he tells her to? If so, I can't blame her. Bryn's controlled her in a pernicious form of grooming, far more subtle than the violent control she suffered from Jamie and Liam.

If Bryn had come for me one year ago, I'd have been neutral about dying. I was weary with the effort of living. But something has changed, and I sense there could be a future. I want to survive.

55

LAURA

SUNDAY

Summer nights rarely darken to inky black, and I see flecks of orange through the campervan's windows. It can't yet be dawn, but today is the third anniversary of Ellie's death.

On that day, it rained. Fat, grey drops beating against the window of our pebble-dashed semi as I howled out my grief and agony. Gareth was still in London. Mum was with me and tried to hold and comfort me, but she couldn't comfort herself. Bryn's attempt to fill my mind with ugly memories of Ellie hasn't worked. My beautiful daughter, her image untarnished, is sharply back in focus: the smiling baby, happy child, the mercurial teenager of the years before she turned sixteen, went to Nantes, and came back changed. Ellie wasn't bad or cruel; she didn't mean to break our hearts, and when she died she was heading home to us. She did love us – I know it now, and I long to tell Gareth. Like Miriana, Bryn had bewitched her, but she'd woken up and seen through him to the darkness of his soul. Bryn admitted stalking her on that final journey and claimed her fall was an accident, but I don't believe him. If there was a crowd surge on that platform, he created it. Intentionally.

It's up to me to get justice for Ellie and honour her memory. Bryn must pay for what he did to her. And to Miriana.

The van is travelling more slowly. I can tell we've left the motorway because there's no longer the whoosh of passing traffic, the road is winding, and Bryn brakes often and sharply. The road surface sounds harsh. My sense of time is muddied, but I'm winning the fight against the tranquilisers. Such sounds as there are don't have a city feel to them, and I urge my addled brain to think. If Bryn is stage-managing my suicide and wants people to believe it's linked to the anniversary of Ellie's death, it will need a symmetry to it. Where would he head for? It has to be Wales.

He turns sharp left, and the hum of wheels on tarmac gives way to a grinding sound as we bump across rough terrain. He mustn't know I'm awake and conscious, so I raise my head cautiously to sneak a glance at him and notice he's reaching for a pack of cigarettes. The van slows to a crawl as he lights up, peering straight ahead through the windscreen into the darkness, and takes his first drag of the cigarette.

The inside of the van fills with smoke. Desperate not to cough, I take shallow breaths. He opens the window and blows his smoke outside. Suddenly, he stamps on the brake and the van lurches to a halt. He opens the driver's door and turns sideways in his seat, and I feel the cold bite of a breeze and smell a familiar tang in the air. When I'm sure he's not looking in the rear view mirror, I hoist myself up and peer out. Ahead of me I see nothing. Only horizon. That, and the smell of salt and ozone, tells me we've reached the sea. And cliffs.

The sky darkens. That orange light I saw must have been faint street lighting before he turned off the highway, because I know now where we're heading. Straight on. To the cliff edge. My chest tightens as I understand his plan for staging my suicide. Bryn's going to drug me some more, put me into the driver's seat and take the handbrake off. I'm going over the cliff.

56

LAURA

All those hours dozing and being flung around in the back of the van, I had a pair of scissors stuffed in my sleeve. Why didn't I try cutting the tape from my wrists? Frantically, I nudge the blades apart but the blasted gag stops me from sticking the handle in my mouth and clamping it between my teeth. How I hate this tape – so efficient for mending leaking pipes, so lethal for me. I poke at my mouth gag with my tongue and feel it stretch, but not slacken enough for me to bite it.

"Laura?" Bryn turns in his seat and glances at me. I freeze. It's vital he thinks I'm still comatose from the sedative. My acting must have convinced him, because he gets out of the van leaving the driver's door open, and I hear a pattering sound – he's urinating against the side of my van. He'll have chosen an isolated spot – who would be on a cliff top at around four in the morning?

I'm no longer woozy, though my head is pounding. I make a mental checklist of my resources: my legs aren't tied, though my wrists are; I have the pair of scissors, but even if I could surprise him, I wouldn't have strength to stab him before he overpowered me.

Bryn's stream of piss has stopped, but he doesn't get back into the van. Keeping my head low, I scramble onto my knees to peer through the windscreen, and my hammering heart skips a beat. The van is less than two metres from the cliff edge, pointing forward on a downward slope. When I move it bounces. Only the handbrake is holding it. I glance through the window to my left. Bryn is twenty metres away, standing on a rocky promontory, staring down at the pounding sea. He must be checking the longest drop, the most lethal rocks.

The sky is brighter now, with yellowish streaks. Bryn's lost the cloak of darkness and I can see him clearly. If I knew how far we were from the road and from houses, I'd clamber out of the van and run, but he'd see me, and his rugby-toned body would outpace me. The scissors are hopeless, not even sharp enough to inflict a nanosecond of pain. There must be a knife amongst my cooking tools. I slide open the under-sink cabinet and ferret around inside feeling for a blade. I find a pack of stainless steel kebab skewers and pull it out, then my hand touches something smooth and cool: the metal bowl of tools, and bits and bobs, I inherited with the van. That's when I see it. The gas lighter – the lethal one that turned into a flamethrower when we tried to light the barbeque and wouldn't go out...

I grip the lighter between my fixed hands and glance out of the side window. Bryn is coming back. I bob down, hoping he didn't see me. He drops something heavy on the ground and bends down in front of the van. As he fumbles around, the van bucks and lurches against the restraint of the handbrake, and I stifle my terror to calculate his next steps. He's placing a rock or log as a chock under the front wheels. The van is already listing forward on a slope. To stage my suicide, he'll need to bundle me into the driver's seat, release the handbrake, and at the last moment unfasten my wrists. Then all he has to do is roll the stone away from under the front wheels, perhaps give it a push from the rear and the van will plunge over the cliff.

Bryn will want me sitting behind the wheel to make it look like suicide. Whatever happens, I mustn't sit there. He thinks I'm still woozy, and probably plans to top up the dose of sedative. He'll have to drag me through the gap between the seats, but it won't be easy if I resist. He might try opening the rear doors and dragging me round the outside of the van, though that's a high-risk strategy if someone comes by. But who would? It's too early for dog-walkers.

Keeping his back to the van, and to me, Bryn reaches in his pocket and lights another cigarette. I can smell the smoke but not see him because he's at the rear of the van on the driver's side. Is he smoking for courage? Are his hands shaking? Perhaps even a murderer has to steel his nerves. Ellie's death was stage-managed from a distance, but is he confident Miriana won't survive her injuries, or does he plan to return to my flat and finish her off?

My eyes roam the van and then I see it – my escape route. He's left the keys in the ignition. If I climb into the front and lock the doors, it'll buy me time. I sidle through the gap and fling myself into the passenger seat. The van rocks as my useless hands fumble to lock the door, and Bryn notices. He runs around the front of the van, pulls open the passenger door and makes a grab for me. This is my final throw of the dice.

Gripping the gas lighter in both hands, I point it at his face, click the button, and watch the flame shoot out and set his beard alight.

57

LAURA

One autumn evening when I was at university, Gareth and I went with a group of friends to a Greek restaurant in Cardiff where tables were set out in long rows, refectory-style, and families mingled with students. We'd been told the evening's entertainment involved getting horribly drunk and dancing on the tables, but when the dancing started, we discovered we were going to stand on our chairs to dance. The men leaned back and carried on drinking, but some of us girls kicked off our sandals and climbed onto our seats. I remember the feel of my bare feet slipping and sliding on the basketweave chair.

That summer I'd spent a week in Santorini, so was showing off my suntan in a white strappy dress. Everyone wanted to recreate fleeting Aegean summer memories. Waiters paused food service to join hands and treat us to their performance of the Zorba dance, arms slung round one another's shoulders, stepping left, then right, swinging their legs, kicking and speeding to a wild crescendo, while we swayed and clapped. The finale was a ritual smashing of crockery against the whitewashed stone wall of the restaurant.

Now they were running late. One waiter leapt to fetch a

broom and sweep up broken china, the others queued at the hatch to collect food orders and fought their way, carrying hot plates, through the rows of diners. My friends and I stayed on our chairs, swaying in time to the music. A waiter, walking behind me, pushed my chair. I overbalanced and fell forward into a candle. The acrid smell of my long auburn hair going up in flames haunts me to this day.

Gareth reacted fast. He poured a full carafe of water over my head, pulled my shrivelling hair out of the flame and pressed a damp napkin against my scorched cheek. Thanks to him my burns were superficial, and the scarring only shows up as a lighter skin tone when I have a bit of a tan. My hair grew back. What I learned from that accident, as well as being deeply grateful to Gareth, was that hair survives singeing but the skin underneath may not.

It's that same sulphurous smell in my nostrils as Bryn's beard crinkles and melts into the skin of his face, which looks black and charred as I flick the flame higher. Pressing his hands over his eyes, he cries out, curses and scrabbles to beat out the flames. I aim the lighter at the crown of his head, his neck and chest. The flame has a long reach, and the fuel makes a satisfying roar. I'm surprised he doesn't run away out of range, but guess he's in shock. He flings himself down beside the van and rolls his face in the grit, sand and grass while flames dance along his right sleeve. I notice he's still gripping his cigarette lighter, and its fuel is feeding the fire. I mustn't weaken, and it's easy to fan the flames with my rage because Bryn stole my daughter from me. He showed me no mercy. So I lean down and point the still-raging flame at the place on his back where his sweatshirt has rolled up to expose bare flesh. I run the flame across his naked skin as if searing a steak. His screams pierce my ears. I flinch. That's enough. I lean out of the van door and grind the gas lighter into the sand and earth until the flame goes out.

Slamming the door, I slide across into the driver's seat, fumbling to start the ignition with trembling fingers. Bryn's lying prone on the path, groaning, his arms covering his face. The flames that lapped his hair and beard have gone out, but his sweatshirt is charred and glowing. His body twitches, so he's alive. I'm not sure how much damage I've done, but I secretly hope those good looks that enticed young girls to fall for him won't serve him so well in future.

58

LAURA

Driving with hands tied is close to impossible, but my instinct to survive is stronger. Sick with terror, I reverse the heavy campervan away from the cliff edge. Bryn's preparations have worked in my favour, because he'd already taken the handbrake off and that would have been impossible for me to do with my bound wrists. I press my foot on the clutch, but need both hands on the gear stick to ram it into reverse while I hold the steering wheel in position with my right elbow. One false move – stalling the engine or pressing too hard on the accelerator – the van could shoot forward and plunge over the edge. Somehow I manage to reverse five metres. I turn the wheel until the van is pointing away from the cliff, drag air into my lungs and weave across grass, through a car park and onto a gravel track.

As I pull off onto the road and turn right, my feeble grip on the steering wheel falters. The tyres spin. I swerve and the van shoots across the carriageway. Luckily, the road's deserted. Has Bryn recovered? Is he chasing me? But soon I'll gather speed and leave him far behind.

The coast road is narrow with a series of bends. I limp along in second gear, not daring to take my hands off the wheel. My mouth gag is still tight, and my nose is running but I can't wipe it. I've no phone, no money, no voice and I'm unfit to drive. With only the vaguest idea of where I am, I crane my neck to look out for road signs. And then I see one: *Cowbridge – 6 miles*. I must be twenty miles west of Cardiff.

A milk lorry rattles past, then a workman's van. I'd noticed him in my rear view mirror, tucked in behind for over a mile. As he finally overtakes at speed, he makes a V-sign and shouts abuse. It's too dangerous to take my hand off the wheel to flag him down, and anyway he doesn't seem the kind who'd help me. So I press on as dawn erupts in yellow splashes across the sky. I head east, blinking into the sunrise, until a sign tells me I'm entering Cowbridge.

The street is deserted. Then I see the illuminated sign of a convenience store. The owner is hauling bundles of newspapers from the kerbside into his shop. I pull over and stamp on the brakes. The man looks startled when I shuffle across to the passenger seat and open the door. From behind the tape that seals my mouth, I whisper, "Help me."

The man's soft brown eyes grow rounder, but he doesn't recoil, and holds out his hand to help me step down. He gasps at my bound wrists, takes my arm and guides me inside the shop, where he pulls out a stool and invites me to sit.

"May I?" he asks, reaching his hand towards the tape across my mouth.

I nod and although he's gentle, I wince as he eases it off. When he sees my red raw skin, he tut-tuts and calls out, "Meera! We have a lady visitor. Come now."

I hear a rustling from behind a curtain at the back of a shop, and a woman's voice says, "One moment."

"What has happened to you?" he asks, in the gentlest voice I've ever heard.

I shake my head and sniff as the tears I've been holding back roll down my cheeks.

A dark-haired woman of around forty appears, shrugging on a felted dressing gown over a gold-trimmed outfit that would be smart enough for a Buckingham Palace garden party.

"Your face looks so sore," she exclaims, stroking my hand as if that will make it better.

Now my gag is off and I can speak, I don't know what to say. "Thank you," I mutter.

Her husband has been examining my bound wrists, and picks up the pair of scissors he was using to snip off the bands around his newspaper bundles. "May I?" He points the scissors at my wrists, and I obediently raise my throbbing arms.

Then I change my mind and snatch them away. "No! Stop!"

He stares at me as if his instinct that I'm a crazy person has been confirmed. He reaches for the mobile phone lying on the shop counter. "I will call the police."

"Thank you." I don't feel strong enough to keep explaining what happened, and that these wrists are my alibi – because less than an hour ago I torched a man and kept on pointing a gas flame at him, as if trying to burn his face off. Maybe I am deranged. I need my tied wrists as proof this crazy woman wasn't simply seeking revenge on a former colleague.

The store owner finishes his call to the police, saying, "She will not let me untie." He shakes his head sadly, edging away from me so his wife can take charge.

Meera smiles. "I will make tea." I watch through the looped red and orange curtain that separates their family accommodation from the shop as she pours cold water into a giant metal teapot, sets it on a two-ring burner and lights it. A few minutes later, she adds teabags and some scoops of sweetened, evaporated milk, and brings everything up to the boil.

When she brings me a cup, I wonder how I'll stomach so much sweetness, but it's drinkable and lubricates my parched throat. I take a few sips, and find words to apologise for landing on their doorstep. "I'm sorry if I seemed rude. I was attacked. I need to show the police my wrists."

Meera's face registers shock, but she covers it with a smile and a nod. She shushes away my apology, and we sit in silence waiting for the police while her husband serves early customers.

Time passes. Half an hour? More? They offer me food. Would I like a share of their own breakfast? A KitKat from the shelves?

"I can't eat, I'm sorry."

At last a patrol car pulls up and two police officers get out. The store owner leads them through the shop and ushers us all into their family back kitchen, drawing the curtain to give us privacy.

The officers introduce themselves, but I can't hold onto their names. Everything that enters my head slips away. The female officer examines the tape and lets out a sharp whistling breath. "Who did this to you?"

I battle exhaustion and stay alert, because there's something I need to tell them. Something important.

"There's a seriously-injured person needing help," I tell them. An image of Bryn, beard and hair aflame, swims in my inner vision. I rub my eyes. "Please send an ambulance. Go fast." I give them the location and tell them I'm worried the person may not survive. I listen to the officer radioing through to Control and giving the address of my London flat, where they'll find Miriana.

Only then do I tell them there's an injured man out on the cliff top, close to here.

59

LAURA

After I've given the officers a brief account of how Bryn abducted and attacked me, they take away the keys to my campervan, telling me it will be examined by crime scene investigators.

"They'll also check it for any mechanical faults, because your attacker might use that as a possible defence," the officer explains. "I'm afraid that means you won't get your vehicle back for quite a while, because the defence also has a right to examine it, if they wish."

"Will my van be left outside this shop all day?"

"No. They'll check the basics here, then move it to a secure covered compound. Where will you be staying?"

I give them Mum's address in Cardiff. Amanda, the female officer, drives me to the hospital and stays with me while my head injury is scanned.

"How long were you concussed?" the clinician asks me.

"I can't be sure. I remember coming round, lying face down on my sitting room carpet and a man's feet pressing down on my calves, but it might have been only a few minutes."

The scan shows no swelling or serious damage, so I'm

prescribed strong painkillers, and cream for the sores on my wrists and face.

"The next part's a bit awkward," Amanda tells me, glancing at a message on her phone. "I'm just checking which room they've allocated us."

"I thought that was it?"

"No. I'll explain in a minute." She leads me along a brightly-lit corridor, passing porters wheeling trolleys, and we turn away from the bustle into a warren of rooms. She pauses three doors along and checks the room number. "This is it."

We sit down on red plastic chairs outside a closed door.

"The scenes of crime officers are coming here to take DNA and toxicology samples from you. You said you were given some kind of drug or sedative?"

I nod. "I think it was prescription medicine."

"We can't delay. Trace evidence and drugs degrade fast." She clears her throat. "They'll need to swab for any traces of DNA on your skin."

"I understand."

"And we'll need to keep your clothes and any possessions."

I'm stunned. "What will I wear?"

"We'll sort something out."

We sit in awkward silence, and I wonder if they'll send me home to Mum's in a hospital gown.

"Th-thank you for staying with me," I say, grateful for Amanda's compassion and support.

"I have to stay. Not that I mind being here and supporting you, Laura. You're the scene."

"How d'you mean?"

She furrows her brow and explains. "The scene of a crime can be a fixed place, but not always, and there can be more than one. If there are multiple victims and someone is hospitalised, we accompany them to hospital and stay with them until they can be interviewed."

"I'm the victim," I remind her. I need to press this point home before they discover the state Bryn's in. "He tied me up, kidnapped me and drove me to a place where he planned to murder me and make it look like suicide."

"Stop, please." Amanda holds up her hand, but I press on, desperate for reassurance and professional advice on my predicament.

"You could say I'm an aggressor because I fought back, but it was in self-defence, and there wasn't much I could do with my wrists tied. I don't know how severely injured Bryn was after I fought him off with the gas lighter, but he didn't look a pretty sight. Do you think I'll be prosecuted?"

"You mustn't say any more, Laura. I don't know – you need to speak to the investigators and maybe get a solicitor. Please."

The brief euphoria I felt at escaping from Bryn to this safe place drains away. I was expecting tough love, but not this.

In my childhood bedroom, one wall is painted a shade of blue that mimics a thunderstorm. Mum insisted on blue walls in every room, so I declared my teenaged rebellion by pushing the palette to its bruised extremities. It reflects my mood perfectly as I lie on my bed trying to recover from a night when I was convinced I was going to die. The morning of hospital checks and toxicology tests, followed by hours of police interviews, tested my resilience and recall to the limit.

Mum makes me vegetable soup and insists I go to bed, but she won't let me sleep. Instead she sits in a chair beside me, asking more questions.

Not wanting to upset her, I give her a heavily-redacted

version of events. But she probes my fabricated story and finds the holes. I have to tell her Bryn drove me to Wales aiming to stage my death.

"He kidnapped me, Mum."

Her face freezes as if she's been caught unawares by a flash photo. I've told her a bit about Miriana, but haven't mentioned the connection between Bryn and Ellie because, well, I just can't. Not yet.

I describe the clifftop showdown, and how I torched Bryn with the faulty gas lighter and engineered my escape.

"Good." She doesn't even flinch. In fact she nods her approval.

"Laura. What happened to you?" Gareth hands me a bunch of freesias and stares at my inflamed face and the red-raw lesions on my wrists.

Mum must have rung him last night while I was asleep, because when I stumble downstairs at midday, he's sitting with her in the kitchen. She must have told him, in outline, about Bryn's attack, and I'm touched by his concern. It turns out the police have already interviewed him, and given he knew nothing of events in the hours following our meeting at the museum café, he must have been bemused. The investigators had warned me not to contact him until after his police interview. Once he'd convinced his interviewer he knew nothing of my kidnapping, the officer had shared brief details of my ordeal on Saturday night.

How different things would have been for him today if I'd gone over that cliff. I imagine the police going to my flat and finding the fake suicide note. Instead of giving a witness statement, Gareth would have been interrogated as a suspect.

"I don't look that bad, do I?" The sores around my mouth have turned an angry red, because my skin reacted to the medicated cream meant to soothe it. The doctor who checked me out was worried about the length of time the blood supply to my hands had been interrupted, but I convinced him I still had feeling in my fingers.

"The emergency services found Miriana unconscious on the floor in my flat," I tell Gareth. "She must have been tied to that chair for at least ten hours. Now she's in hospital and I'm waiting for news."

Gareth and I go outside to sit in Mum's garden, on a bench next to a blush-pink rose bush she planted in Ellie's memory. It's hard to talk about Bryn and Ellie's sordid affair, but Gareth has a right to know. I start at the end with their plan to elope – it sounds quaint and old-fashioned – and work my way backwards to the French exchange trip and explain how he'd preyed on her. Over the past couple of days I've remembered several girls at school were infatuated with the young French teacher when he first arrived. They used to mooch around outside whatever classroom he was teaching in, and blush and giggle. How lucky those girls and their parents were that his gaze settled elsewhere.

"You're telling me Bryn was Ellie's lover? That she ran away to London to be with him?" Gareth's eyes widen until his eyelids seem to disappear inside their sockets. "I'll fucking kill him."

"Bryn wasn't your friend, Gareth. He stayed close to you to make sure you didn't uncover his grubby secret. I guess you could say he was grooming you, just as he groomed Ellie. And Miriana."

It's clear to me now that seemingly chance events came about because Bryn cultivated a friendship with Gareth. When Gareth confided that Rosie might know the identity of the mystery man seen with Ellie, it spurred Bryn to act. It was Bryn, playing for time, who persuaded Gareth to talk to me before approaching Rosie. Mum must have told Gareth which campsite I was heading for, but why did he tell Bryn? I picture the scene in the rugby club bar, probably on that same evening when I'd called in on Mum: Gareth mentioning my plans, Bryn feigning interest because he and I were former colleagues. *She's going to Tenby, is she? I've stayed at a few campsites there. Which one? And she has a campervan – what make?* Even if Bryn didn't get my registration number from Gareth, a metallic red Volkswagen couldn't have been too hard for Miriana to find.

Mum brings us a tray of tea and a plate of scones.

"She's desperate to fatten me up," I say, and Mum laughs.

"Well, you do look a bit skinny, if you don't mind me saying." Gareth knows that will please Mum. I don't mind; I'm happy there's a rapport between them. I'm glad they were able to support each other in the years I was hiding away from life. Mum goes back indoors so we can talk freely.

Half past one is an odd time for a cream tea. "I'm not sure I can eat this," I say, "but I do fancy a drink. Could you fetch me a beer?"

While he's gone, my thoughts turn to Miriana. Though I'm not religious, I offer up a silent prayer of thanks that she's now recovering in hospital. Ever since Bryn bundled me out of my flat and into the van, my anxiety for her drove me to fight to stay alive. I'll probably never see her again, but I'm glad she's safe. It would have been beyond terrible for Miriana to die on the third anniversary of Ellie's death.

Gareth strolls back with the beers and a bowl of crisps. "Your mum insisted," he grins, setting the crisps down on the bench between us. "Eat up." I take a handful and stuff them into my mouth, enjoying the saltiness.

"The police officer who interviewed me told me self-defence is a complete defence, as long as I grabbed the first thing to hand and didn't tamper with the lighter to make it into a weapon," I say. The police have told me Bryn's alive but haven't revealed the extent of his injuries, and I haven't enquired. "D'you think I'll go to prison for GBH or attempted murder?"

"I don't." Gareth puts his arms around me and I'm glad we've forgiven each other because that's a start. Our healing won't begin until we can forgive ourselves.

60

LAURA

The police found my handbag in the van under the front passenger seat. Bryn must have taken it from the kitchen. When they tell me he probably put it there as evidence to speed up identification of my body, I almost laugh. What self-respecting woman would set off to kill herself and not take her handbag with her?

My laughter turns to irritation when the officer tells me I can't have it back.

"We need to swab it for DNA and fingerprints. If there are traces of Bryn on its contents, it will become a court exhibit."

"But I need my house keys and my phone!" Panic grips me. I haven't had a chance to let Bill know what's happened and explain why I haven't returned his call. He doesn't do social media, so if I can't get my phone back, how will I find him?

"Sorry. Your phone will be examined for messages or data that might become evidence, so we have to retain it. Your house key, too – you'll have to use a spare or get a locksmith to let you in."

"Listen." I try to stay polite. "If you won't give me back my phone, there are two numbers from my Contacts I urgently need. Can you get them for me?"

"I suppose so," he says reluctantly.

The first number is for Callum upstairs because he has a spare set of keys to my flat. When I ring him he seems happy to hear from me.

"How are you, Laura? I've been so worried." His tone belies his words, because it sounds to me as if he's buzzing with voyeuristic excitement. "Your flat was a crime scene. An officer was posted outside your front door for two days. When I got back from Brighton on Sunday afternoon, he pounced and whipped me into a patrol car for a chat. I was shitting myself. They were asking questions like, when had I'd last seen you, did I know Miriana, and had I heard any disturbance. That sort of thing."

It's irrational of me to feel annoyed, but Callum rarely goes away – so how come he chose that weekend to go to Brighton? If he'd been home, he might have heard me shouting and fetched help.

"Did they kick my front door in?"

"I don't think so. There's incident tape stuck on it, but they broke in the back way. Hang on a minute – I'll go and check."

I listen to his feet thudding down the stairs, imagine him going around the side of the house and into my patio garden. Despite what happened there, I'm nostalgic for my flat and I want to go home.

When he returns, he's breathless from running. "It's all good, Laura. They broke in through your kitchen door but they've repaired it. Your front lock hasn't been tampered with."

"I'm coming home on Friday evening," I tell him. "The police have given me clearance to return to my flat, but they've kept my keys so I'll need to collect my spare set from you."

"No problem. I'll be in – see you then."

I stay on at Mum's for two more days. She and I have found a way of blanking out recent horrors and bringing Ellie back into our conversation and our lives. We talk about her and share happy memories.

"You should have been a counsellor, Mum." I'm beginning to feel better.

"I was, in a way," she replies. "Citizens' Advice counsellors don't just deal with practical problems, you know. If someone's struggling with debt or marriage problems, the box of tissues comes out at the meeting."

Spending time with Mum is a small repayment for the years when I left her to cope alone with grief, and I'm grateful to Gareth for helping her through. As my physical wounds scab over and turn a healthy shade of pink, I know I'm healing from the inside.

Mum's not happy when I tell her I'm going home. "It's too soon, Laura. Stay a bit longer."

"No, Mum. I'll visit again soon, but routine will help me now."

I don't feel like taking the train to London, so I hire a car and arrange for it to be delivered to the house. I've no packing to do because I landed on Mum's doorstep empty-handed. Even the clothes I'd been wearing had been taken from me for forensic examination and kept as evidence. I've been borrowing her clothes and toiletries, and she's made a supermarket trip to buy me underwear and a few essentials. Gareth has visited us a couple of times, but I haven't felt like going out.

My hire car will arrive at two o'clock and I've no reason to delay setting out for London. I stand in the hall grasping a piece of paper with a phone number written on it, and turn it over in my hands. Have I left it too late? It's days since I promised Bill I'd ring him. My phone – like my campervan – is still with the forensics team. He must have decided I'm ghosting him. What else could he think?

Around midday I dial Bill's mobile, reasoning that as I'm calling from Mum's landline, he won't recognise it and might pick up. He doesn't.

I'm ridiculously disappointed. What did I expect? It's late July, so he's probably left the country to take that trip to Scandinavia he was enthusing about.

"Have some lunch before you go," Mum calls. I'm about to say I'm not hungry, but she's set up a picnic table in the garden next to Ellie's rose bush, so I can't disappoint her.

I'm biting into my sandwich when I hear the phone ringing. I stumble to my feet and run indoors, grabbing it from its cradle on the hall table.

"Who is this?" asks a voice on the line, unmistakably Bill's. "I've a missed call from your number."

My chest feels tight and it's a struggle to speak. "It's Laura."

"Laura! It's been ages. I didn't expect to hear from you again." There's a slight catch in his voice, but his tone isn't particularly warm.

"I'm sorry. I want to explain but... It's complicated." What's the point? I've left it too long. It's a sunny day, but I've come inside from the garden to the cool dark hall and I start to shiver.

"After you told me to leave I thought we were over, but I couldn't stop thinking of you. I got your messages saying you'd call, but then you didn't..."

"There's a reason."

"Don't mess me about, Laura."

I tell him the truth. "I was attacked."

For five seconds the line goes silent, then he gives an audible gasp. "Are you all right?"

"I am now. The man's been arrested. I've been staying with my mum while I recovered, but I'm going back to London this afternoon. There's so much to tell you, but I can't explain it on the phone." I cross my fingers hoping he'll suggest meeting soon.

"I'll be there," he says.

"On Saturday?"

"No, not Saturday. Tonight. I can't risk you changing your mind again." We both laugh, and it breaks the tension. "I'm working on a photoshoot in Stratford-upon-Avon, but it's wrapping up soon. I'll head home and collect the van. I should be with you between seven and eight."

My heart lifts. This is what I hoped he'd say.

"I can't wait to see you. I'm setting off soon and I'll pick up something for supper on the way."

"Great. Your phone seems to be disconnected. Do you have a new number?"

"No. The police are keeping my mobile as evidence. I had to beg them to give me your number." I think of all the other numbers in my Contacts that I've lost. Most will be easy to find again – except one. Damn. I forgot to ask the police officer to give me Miriana's number. I doubt I'll ever see or hear from her again.

"Make sure you listen out for your doorbell," says Bill. "I don't want any more missed communication, okay?"

We both laugh.

I was a little bit spooked about returning to my flat, but knowing Bill will be there later this evening eases some of my apprehension. Will it look like a war zone? Or trigger terrifying memories of the night Miriana and I were held hostage? Will my flat ever feel like a safe haven again?

61

LAURA

Callum greets me with a friendly hug and seems genuinely happy to see me. "Do you want me to come in with you?" he asks, handing over my keys.

"No thanks. I'll be fine, and a friend's coming over later."

"What happened to your lodger?"

"Lodger?" My head is brimming with thoughts of Bill. Then I remember. "You mean Miriana? It's a long story. I'll tell you another day."

Shreds of blue and white incident tape are still stuck to my front door. When I pull them off, blue gloss paint flakes away. I insert my key, and it's no surprise to find it's single-locked and the burglar alarm's not activated. I can hardly blame the police, because they wouldn't have known the code to set it after they'd finished examining the crime scene.

My shopping bags are clinking with bottles because the supermarket's alcohol aisle signalled to me: *Time to celebrate!* I hurry to the kitchen to put everything in the fridge.

Sunshine filters in through the honeysuckle and stencils a pattern of light and shade on the worktop. Everything looks bright and orderly. I swallow. How could I have dreaded returning home? The counter is gleaming; nothing looks out of place, yet the forensics team must have examined every crevice. In my police interview I'd stressed that the tape Bryn used to bind my wrists came from my own cupboard, and the knife from my kitchen drawer. I speculated aloud about how premeditated Bryn's actions were. *Stick to the facts*, the interviewer reminded me, but I couldn't help wondering if he came planning to attack Miriana and me. Did he bring other weapons? Using my roll of tape on Miriana would fit with his scenario of me as the aggressor.

I finish unpacking, and put the food I've bought for supper in the fridge. The orderliness of the kitchen soothes me. Perhaps the investigators will have cleaned up my sitting room and dealt with the stains and overturned furniture? There's only one way to find out.

As I dawdle towards the sitting room, my heart is pounding. An image of Bryn, the knife, and Miriana keeled over on the floor, takes shape as I turn the knob and push the door open.

I step inside – and recoil. That fleeting vision was no dream or flash of PTSD. In this room, time has stopped. I'm dragged back into the terror…

Outside the streets are mellow in evening sunshine, but here the curtains are tightly-drawn so the light penetrating is dirt-grey.

Miriana is sitting in the straight-backed chair, sideways on to the window, her face in silhouette. She doesn't speak, smile or stand to greet me. Mesmerised, I take a step towards her.

"What are you doing here?"

"You gave me a key. Remember?" She turns her head and says in a slow drawl, "So you didn't die. But he did. You'll be sorry for that."

"Who are you talking about?" I stare wildly around the

room as if someone else might be hiding. "Who do you mean? Who's dead?"

"Gareth." She spits the name at me, and I see a single tear gleam on her cheek.

"You mean Bryn, don't you?" I keep my voice calm and even. "He's not dead, Miriana. What makes you think that?" I reach for her hand, but she snatches it away.

"He said he'd come back for me," she whispers, "but he never did. If he's not dead, he'd keep his word. I was asleep for a long time. It was so very cold. When I woke I was in hospital. The doctor checked me over, nurses gave me painkillers, but no one explained anything. The police were waiting to ask me questions. So many questions: about him, about you, and why I was living in your house…"

She pauses. I'm about to speak when she lifts her head and shouts, "I thought *you* had died. I wish you had."

I reel back as if I've been punched. Miriana flicks her hand dismissively, as if I'm nothing, my life of no consequence.

"Gareth – the man you call Bryn – warned me about your fragile mental health. Why do you think he sent me to find you at that campsite? It was because the third anniversary of Ellie's death was coming up and he wanted to protect you."

I hang my head and stay silent.

"He knew you didn't want to go on living. He told me he was going to take you away from London and keep you safe until the anniversary had passed." Miriana's eyes search for mine and lock on. "He said he couldn't be sure he'd be able to stop you if you were, you know, determined to kill yourself."

My jaw drops. "Is that what you told the police?"

"Sure. He was your man, Ellie's father. I didn't believe you when you said he was called Bryn, and I told that to the police officers who interviewed me." Miriana shrugs. "When I asked about him, they said there'd been an accident then they clammed up. I begged and begged, but no one would say anything and his phone was disconnected." Her tears flow freely now, and she doesn't try to stem them. "I thought he must be dead. What else could I think?"

It dawns on me with a sickening realisation – Miriana was part of this charade from the outset. Bryn was a monster of manipulation. If he could groom Ellie, who had a strong family, confidence and self-worth, how much easier must it have been to coerce Miriana, who had no one in her corner?

"But, Miriana, he hurt you. Don't you remember? He tied you to this chair and struck you so hard you lost consciousness." I dredge through memories of our ordeal in this room, Throughout it, Miriana didn't seem lucid. I assumed she was woozy because he'd hit her, but perhaps he'd given her a sedative too. Perhaps she was never aware of what was going on, or of the things he said.

She shrugs. "That was nothing. He didn't hurt me. I was acting. He explained everything and gave me pills so I wouldn't feel pain. He told me you and he might argue, and he didn't want me remembering any quarrel."

I bet he didn't, I think grimly, but Miriana's reframing of truth is making me desperate.

"What about the fake suicide note?" I ask. "The blog diary he wrote in your name, saying I was abusing you?"

"Honestly, Laura, I've no idea what you're on about."

"You didn't care what might happen to me if he took me away?"

Her voice has a harshness I've not heard before. "Why would I? Who has ever cared about me? My parents left me. My boyfriend pimped me over to his brother to run drugs. Only Bryn ever cared for me. I'd do anything for him."

With a sickening tightness in my chest, it dawns on me –

she's in love with him. Just like Ellie, and who knows how many other naïve girls before her.

The oppressive greyness in the room weighs down on me. I've spent too long in the shadows not wanting to know the truth. It has to end.

I lash out at her. "Bryn might not be dead, but he won't be around to harm me, or you, or anyone else. He tried to murder me, and he'll be going to prison for a long time."

Striding past her, I pull open the curtains and let evening sunshine pour in. My patio garden is a riot of colour. The scarlet geraniums, with a few drooping blossoms in biscuit-brown, continue their cycle of birth, death and renewal. I hear Miriana rising from her chair and walking to the door. She's leaving. Good. But when I turn around, she's still there. Now she's sitting cross-legged on the floor, leaning against the door and nursing a cushion on her lap.

My doorbell rings. I jolt and Miriana flinches. "Who's that?"

It must be Bill. I take two paces towards the door, expecting her to move aside.

"Get back!" she orders.

"Don't be ridiculous. It's my friend."

The bell rings again.

"I'm serious." She slides her right hand beneath the cushion and produces a knife.

I gasp. This is no ordinary kitchen knife. It has a red handle and a long, pointed stiletto blade – the kind designed to reduce friction on contact and cause serious harm, or death.

"Miriana. Where the hell did you get that?" Bile rises in my throat.

She turns the knife over so sunlight glitters on the blade. "Cool, yeah? It's the real deal. Liam gave it to me before my mission to Wales."

I call on my years of teaching experience and try to sound calm. I've had practice at removing knives from students.

"Put the knife down on the floor and slide it towards me. **Now**. I'm going to walk towards you, and you are going to move out of the way so I can let my friend in."

The bell has stopped, and now there's a continuous staccato knocking. What must Bill be thinking? That I've enticed him to drive all the way from Birmingham to London and now I'm ghosting him? He won't even know I'm at home, because my campervan isn't outside and he won't recognise the Peugeot I hired to drive back from Cardiff.

I hold up my hands in a gesture of surrender and inch forward. "Listen, Miriana. I'm coming through to answer the door. Okay?"

Miriana adjusts her grip on the knife and slashes a figure of eight in thin air, like a child brandishing a sparkler. I move back, but I won't stay silent.

"Bill!" I yell in my loudest voice. "I'm here. Help!"

"Shut up!" Miriana tilts her head on one side and appears to be listening. "He's gone."

She's right. The knocking has stopped.

I take a breath. He'll wait, won't he? Or use his initiative to find a way to get inside? Perhaps he'll knock on Callum's door. But Callum no longer has my spare keys, because I've just taken them.

I play for time. "Put the knife down, Miriana. Listen to me – you've done nothing wrong. So far. I don't believe you want to hurt me, but an accident would be easy with that knife. Give it to me." I flatten my palm and hold my hand out.

She gives me a blank stare.

"There are services who can help you and find you a place to live. You can study or work and make a fresh start. You said you wanted to work with animals…" I step towards her. Could I use my greater strength to shunt her sideways, away from the door? But the slightest nick of that knife and I could bleed to death.

"I don't care," she retorts. "If he's going to prison it's your fault. And if he's not here, I don't want to live." Her voice quivers but her hand is steady. With a deft wrist movement, she turns the knife away from me and points it at her own throat. "It's your fault. If I kill myself, they'll know what you said about him is a massive lie. How will you get out of that one?"

With a sick, sinking feeling, I retreat towards the window, not taking my eyes off her. "I'm not going to hurt you. Miriana. I want to help you."

I run my hand along the sill, feeling for the key to the window lock. She can't guard the door and window at the same time. If she runs at me with the knife, can I pick up a chair and fend her off while I open the window and climb into the garden?

I hear snuffling like a distressed animal – Miriana is weeping. What brought that on? Her hand, holding the blade, is shaking. Her knees are bent up, her head is bowed. She isn't watching me. As my fingers make contact with the key, I glance out into my garden and gasp! Dangling over the flat roof of my kitchen are a pair of suntanned legs in khaki shorts. Bill. He kicks the air, his feet scrambling around for the window ledge, then grips the drainpipe and lowers himself onto my patio.

62

LAURA

From her seated position by the door, Miriana can't see the drama unfolding in my garden. I don't believe she wants to die. She's overwrought with emotion. Even if she still has murderous intent towards me, I don't want her plunged into the lottery of the youth justice system. I used to be so persuasive and rational, but with all that's happened I've turned inwards. For this to end well, I need to find my voice.

"Miriana, I know you hate me, and I'm sorry," I say. "But I've only ever wanted to help you. I didn't understand your feelings for Bryn. But there are other people who care about you. Think of your mum. She loved you so much she left you behind though it broke her heart. She wanted you to have a chance of a better life where you wouldn't have to obey your father or answer to any man."

Her expression's sullen, but she seems to be listening.

"You can reach out to your mum without going to Albania. You can stay here and make a fresh start."

Miriana sobs harder. Her nose is running and she wipes it on her sleeve. She puts the knife down on the floor in front of her. I take a half-pace towards her. Then another, keeping my eyes locked onto her face.

"I was a mother too, Miriana. I always will be, even though Ellie's no longer here. There's nothing worse on this earth than losing a child. I promise you, your mum will be thinking about you. Every day." I make the final step and cover the knife with my foot. I bend down to pick it up and carry it across to my desk where I lock it in a drawer.

"Now I'm going to open the window. My friend's arrived and I need to let him in, but I'm here for you. Think of your mum, and imagine it's her standing beside you in my place."

"My mum." Miriana takes hold of the door handle and pulls herself up to standing. "I'd love to see her."

Outside the window, Bill crosses the garden, followed by Callum. "Who's that?"

"It's Bill, the friend I told you about." She narrows her eyes and glares, but as they approach the window she notices Callum, behind Bill's right shoulder.

His familiarity seems to reassure her, and a smile tugs at the corners of her mouth.

"Callum!" she calls out, and he gives his gap-toothed grin and a hand gesture somewhere between a wave and a salute. In that moment I forgive him anything. He can use my roof as his sun terrace in perpetuity. I unlock the security bolts, and the sash creaks as I slide it up, but after a few inches it gets stuck.

"Laura – what's going on?" Bill has to bend to speak through the gap. "Are you all right?"

"We're fine now," I say. "This is Miriana." I smile and put my arm around her shoulders and we stand side by side, facing the men in awkward solidarity. Miriana glances across at my locked desk drawer and whispers to me, "Will you tell them?"

I shake my head. "Come on, help me get this window

properly open." We each take hold of opposite sides of the frame and push, our four hands working in unison; it judders, then slides up till it's wide enough for Bill to clamber over the sill, into my home and, perhaps, into my life.

63

LAURA

My relationship with Miriana was complicated from the start I'm not best-placed to support her through rehabilitation and signpost her to an independent life, away from men who want to exploit her. I've blurred too many boundaries because of Ellie.

In the turmoil of that evening, I phone round Social Services and other agencies seeking help for Miriana. Bill and Callum retreat to the kitchen; Miriana sits with me while I make the calls and relay everything to her exactly as it's explained. It turns out that because of the way she was exploited by Liam, she might qualify for support as a potential victim of human trafficking.

"Are you happy with that?" I ask her. "They'll keep you safe and help plan your future." I don't mention anything that sounds intrusive like counselling.

She shrugs. "I guess so, if they'll find me somewhere safe to live."

While we wait for a worker from an anti-slavery charity to come and take Miriana to a safe house, we join Bill and Callum in my kitchen and I fend off their questions while making tea and snacks. Callum offers Miriana a cigarette, and they stroll outside into the garden to smoke.

When the support worker from the hostel arrives, Miriana goes with her willingly. She says a brief goodbye to me, but it's Callum who walks with her to the woman's car. I close my front door on this girl, who has stirred up such emotion in me. I've been protective, angry and sorrowful – for her and for myself. Although Miriana was manipulated and didn't understand her role, she's led me back to Ellie. Knowing the brutal truth of what happened is hideous, but not knowing was far worse.

Callum lingers on in my kitchen, drinking beer as the sun sets. I don't have the energy to cook the supper I'd planned for Bill and me, so I open a bottle of Merlot.

"Where did you meet that girl?" Callum asks.

"Sorry. I can't deal with any more questions today."

"Fair enough. She's given me her number. I'll ask her myself."

By the time Callum stands up to leave, the bottle is half-empty. I switch to water, but Bill carries on drinking, sipping his wine slowly.

"Now he's gone, are you going to tell me?" he asks.

I nod, and explain about the relationship between Ellie and Bryn and how that led him to attack me. Bill's eyes fill with anger as I describe what happened on the cliff top.

"That bastard, I'll kill him." He reaches for my hand.

"No need. He won't be hurting me or anyone for a long time. Do you mind if I don't talk about that? It's lodged inside my head and won't go away."

"Tell me about Miriana."

"Her boyfriend's brother, Liam, sent her from London to South Wales to deliver drugs."

"Is that like 'county lines' where criminal drug dealers exploit young people?"

"Yes. Often they use children even younger than Miriana. It was already happening when I was still in teaching. Criminals use children because it's easier for them to stay under the radar. Miriana was ordered to move into Tinker's home, and that's called cuckooing, where dealers take over the property of a vulnerable person as a base in a new area. You can guess what happens next."

Bill grimaces. "Some kind of violent takeover of territory. But it sounds like Liam underestimated Miriana. You told me she walked away."

"She did – but straight into the clutches of Bryn, whose expertise in grooming teenage girls was right off the scale."

When I'm too exhausted to talk any more, we go to my bedroom and Bill holds me until I fall asleep. He dozes while I drift in and out of consciousness and wake screaming from a nightmare where I'm bound and helpless in my campervan, minutes from plunging over the cliff.

Over the next few weeks, I succumb to the grief that's been building inside me for three years like a debt earning interest that needs to be paid back. I keep reminding myself that Bryn's hold over Ellie had snapped, that she was leaving him to come home to us and was sorry for the pain she'd caused. I need to believe this.

My boss signs me off on sick leave. Some days I can't get out of bed. I curl up into a tight ball, staring at the wall. Anguish comes in waves, but mostly I'm silent, no thrashing limbs or weeping or moaning. My chest feels tight and I'm drenched in sweat, yet my face, hands and feet feel frozen.

I feel as if I'm lost in a mist, searching for Ellie, while Bill stays on in my flat, taking care of me. He brings tea and makes simple meals of soup or a cheese omelette. I thank him and force the food down, but later when he's left the room, I tiptoe down the hall and throw up in the toilet, hoping he doesn't hear.

"There's a letter for you," Bill says one morning, bringing it to me on a tray with coffee and toast cut into fingers. It's 10.30 but I'm still in bed, woozy from pills prescribed by my doctor and meditating as I prepare to face the day.

I recognise the postmark and rip the envelope open with my forefinger. "It's from the police," I tell him, reading rapidly. "It says I won't face charges for assaulting Bryn."

"It's over." The tension briefly leaves Bill's face. Both of us have been feeling the strain.

But for me it isn't over, because the investigation into Bryn's abduction and attempted murder of me ticks on. I wonder if he'll face charges over his relationship with Ellie and abuse of his position of trust. I want justice for her, but reopening it all would break me.

Gareth keeps me updated. He's been told it would be tricky to prove sexual activity, as Ellie can't give evidence and Bryn's sure to deny the confession he made in my flat.

Gareth also told me Rosie had identified Bryn as the man she saw with Ellie on the coastal path at Southerndown. I still don't understand why she kept quiet until now. I suppose she didn't connect Bryn with Ellie leaving home. Or perhaps she wanted to punish me for storming into her room when I was wild with fear for my missing daughter? I know Ellie would never have been so petty if it had been the other way round, but who knows how some teenage girls think?

August passes by without me, but one sultry morning in early September I wake and the mist in my head has cleared. I potter in the garden, reviving neglected plants, and over supper I say to Bill, "I'm ready to see Miriana, but I don't have her number. It's on my mobile that the police are keeping for evidence."

"I think I know a man who does," he replies.

"Who?"

"Callum." Leaving half his tagliatelle uneaten on his plate, Bill springs to his feet and heads for the door as if having a mission gives him purpose. How tough it's been for him stuck in one place, inhabiting the darkness of my despair when he could have been touring Scandinavia in his campervan.

When I ring Miriana she sounds surprised to hear from me, but agrees to meet and says she'll bring her support worker. Perhaps she feels as awkward as I do about our connection. We agree to meet at a café near to Clapham Junction station.

"I'm not allowed to tell you the address of the safe house," she explains. "But I'm still in London. They've told me some slavery survivors are sent hundreds of miles away for their own protection."

64

LAURA

The air is chilly with a faint aroma of autumn when I set off to meet Miriana. Bill wanted to drive me. His campervan's been parked outside my flat for weeks, going nowhere more exciting than the supermarket. But this is something I need to do on my own.

I catch the bus but it hits a traffic jam alongside Tooting Bec Common, and I arrive hot, bothered and twenty minutes late. The café windows are steamed up so I can't peek inside, but when I push open the door and glance around I don't recognise anyone. How old is Miriana's support worker? There are mother-and-daughter combinations, but none of the girls looks like her. As I sweep my eyes round the room again, a young woman with spiky black hair waves to me from a table by the wall. I was looking for a girl with fair hair, but of course, Miriana's natural hair colour is dark. She's no longer bleaching it and has returned to her original self.

The key worker, a woman in her thirties, introduces herself as Agnes. She offers her hand, but before I can take it, Miriana barges between us and hugs me.

"Laura saved my life," she tells Agnes. I blush, but the compliment sets a positive tone. The counselling she's had must have helped her sort out her feelings. At least she no longer hates me. They've finished their drinks, so I ask the waiter to bring a fresh pot of tea, and coffee for Miriana.

"You've started college – I'm so pleased," I say, as we wait for our drinks.

"Yes. I'm studying Animal Care." A smile breaks through her usual guarded expression, and I see a young woman with a passion for life. "I'll have to resit Maths and English, but I'm sure I'll get the grades now I have less to worry about. Thanks, Laura. If you hadn't driven me to London that day, I'd still be in that flat in Penarth with Gareth – sorry, I mean Bryn."

My pulse slows. Some young people in her situation don't even realise they're being exploited, but she gets it now and refuses to be a victim. With no place of safety, she was ricocheting from one inappropriate relationship to the next. Even the way she behaved around Callum suggested she still has some learning to do about relationships with men.

"Will Miriana be allowed to stay to complete her course?" I ask Agnes. "What's her UK residence status?"

"We're working on it." Agnes puts down her mug with a firm clunk. Miriana stares at the sunflower pattern on the tablecloth. "Her parents entered the country illegally, but she was born here. Show Laura the photo of your birth certificate."

Miriana taps her mobile and shows me the screen. I remember her telling me she took this photo while her father was sorting through family documents. It shows her place of birth as Croydon. It also solves the question of her age, which bothered me when she was staying at my flat. "So you've just turned eighteen."

She meets my eyes with a steady gaze. "You see, Laura. I told you the truth."

"Our immigration lawyer thinks she'll qualify, because her parents' status when she was born gave them indefinite right to remain," says Agnes. "We'll get a certified copy of her birth certificate and she can apply for a passport, but if there's a query, it might be hard to get other documents."

"And if that doesn't work?"

"She lived in the UK for the first ten years of her life, so she can register for citizenship if she didn't leave the country for more than ninety days."

"I've never been abroad." Miriana cuts in, her eyes flitting from Agnes to me.

"There you go then. It'll work out."

Miriana rests her head on her forearms on the café table, and her narrow shoulders shake. I lay an arm across her back to comfort her until her crying stops. She's not as skinny as she was. The spiky black hairstyle suits her. She no longer bears even a passing resemblance to Ellie, and I'm glad. Miriana now looks like the girl she was meant to be.

She takes a paper napkin from the holder on the table and dries her eyes. "I rang my mum," she tells me. "Like you suggested. She was so happy to hear from me. She said she loves me and we'll meet again soon."

It's hard to take in so much good news. After everything she's been through in her short life, Miriana can look forward to a safe future.

"Once you have citizenship and a passport, you can go to Albania and see your mum and it'll be up to you whether to stay or leave."

"I'd like that." Miriana props her chin on one hand. "To see Mum and meet my grandma, knowing I can still come back for my studies. Who knows, maybe Dad will forgive me?"

My eyes well with tears, and as I return her smile a feeling of calm washes over me. For the first time in three years my shoulders relax, knowing that sometime in the not-too-distant future, another mother will have her lost daughter restored to her.

THE END

ALSO BY HELEN MATTHEWS

Girl Out of Sight

The Sisters

ACKNOWLEDGEMENTS

The popular image of an author grafting away alone in a garret is only part of the story. In reality, getting a book written and out into the world is a collaborative process and wouldn't be possible without a team.

Grateful thanks to Betsy Reavley, Tara Lyons, Hannah Deuce, Lexi Curtis and everyone at Bloodhound Books for bringing this second edition of The Girl in the Van into the world, and for the stunning cover design. This novel was previously published by Darkstroke Books and I'd like to thank Steph, Laurence and my eagle-eyed editor, Sue Barnard.

Massive thanks to novelist and editor, Joanna Barnard for an excellent manuscript critique and for enthusiasm and encouragement when this book was at draft stage.

Thanks to my beta readers Gill Swales, Susan Corfield and Fran Morgan, who enjoyed the story, offered thoughtful feedback and spotted some glitches I hadn't picked up.

This book was written during the Covid pandemic when my critique group had to meet on Zoom. Sherron Mayes, Katharine Johnson and Jane Risdon's insights improved this novel and their friendship helped me through bleak months of lockdown. Sherron tragically died in August 2023 and we feel her loss keenly.

My friends in Ark Writers (Katrina, Sue, Jenny, Di, Jenni and Mark) have been unstinting in their support, as have the brilliant writers I met on the MA Creative Writing course at Oxford Brookes University. Thank you Annie, Benedicta,

Helen, Yvonne, Rachel, Rose, Claire and Patrick. A shout out is also due to Rushmoor Writers for helpful critiques over almost two decades.

While researching and fact-checking The Girl in the Van I've been lucky to have answers to my research questions from anti-slavery charity Unseen for which I'm an Ambassador. I donate a percentage of my royalties, and all fees I receive for author talks, to this inspirational charity. If your book club would like to read my novel and learn more about modern slavery, please get in touch.

I'm grateful to crime and police procedural adviser, Graham Bartlett, who cast his forensic eye over sections of the story involving police investigations and answered my questions.

The action in The Girl in the Van takes place in London and along the South Wales coast in Tenby, Penarth and Cardiff, where I grew up. The novel also features a family with roots in the Balkans. I visited Albania in 2017 but I'm acutely aware that much about that fascinating country is unknowable to an outsider. I'm grateful to journalist and author, Teuta Metra for answering my questions and putting me straight on some details. Any remaining errors in the book are mine.

Thanks to my family for their continuing support: my husband, Alan; Alex, Bronwen and their partners, and my sister Fran.

A NOTE FROM THE PUBLISHER

Thank you for reading this book. If you enjoyed it please do consider leaving a review on Amazon to help others find it too.

We hate typos. All of our books have been rigorously edited and proofread, but sometimes mistakes do slip through. If you have spotted a typo, please do let us know and we can get it amended within hours.

info@bloodhoundbooks.com

www.ingramcontent.com/pod-product-compliance
Ingram Content Group UK Ltd.
Pitfield, Milton Keynes, MK11 3LW, UK
UKHW041342130525
5888UKWH00027B/246